Praise for *In the Field of Grace*

I had a long business trip and planned to scan *In the Field of Grace* while on the road. Well, forget that—I was hooked from the first page! This is an amazing narrative. I was overwhelmed by the beauty of Ruth and Boaz's story. The biblical account came alive as the love story of Ruth and Boaz unfolded. I feel blessed to have read this book. **I devoured it, reading late into the night.**

—Debbie Macomber, *New York Times* bestselling author

Packed with spiritual truth, impeccable research, and well-placed humor, *In the Field of Grace* takes your heart on a journey of love, loss, and triumph. **This powerful retelling of Ruth and Boaz's story is my favorite novel this year.**

—Mesu Andrews, author and ECPA Christian Book Award winner

Tessa Afshar is a brilliant writer and a beautiful soul. With a strong, poetic voice, Tessa brings biblical stories to life in a way that makes me want to kneel, pray, shout, and sing, all at the same time. In Tessa's latest novel, *In the Field of Grace*, she explores the story of Ruth and Boaz, their hardships and their breakthroughs. **I finished the book feeling grateful again for God's intimate goodness and grace, and I remembered afresh how He sees us, loves us, and cares about every detail of our lives.** Tessa crafts such beautiful books; I never want the stories to end! And the beautiful thing is these stories have the power to shape us and change us when we give God access to our own stories. Well done, Tessa. I can't wait for your next book!

—Susie Larson, national radio host, speaker, and author of *Your Beautiful Purpose* and *The Uncommon Woman*

Tessa Afshar offers readers one of the most cherished love stories from the Scriptures! Wonderfully researched, *In the Field of Grace* brings to life the tenderhearted and vulnerable Ruth, who is **sure to captivate biblical fiction lovers**!

—Kacy Barnett-Gramckow, author of The Genesis Trilogy and *Dawnlight*

The love story between Ruth and Boaz is reimagined with truths as timely today as they were thousands of years ago: reminders of faith, love, and the sovereignty of God.

—Tracy L. Higley, author of *The Queen's Handmaid*

A beautifully told story that will truly capture your heart. A must read for biblical fiction fans!

—Ginger Garrett, author of *Chosen, Reign,* and *Desired*

In the Field of Grace

a novel

TESSA AFSHAR

MOODY PUBLISHERS
CHICAGO

Published in association with the Books & Such Literary Agency, 52 Mission Circle, Suite 122, PMB 170, Santa Rosa, CA 95409-5370; www.booksandsuch.biz

Edited by Pam Pugh
Interior design: Ragont Design
Cover design: DogEared Design, LLC
Background image: iSrtock / 000011390255
Phoro of couple: Kirk DouPonce
Author photo: Christine Richenburg

Library of Congress Cataloging-in-Publication Data

Afshar, Tessa.
In the Field of Grace : a novel / Tessa Afshar.
pages ; cm
ISBN 978-0-8024-1097-9
1. Ruth (Biblical figure)—Fiction. 2. Naomi (Biblical figure)—Fiction. 3. Women in the Bible—Fiction. 4. Bible fiction. 5. Christian fiction. I. Title.
PS3601.F47H66 2014
813'.6—dc23

2014002833

We hope you enjoy this book from River North Fiction by Moody Publishers. Our goal is to provide high-quality, thought-provoking books and products that connect truth to your real needs and challenges. For more information on other books and products written and produced from a biblical perspective, go to www.moodypublishers.com or write to:

River North Fiction
Imprint of Moody Publishers
820 N. LaSalle Boulevard
Chicago, IL 60610

1 3 5 7 9 10 8 6 4 2

Printed in the United States of America

To Rebecca Rhee, dearest friend through joy and sorrow;
your friendship is like coming home.

Prologue

Those who walk uprightly
Enter into peace;
They find rest as they lie in death.
ISAIAH 57:2

Death squatted at Boaz's door, waiting like a vulture, biding its time. He could sense its presence—inexorable, hungry, patient.

Judith—the wife of his youth, the woman he had married for love, his doe-eyed companion, lay dying.

Boaz leaned over to smooth the dark, sweat-stained hair from her brow. Alerted by his gentle movements, her dog, Melekh, lifted its long snout and inspected Boaz's movements with suspicious intensity before settling its muzzle on its paws again. The dog's gaze shifted back to the emaciated woman on the bed. It was a mark of the drastic circumstances that the beast had been allowed on the bed. Normally, it didn't even make it through the chamber door. Yet as soon as Melekh had come limping in through the threshold, the beast had claimed the place like it had every right of ownership. With profound indifference, Judith's dog treated Boaz as an annoyance rather than the master.

Boaz ignored Melekh and lifted his wife's hand, holding it tightly, willing her not to give up. The woman on the bed had thinning, oily hair, and a face that looked like it had melted in the sun on one side, but that wasn't what Boaz saw. He remembered Judith as she had been when he had met her for the first time, with thick hair that fell below her hip, and a smile that could melt rock. Not that he had melted. He had been sixteen, a man in his own eyes. His father had sent him north to examine a parcel of land owned by Judith's father. She had offered him wine and cheese when he arrived. He took the cup from her hands and turned his shoulder on her lingering gaze. He had no time for young girls. This was the first time he had been entrusted with an important mission on his father's behalf and he intended to do well. The land proved fertile, and his father purchased it based on Boaz's recommendation. The trade went smoothly, and the two families became friends as a result of the new connection. For years, Judith wove in and out of Boaz's life, though he took his time getting around to noticing her existence.

Judith acted as a shepherdess for her family. Her father had assigned a herd of his best sheep to her care, knowing her competence with the animals to be equal to any man's. In the end it was her handling of the herd that had first drawn Boaz to his wife. She often teased that he had needed dumb sheep to act as matchmaker between them. True enough. He had admired her ability with the beasts before he had ever taken notice of her beautiful black eyes or her midnight-dark hair.

"How do you keep them so fat in a drought year?" he had asked one day, addressing her directly for the first time.

She had laughed at him, making him redden with self-consciousness, wondering what he had said that could be construed as funny.

"What?" he said, not bothering to curb the annoyance in his voice.

"They are not fat."

"They are, compared to my father's sheep." And that had been the start of their attachment. Later, she had confessed that she had loved him the first moment she had seen him.

He had frowned. He knew he wasn't a handsome man. What would make a pretty young girl set her heart on his crooked nose and ordinary face? But she insisted that to her, he was beautiful. That was the moment he had truly fallen in love with her, he thought.

He brought her hand to his lips and gave it a light kiss. A kiss she could not feel. Her dog growled. Melekh never liked when Boaz touched its mistress, not even after fourteen years of witnessing them together. The beast wasn't usually this touchy, Boaz had to admit. Judith's sickness had multiplied the animal's possessive instincts.

Melekh was born the year before they married. Judith was present when the little golden pup first opened its eyes and she liked its spirit from the start. She picked up its wriggling body and held it against her, and they belonged to each other from that moment. They welded together in an affection that surpassed the usual bonds of duty between a dog and its shepherd. She named the dog Melekh, *king,* and as if understanding the exact significance of the name, that animal had never stopped behaving as if it carried royal blood.

Boaz owned enough sheep to understand dogs were necessary to mind the sheep, to keep the wolves at bay, to warn their masters of potential danger. They had a prominent place in the life of a shepherd. And no part of that place included coming into the house and being caressed and cuddled like a baby. Not from Boaz's perspective.

"Where I go, Melekh comes," Judith had said the day they were betrothed.

"Of course. I have a nice field behind the house where he can roam freely."

Her rounded chin lifted mutinously. For a woman unaccustomed to shrill arguments, Judith could be fierce. "If you want me to sleep inside, Melekh sleeps inside."

A picture of Judith sleeping in the fields at night, with the dog on one side and him on the other, flashed before Boaz's mind. "It can come inside." Her dark eyes lit up with joy. Boaz decided he had made the right decision. He cleared his throat. "Never into our chamber, mind. That's just for you and me."

Judith had sealed her acceptance with a wide smile. For fourteen years the beast had shared Boaz's roof and eaten the scraps of his dinner. Boaz had never warmed to Melekh enough to cuddle it and speak to the dog like it was a child the way Judith did. But he had learned to tolerate the beast. For its part, Melekh ignored him most of the time. They had moved past being enemies. But they had never grown into becoming friends either.

The room smelled like fresh blood and the musky scent of spikenard. The servants had used the expensive oil in an attempt to cover the scent of sickness. Instead, the room reeked of a mix of bodily emissions and the pungent odor of perfume. It made his stomach turn.

They should be celebrating, not mourning. Only four days ago, Judith had been large with child, weeks away from delivery. She glowed with happiness even though it had been a difficult pregnancy. Judith's pregnancies were always difficult. When her hands and feet started to swell, she and Boaz paid little heed. Even the midwife had shrugged her shoulder.

On the morning of the Sabbath, while dressing in her mantle, Judith fell to the floor without warning. In horror, Boaz watched her body convulse, limbs jerking about in uncontrollable spasms. Spittle frothed around her mouth. Finally, the forceful movements of her muscles relented, leaving her unconscious for over a day.

She awoke with a blinding headache, unable to move half her body. Then the birth pains came. How could a woman, half paralyzed, manage to give birth? Boaz could not understand how she had survived. The baby, when he finally emerged, blue and silent, lingered on this earth for mere hours and even that was a miracle. He never cried. He simply closed his eyes and gave up the fight.

Boaz did not tell Judith when she awoke for a brief hour. He did not have the words. He forced his mouth to stretch into a smile and tried to protect her from one final horror, worried the knowledge of it would be her undoing. Sick as she was, paralyzed in the right half of her body and out of her mind with a headache that never left, she knew. She knew her little one was gone.

It proved too much for her. She could not cope with a shattered body and a broken heart at the same time. She gave up. Boaz left her side for an hour to see to their son's burial. He returned to find Judith slipping away from him, one shallow breath at a time, Melekh lying by her side, watchful as if it counted her breaths.

For the first time in fifteen years, Boaz reached out and patted the dog. Love for Judith bound them together in her dying hours. They were crushed under the same weight. Unspeakable horror. Grief. Loss. Unaccountably, touching Melekh felt like a comfort. It met a need deep inside Boaz, as he sat next to his wife, terrorized at the thought of losing her. Melekh looked up, its grey eyes filmed over by old age. Then it did something unaccountable too. Something it had never been moved to do. It licked Boaz's hand.

Boaz swallowed a sob and fell on his face, praying that God would spare Judith. But he already knew the answer. She was going to their children.

She opened her eyes and called his name. Boaz sprang to his feet and ran to her. She tried to smile. Only one side of her lips lifted, the other limp, sloped down, like a permanent grimace of pain. Her face had become divided—half dead, half alive; half grieving, half smiling. He would keep her like this and be happy. If only she would stay with him.

She mumbled something he could not catch. It was difficult to make out her slurring words since she had been struck down. She tried several times and finally he understood her words. "I'm sorry I wasn't always the wife I hoped I would be. I'm sorry I failed you."

"Stop, Judith. You never failed me."

"I let sorrow take me from you. I'm sorry for that."

Boaz wept. He had left a bit of his soul in the dark, shallow grave, next to his son's pitifully tiny body. At least the babe wasn't alone. He was buried next to his older sister, Sarah. And soon, his mother would join them.

It seemed impossible to accept. *Judith!* Her name reverberated through his mind, a soundless scream of anguish.

They had been happy together for many years even though Judith had been unable to bear children. She had suffered five miscarriages in as many years. For every baby, she had shed endless tears. Every one of her tears had lashed his heart like an iron-tipped whip.

"You are an honored man. You belong to the lineage of Nahshon, the famed leader of Judah. God has enlarged your land and prospered your cattle," she said to him one night, holding on to a tiny garment, never worn. "You deserve children so your name can go on. Instead you have become an object of pity among our people."

"I don't want children. I want you."

She shook her head, dark curls spilling down the small of her back. "I am barren. Take another wife, Boaz."

"I will not! Be patient. Didn't Abraham have to wait long years for a son? Didn't Isaac? We have a long time before we match their patience."

"Take another wife."

He resisted. He couldn't imagine sharing his heart and body with another woman. Judith was his wife. His love.

God blessed his patience. Judith became pregnant and this time carried the baby to term. They had a little daughter, with Judith's beautiful face and a sparrow's delicate voice.

For six years Boaz was enchanted by his precious girl; he heard her first words, comforted her through her tears, watched Judith put her to bed at night, and laughed at her precocious antics. For six years Sarah charmed him, cuddled him, loved him, filled him with joy.

It took only six days of fever for her to be taken from him. Was it a mere year since he had lost her? It felt like a lifetime.

He only knew that he survived that season by clinging to the Lord. His heart was crushed, but his faith grew.

Judith fell apart. The loss proved too much, robbing her of health and hope. Boaz fought for her with a tenacity he had not realized he possessed. He fought for her to go on. To cling to life and persevere.

"For my sake, please Judith, for my sake! Don't you love me as much as you loved our child? Please fight for us. Don't give up on me, beloved." He begged and cajoled. He prayed. He pushed. Anything to get her to hold on to living.

"I can't bear it, Boaz," she said one night as she sat on the roof, her feet dangling from the edge, her eyes locked on the bright stars. "I can't bear this loss."

Boaz felt a shiver go through him. He grabbed hold of Judith's fingers and squeezed with desperation. "Judith, life often brings us more sorrow than we think we can bear. But God is greater than every desolation. He is greater even than death. He will see us through."

Judith shook her head. "I don't have your faith, Boaz."

Months passed, months of slow agony as Boaz watched helplessly while his wife grew weaker in soul and body, unable to get a foothold in life, unable to hope and be restored. One night she came into Boaz's bed. "Give me another child," she said. "Give me comfort in my despair."

He didn't fight her. He should have, knowing how physically weak she remained. Instead he gave in. He kept her in his bed until she became pregnant for the last time.

And now, he was paying the price of his weakness. She lay dying because he couldn't refuse her.

"Boaz!" she called out in her weak, mumbling voice.

"I'm here."

"Promise me."

"Promise what?"

"You'll be happy? When I'm gone."

A fly tried to land on her arm and he swatted it away. No matter how hard they tried to repel them, the flies always came, attracted to the putrid scent that had begun to rise from her flesh. "How can I be happy? You have to stay with me, Judith."

"I can't, my love. It's my time to go. But I want you to find happiness. I want you to know joy. Please try. For me."

Her dog started to howl. Boaz was horrified by the sound. It reflected the scream that had been trapped inside his own heart too closely. He reached out his hand and softly, comfortingly caressed the thinning fur. "It's all right, boy. It's all right." Melekh's howling subsided. It gave one last wail and placed its muzzle on Judith's chest.

Judith gave her lopsided smile. A single tear ran down her left cheek. "I've finally managed to turn you two into friends." She closed her eyes, took a deep breath, and said, "I love you, Boaz. Always."

They were her last words.

Chapter One
FIVE YEARS LATER

To whom do you belong? And where are you from?
1 SAMUEL 30:13

Everyone in the city of Kir-hareseth seemed to have descended upon the marketplace, making final purchases before the stalls closed down. Crowds. Why couldn't they just stay home? Ruth tried to ignore the jostle of too many bodies. Dragging a perspiring hand down her worn tunic, she took a deep breath to steady her jangled nerves; the scent of sweat covered thinly by oily perfumes hit her with the force of a blow.

Ruth's mother had sent her to buy dates. She eyed the mounds of brown sticky fruit in a stall, trying to calculate how to get the best price so she could avoid one of her mother's blistering set downs. Bending forward, she picked one and examined it with intensity. It looked like a date to Ruth, which exhausted the breadth of her knowledge on the topic. About to open her mouth to ask for the price, she was surprised when a gentle hand caressed her arm.

"You can find better," a soft voice whispered in her ear. Startled, Ruth turned to find the source of the advice. The woman was in her middle years, with smooth skin and thick grey hair that peeked from beneath her ivory headdress. Her faded blue tunic appeared clean, the only good thing that could be said for it. The leather of her sandals, visible beneath her ankle-length tunic, showed signs of long wear.

Brown eyes sparkled at her. "What a lovely young woman. May the Lord bless you, child."

Compliments and Ruth did not go together. Certainly, no one had ever called her *lovely*. Her eldest sister was the acknowledged beauty of the family. Ruth was the last born and the Great Disappointment. The last chance at her parents' hope for a son, unfulfilled.

Too tall. Too quiet. Too female.

"Pardon?" she said, fumbling with the empty cloth bag she held, trying unsuccessfully to swallow.

"Forgive me. My sons tell me I am too free with my tongue. But you are such a pretty creature, I had to tell you."

Ruth gaped at her like one of the cows of Bashan.

The stranger flashed a wide smile, displaying a full set of startlingly white teeth. "I've embarrassed you. I'm sorry. We are more forthright with our thoughts in Israel. I've never lost the habit."

That explained the odd lilting accent. And the strange blessing she had given Ruth. What had she said? The Lord. Not Chemosh, but the Lord bless you. "You are an Israelite," Ruth said, forcing her tongue around the words.

"Yes. My sons and I have lived here for some years. We came when Bethlehem went through a famine and we feared we might starve. My husband was with us then, but he died of a wasting disease some years ago."

"That must have been hard to bear," Ruth said. "Having to raise your sons alone and in a foreign land."

"Hardest thing I've ever done. But the Lord has seen us through."

Ruth, who knew nothing about this Lord other than a vague recollection that He was the deity worshiped in Israel, gave a short nod.

"I am Naomi. Naomi of Bethlehem, in Judah. And you, my sweet girl? What do they call you?"

"Ruth."

"Ruth." Naomi nodded. "I like it. Have you brothers and sisters?"

"Four sisters, all older."

Naomi raised her brows and made a gentle humming sound in her throat. An odd silence settled over them; Ruth felt the crowds receding from her senses, their incessant sounds and smells muted. She had a strange notion that the woman had gazed into her life and seen it, known its pains and sorrows, just from that one sentence. As if Naomi knew that four older sisters meant Ruth had grown up invisible. Unwanted. Never quite managing to please anybody.

Yet she had uttered no words. Just that gentle humming in her throat.

As if coming to a sudden decision, Naomi said, "You must come to my home and share supper with us. My sons will be delighted to meet you."

Ruth's jaw dropped open. "I . . . thank you. But I must buy dates. For my mother."

"Ah. Try that stall over there. Mesha is almost an honest man. And his fruit is fresh. Don't let him pick for you, though. Insist on picking the ones you want. He'll grumble, but pay no mind. Your mother will be happy with what you bring home."

You don't know my mother.

"That's kind of you. Thank you, Naomi."

Before Ruth settled on a price with the vender Naomi had recommended, the woman herself showed up again, stationing herself at Ruth's side. "Come, Mesha. What kind of price is that for a daughter of Moab? You can do better."

Mesha complied by lowering his price a fraction. Ruth, who had no talent for haggling, gave the Israelite woman a grateful smile. "For once I'm returning from the market with a decent purchase. Not only do I thank you, my whole family thanks you."

Naomi laughed. Ruth liked the sound of it, clear and pleasing, without drawing needless attention. She could imagine the hardships of the woman's life. And yet Naomi had not lost her ability to find joy in small things.

"Will you come and visit me after you deliver the dates to your mother? It's only my sons and me, and our house is simple. But you would be most welcome. I'll give you supper and afterward walk you home so you won't have to worry about finding your way in the dark."

Ruth felt her skin turn warm as blood rushed to her cheeks. "I would like to."

Naomi patted her hand and told her how to find her house.

Before delivering the dates to her mother, Ruth hid two of the plumpest in her sash. For once, her mother had no sour comments when she examined her daughter's purchase. It never occurred to Ruth to expect praise for her success. Praise and her mother were not frequent companions. Not when it came to the woman's fifth daughter.

"Where is Grandfather?" Ruth asked.

"Where else? Slumbering on his mat as usual, expecting everyone to take care of his lordship."

Ruth flushed at her mother's bitter complaint. The only true kindness Ruth had received growing up was at the hand of her grandfather. Though everyone else in her family had found her wanting, her father's father acted as though Ruth were the most precious member of his brood.

In fond remembrance, Ruth fingered the luxurious linen sash tied at her waist. The old man had bought it for her years ago, after Ruth's sisters had teased her more mercilessly than usual. Unable to bear their mean words another moment, she had run into the field behind their house and hidden through the night, shedding her tears in private. No one had bothered to try to find her. Except Grandfather.

Late the following morning he had come upon her, crouching in order to see into her eyes. "There you are. I've been looking everywhere for you."

"I was here."

"So I see."

"Is Mother very angry?"

"No more than usual, shall we say? So long as you finish your chores, I believe she will grow calm. Now, I have a present for you."

"For *me*?"

"Yes, indeed. Because you are my adorable granddaughter and I am proud of you." He proffered the most exquisite sash Ruth had ever seen. It had white and dark blue stripes, with lighter blue flowers embroidered through the edges.

She gasped. "This must have cost a fortune."

The old man smiled. "It did. And you are worth it."

Ruth let the memory fade, blinking back tears.

The grandfather she held dear had disappeared in the past few years. His mind had grown dim with time. Often he didn't seem to recognize any of them. He had grown tangled in a shadow world, isolated, unable to grasp the ordinary things of life. He was with them and yet lost to them.

Ruth knelt by his mat and caressed his shoulder with a light hand. His eyes opened, faded and unfocused.

"I have a present for you, Grandfather." Ruth handed him one of the dates, trying to keep the exchange hidden from the rest of the room with her slim body.

The withered man stared at the date in the palm of his hand, his expression blank. "Put it in your mouth," Ruth encouraged. "It's sweet." She moved his hand toward his mouth, and obediently he took a bite.

He made a small sound of appreciation. "I told you you would like it," she whispered. "Don't let Mother catch you, or there will be great gnashing of teeth."

A smile broke on the old man's face and for a moment he looked like his old self, understanding and humor twinkling in the filmy eyes. Sometimes lucidity broke over him like the summer rains, sudden and inexplicable, and he became again the man she loved and missed like part of her own heart. But those moments were growing rarer with each passing day.

"Oh Grandfather." Ruth gave him a hard embrace; by the time she moved away, the empty look had taken the place of the momentary clarity. Ruth's shoulders slumped. Gently, she fed him the last date before leaving his side.

Her mother made no demur when Ruth spoke of her intention to visit Naomi. In truth, no one cared much if Ruth remained in the house or left it for hours, so long as she fulfilled her endless list of duties.

Ruth enjoyed the walk to Naomi's house. The streets were empty save for a few children lingering late to play one last game before being called home. It was her favorite time of day, just before twilight when the world became more still, when the intense bustle of the day drew to a close and the noise of the rushing crowds ceased.

The sycamore door to Naomi's house stood open, revealing one narrow room, the only chamber that the house boasted. The high lattice windows had been thrown open, allowing the pale, dying rays of the sun into the chamber, giving the place a cheery look. A few handwoven mats covered most of the bare, earthen floor, and two cushions with faded weaving sat against the far wall. A cluttered cleanliness marked the small space.

Ruth felt an odd peace as Naomi welcomed her inside. She could not explain it. But here, in this stranger's home, she felt more settled than she ever had in the house where she had spent her whole life.

Naomi took her hand and drew her farther into the chamber. "Aren't you tall? I have to tip my head back to look into your eyes."

Ruth bit her lip and lowered her face. Her height had been a source of unrelenting shame since she had turned ten and, without warning, grown into a pole. She managed to be taller than everyone in her family, even her father. Her sisters tormented her with names like *tree trunk* and *rooftop*.

Naomi gasped. "Oh my dear, I meant it as praise. You are like a willow, soft and full of grace. In Israel, tall women are much admired."

Then I should have been born in Israel. But she swallowed the words.

"Sit down here, dear Ruth. The cushions have gone flat, I'm afraid."

Ruth sat, tucking her feet up to the side of her hip, arranging her loose tunic to cover her toes. "They are very comfortable."

"My sons aren't home from the field yet. They leave early and return late. Poor lads. Their work is hard. We'll eat when they come. Do you like lentils?"

"My favorite," Ruth said, as if she didn't have to eat them every day. "May I help you with the bread?" Before Naomi could respond, she rose to go to her. Naomi was making cakes of dough with ground barley flour, and after rinsing her hands with water, Ruth took a large handful to knead.

"Such light flour," she said, allowing admiration to color her voice. She knew the effort it took to grind the barley grain into a fine powder. With Naomi the sole female occupant of her house, she could not share the burden of grinding with another woman, which would allow her to use a larger, more efficient hand mill.

Naomi smiled. "I fear I'm vain when it comes to my cooking. So if you want to win my heart, you've started on the right foot."

Another compliment? Ruth was losing count of them. She looked down and kneaded harder.

"The stone is hot. As soon as Mahlon and Chilion return home, we will bake the bread, so we can have hot barley cakes with our soup. Won't they be surprised to see you?"

Ruth gave Naomi a sharp look from under her lashes. "So you don't bring the daughters of Moab to supper every day?"

The older woman dissolved into peals of laughter. She wiped a hand against her cheek, leaving a white trail. "Not every day, no. But a woman with two unmarried young sons can't sit about doing nothing. The boys toil in the fields of their master most of the day long. What chance have they of meeting eligible young women?"

Eligible young women? Unmarried sons? What had she entangled herself in? Ruth swallowed a deep breath and pointed to Naomi's face. "You have flour smudged on your cheek."

Naomi lifted a cloth to wipe away the smudge of flour.

"I don't think this will work." Ruth tried to keep the panic out of her voice. The thought of meeting two strange men for the express purpose of being weighed as a possible bride turned her stomach into a big knot. They would only reject her. "Perhaps I should go home." She started to wipe her hands on the cloth next to her when the sound of conversation made her freeze mid-swipe. She frowned as she heard a feminine voice, softly responding to a man's comment.

The older woman spun toward the open door, her hands fluttering in the air.

"Mother, we have brought you a guest," said the shorter of the two young men. "This is Orpah. We met her at the field and asked her to supper. She . . . She . . ." His voice trailed as he spotted Ruth.

Naomi broke the tension by bursting into peals of laughter. "The Lord be praised. I have also asked my friend Ruth to supper. What a blessed night, to have two new friends join us."

Ruth gulped. It would be offensive to leave now. She would have to stay and see the evening through. At least the other girl, Orpah, would share the burden of attention. She was a pretty girl, no older than seventeen, with rounded cheeks and thick, long black lashes.

They sat on the floor around a well-used mat to eat supper. When Naomi introduced her sons, Ruth did not even lift her chin far enough to see which name belonged to whom. She busied herself with dipping her warm bread into the bowl of aromatic lentils and listened carefully to the conversation flowing around her.

Her attention strayed to Orpah as the girl fanned her face. "I can't abide the heat. This afternoon, I thought my head would bake in my headdress and drop right into the field. That would have been a mess. Knowing the foreman, he would have made me clean it up myself."

Ruth laughed, her outstretched hand forgotten where she had moved to dip her bread into the olive oil. To her surprise, her fingers bumped into solid flesh. She raised startled eyes and collided with a warm brown gaze.

Chapter Two

A friend loves at all times.
PROVERBS 17:17

His skin shone pale as bleached ivory against his dark beard. It was his smile that first caught Ruth's attention. His mouth, too wide for beauty, softened his otherwise ordinary face into the sort of friendliness that made her feel welcomed to the soles of her feet. As if she had known him for years. And she could not even tell his name! Mahlon or Chilion?

Guessing her thoughts, he said, "Mahlon."

With a sudden jolt, she found herself wanting to giggle. "I was going to guess Chilion," she confessed.

"I forgive you. Which is generous of me, considering when we were introduced, you disdained to look upon me even once."

"I thought it polite not to stare."

"Don't worry. I did enough staring for us both."

Ruth felt the rhythm of her pulse speed, making her breathless. "I don't think your mother has the measure of you."

The wide mouth flashed another winsome smile. "How so?"

Ruth nibbled on her lower lip, caught between laughter and embarrassment. "She believes you are helpless and lonesome. I think you know your way around many a Moabite maiden's heart."

He shook his head, looking tragic. "I hardly know any Moabite maidens."

"How many?"

"Counting you and Orpah? Two."

Chilion, overhearing his brother, shoved a shoulder into his brother's arm. "Not for lack of trying."

Naomi and Mahlon walked Ruth most of the way home. They finally turned back when she pressed them, just before she arrived at her house. As the outdoor enclosure of her home came into view, Ruth could hear the screech of her mother's raised voice. Frowning, she picked up her steps. Though her mother's temper bore a legendary sting, it rarely grew so noisy as to rouse the interest of the neighbors.

She shoved open the door, which someone had had the forethought to close. A wave of nausea pressed in on her as the scene inside unfolded.

Her mother was screaming, midsentence, " . . . and cannot abide it one more day. You are a disgusting old man. What is the matter with you? Why won't Chemosh strike you down?"

Her grandfather stood with his head bowed, his sparse lashes lowered. His fragile hand, resting against the wall, trembled so hard that Ruth could hear the sound of his flesh beating a rhythm against the mud brick in spite of her mother's thundering voice. On the back of his old tunic ran a long, wet stain, extending from below his waist to mid-thigh.

"You stink, old man! You're reeking up my house."

For an infinitesimal moment, Grandfather lifted his eyes. They were clear and filled with so much shame, Ruth stopped breathing. She wanted to beat her head against the wall. Of all the times for him to regain self-awareness!

"I'll clean him, Mother." She tried to inject a soothing tone into her soft voice. "It's all right. I will take care of him."

"You! What do you know about it, an unmarried girl?"

"I'll manage. You're tired. Rest. Leave him to me."

For a moment the older woman seemed disconcerted. She smoothed back her hair, once. Twice. "It's not my fault. He drives me to it. Worse than a baby, he's become. And with your father never home to give a hand, everything lands on me."

"I'll take care of him," Ruth whispered again, and took her grandfather by the hand and drew him outside, grabbing a towel, pitcher of water, basin, and a fresh tunic on her way. No one else offered to help. They never did. Her sisters had no interest in an old man who had little to offer them save exasperation and extra labor. Their mother, protective of them in a way she never had been of Ruth, did not insist that they help with Grandfather. They had their chores, of course. Sewing, mending, cooking, and washing. Lighter work compared to Ruth that left their hands soft and feminine, free of the calluses that plagued Ruth's palms.

She was grateful for the lengthening darkness, which gave her work a semblance of modesty. "I'm sorry, Grandfather," she said. But to her relief, the old man had retreated into his shadow world again. After cleaning and changing him, Ruth took him back into the house and helped him to lie down on his mat. She covered him with his old cloak and returned outside to wash his tunic with lye.

That night as she lay sleepless on her mat, the discordant snores of her sisters filling the hot chamber, Ruth thought of Naomi's welcoming manner and Mahlon's encompassing smile. It occurred to her that if Grandfather lived with *them,* they would treat him with kindness. They would seek to comfort him as he grew increasingly lost in the twilight of his waning mind.

Instinctively, she knew that Naomi would bear the burden of a man who had become so much less than himself. And Mahlon would not run away to avoid the unpleasantness of it, as her father did. He would not hide in the fields, seeking the excuse of work as a way to shirk the hardship of caring for an aging parent. Life with Naomi's family would be very different from her experience in her own home.

Ruth pushed the thought aside. It was an impossible dream. *The only thing I ever wanted was to belong.* She sighed, and buried the rising tide of that impractical longing as best she could.

For the next five days, she had little time to dwell on dreams. Grandfather took a turn for the worse, and she spent every spare moment trying to make him comfortable, trying to lift some of the weight of his care from her mother's exasperated shoulders. On the sixth day, close to the noon hour, an unexpected knock on the open door arrested everyone's attention.

Naomi stood near the entrance, her pleasant face wreathed in a tentative smile. "Peace," she called out. "I am Naomi. I have come to ask after Ruth."

Ruth ran to the door. "Naomi! Come in. How good of you to come."

She shook her head, remaining outside. "I won't intrude. You seem busy. I have brought your mother a fresh loaf of bread to thank her for allowing you to visit us."

"How thoughtful." Ruth took the cloth containing the still warm loaf. The aroma of freshly baked wheat made her mouth water. "I doubt the pharaoh of Egypt has bread so fine. Won't you come inside and meet my family?"

Naomi's gaze met with a frosty reception from the mistress of the house, who was crouching by the indoor fire, stirring an old pot while coldly surveying the scene before her. "Another day, perhaps," she said.

"My grandfather has been very ill. I have had no time to visit again."

"I am so sorry to hear it. Looking after a sick relative can be a heartache. But it can be a comfort too, knowing that you can help carry a little of their burden in their time of need."

"Thank you. And for this, also," Ruth said, holding out the bread. "I know my family will enjoy your baking as I did."

"Come back and tarry with us when you can."

As soon as Naomi left, Ruth's mother pulled her to the side. "That woman does not hail from Moab. Not with that bumpkin accent. Where is she from?"

"Bethlehem of Judah, in Israel."

"Israel? Have you lost your mind, running about with those people? They are backward, Ruth, and worship a strange God no one but they understand. More importantly, did you see her clothes? Ragged as a beggar's. I don't want my daughter associating with such people."

"She is kind." Ruth's words came out stiff as a wooden plank. "She sent you this bread."

Her mother rolled her eyes and turned away.

Every day after that, Naomi made the time to visit Ruth, always with a present in hand: a cake of raisins, a small earthenware pot of pickled capers, an armful of wild onions, loaves of barley bread. At first she refused to enter. Although she did not say so, Ruth knew that the Israelite woman could sense her mother's hostility. In time, her mother was softened by Naomi's persistent generosity, and while she did not descend into true hospitality, she did invite her in. The older woman's visits became so regular that no one save Ruth paid her much heed anymore.

Naomi would bide with Ruth next to Grandfather, sometimes in comforting silence, sometimes sharing fascinating memories from her native land.

"It's true," she told them one late afternoon. "Once, long before my time, a woman ruled in Israel. Her name was Deborah."

Ruth, who had learned that the Israelites had no king or prince, sucked on her lower lip. "A *woman* reigned over you?"

"She proved herself one of our best judges. We had forty years of unbroken peace thanks to her wisdom. She would sit under her palm tree in Ephraim and help people resolve their conflicts."

"What if there had been war? How could she have coped?"

"War did come. Jabin, king of Canaan, had cruelly oppressed the Israelites for twenty years, and the commander of his army, Sisera, remained undefeated. He had nine hundred chariots fitted with iron, if you can imagine such a wonder. Who could stand against that army?

"Then Deborah, who was a prophet as well as a judge, heard

from the Lord concerning the hardship of our people. God wanted Barak, the head of Israel's army, to go up against Sisera. It was time for Israel to vanquish its enemies. Do you know what Barak said?"

"*What?*" Grandfather cried without warning. Ruth and Naomi stared at each other with round eyes.

Naomi cleared her throat. "Barak said he would go, but only if Deborah went into battle with him."

"A mouse?" Grandfather interjected.

Ruth and Naomi looked about them, alarmed.

"Or a man?" Grandfather continued.

"Oh, you mean Barak?" Naomi laughed. "A cross between the two, I imagine. This war required faith. Faith that the Lord had more power than the iron chariots of Canaan. Faith that God could overcome in the midst of an impossible situation. Deborah had enough faith to cover Barak's lack. She told him that she would certainly go. But she also foretold that he would lose the highest honor in spite of winning the victory."

"She rode into war?" Ruth's voice came out high. "What happened?"

"Deborah didn't actually fight in the battle, but she went with the army and gave them the confidence of her faith. Sure enough, as God had promised, Israel routed Sisera's army in spite of his nine hundred unconquerable chariots."

"That's an astounding victory. Did she offer a great sacrifice to the Lord? One of her children, perhaps?"

Naomi's face scrunched as if she had drunk sour milk and desperately wanted to spit it out. "We don't sacrifice humans in Israel. Life belongs to the Lord. It is not for us to destroy."

Ruth gave a slow nod of her head. "You serve a merciful God."

"Yes. Thankfully."

"Tell me, what became of Sisera and Barak?"

"In the midst of the melee, Sisera managed to flee on foot. His heart must have brimmed with relief when he made it unharmed to the tent of a woman named Jael. Sisera imagined himself safe, surviving to fight another day, because Jael's absent husband was on friendly terms with King Jabin. But he miscalculated. Exhausted, he fell asleep, and Jael killed him with a tent peg. So you see, the great commander lost his life to a woman, and Barak lost the glory of vanquishing his greatest enemy."

"So Deborah prevailed?"

"She did. The name of Deborah lives on for all generations as a woman raised up by the Lord to deliver our people."

"Your God used a woman to fulfill His plans for your people?"

"You never know who the Lord will use. Perhaps one day, it will be you, Ruth."

Ruth chuckled. "Not unless He is very desperate. By the sound of Him, I don't believe He is. What do you think, Grandfather?"

"The Lord," he said.

"Yes indeed," Naomi said, giving a broad grin of approval.

The interaction seemed to have exhausted the old man and before long he had sunk into a deep sleep.

The next day, Ruth rose before sunrise to fetch water. The well, located an hour's brisk walk from their house, would congest with long lines of chattering women later in the morning. To avoid the lines—and the crowd—Ruth had grown accustomed to awakening early each day, and arriving at the well when most women were just rising out of bed.

She drew water into her large clay pot, grunting as she swung the heavy jar over and up to settle snugly against her slender hip. She had performed this chore so often since childhood that she could manage it with a wool blindfold.

Her mind roamed as she walked home. She thought of the chores that still awaited her: weeding and tending the garden, making bread for the evening meal, washing the floor mats, which had grown dusty with use. No doubt her mother had more work in store for her as well.

She wondered if she would be able to sneak a few raisins to her grandfather with his noonday meal. He had slept through the night without having an accident. Ruth could not help but feel that Naomi's visits had somehow helped the old man.

After washing the mats and sweeping the floor, Ruth turned to the hard work of helping her mother grind flour in the hand mill. When she finished, she checked on Grandfather and found that he had dragged in mud all over the newly washed mats. She groaned and threw her grandfather a vexed glance where he lay in the corner of the room. Bending, she started to wipe the mats clean again before her mother saw the mess and lost the last of her patience.

In truth, on occasion, even Ruth found it a challenge to contend with Grandfather's unintended disarray. Love alone tethered her frustration and made bearable the numerous inadvertent blunders of the old man, which increased her already heavy workload. She cherished him too much to give in to anger. Because of that love, her heart never grew cold and resentful toward him the way her mother's had done.

At noon, not only was Ruth able to bring Grandfather a small pile of raisins, but she also managed to fill his bowl with an extra portion of lentil stew, skimmed from her own share.

As she placed the raisins in Grandfather's hand, the old man turned and looked full into her eyes. "My beautiful Ruth," he mumbled and patted her cheek. "I missed you."

Ruth felt her throat tighten. "Oh, Grandfather. I love you so dearly."

The old man stuffed all the raisins in his mouth at once. "Good!" he declared after he had swallowed them.

Ruth wiped a thin rivulet of spittle from the side of his chin. "Sweet, aren't they?"

A gnarled hand rested on her head for a fleeting moment. "Like you."

Grandfather had not spoken so many clear words together in months. Ruth swallowed tears of joy. He was improving.

"Naomi will come and visit you this evening. Perhaps she will tell us more amusing stories."

"The Lord," Grandfather said.

"Yes!" Ruth felt a smile rise up from deep inside. "She will tell us stories about the Lord. Now, would you like me to tell you about Chemosh?"

"The Lord," he said again. He laid his head against her shoulder. "My Ruth."

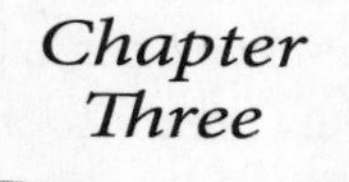

Chapter Three

Even if my father and mother abandon me,
The LORD will hold me close.
PSALM 27:10

The next morning Grandfather did not wake up at his usual time. Nor could they shake him out of his slumber. The sleep deepened. Lengthened. Lasted from sunrise to sunset and back around again.

And dissolved into death.

Ruth felt like someone had stolen the ground from under her feet. Her heart had turned into a gaping hole. Grandfather had seemed well toward the end, speaking so tenderly that she had convinced herself he was improving.

Instead, those words had been his final declaration of love and approbation. He had risen out of the ashes of his illness for one last blessing. A bittersweet goodbye.

She felt lonelier for him than she had thought possible. She had been losing him for years, bit by precious bit. His death should have been easy to bear in the circumstances. But she found herself missing even the shell, missing the hope of catching a momentary glimpse of his true nature flash out like lightning, fast and powerful. Now there would not even be a glimpse.

Mahlon and Chilion accompanied their mother to pay their respects to Ruth and her family. Mahlon looked at Ruth with eyes so warm they felt like the comfort of a fire in the dead of winter.

"Come and see us soon," he said. "Come and see me."

Ruth drew a perspiring hand against her sash. All her sisters had gathered in the house. Her eldest married sister, doe eyes darkened with kohl, moved about with her lush hips swinging languidly, serving guests honey-soaked bread. To her surprise, Mahlon's gaze never strayed her way. He kept his attention on Ruth as if no one else existed in the world. It was a new experience for Ruth to be in the same room with her eldest sister—any of her sisters—and take precedence. They were so much prettier than she was that they left no room for her to be seen. Except by Mahlon and Naomi.

She gave a quick nod. "I'll come when I can."

Ruth found a refuge in Naomi's house. Often, after her duties at home came to an end, she made the familiar trek to the Israelite woman's home. Together, they would weave or bake as they chatted until the men arrived. Sometimes Orpah would join them, and the evening would pass in pleasant conversation.

Having so recently been touched by death, Ruth grew curious about Naomi's loss.

"Do you still miss your husband?" she asked one afternoon.

Naomi twirled her spindle with mindless grace. "I will miss Elimelech all the days of my life. But the ache has become bearable. There are times I even forget it's there."

"I am glad he made you come to Moab."

"Sometimes I wonder if we made the right choice." Slender fingers worked the spindle. "House of Bread—that is what the name of our city means. But there was no bread to be found in Bethlehem. We could have lingered. Trusted the Lord for a miracle. Or taken the solution into our own hands.

"Elimelech was not a waiting man. He was strong and capable. He wanted to give our family the best. You never saw so much frustration in one man the year the famine hit Judah. All his effort availed nothing; what can you do to a land parched as the desert? You can work as hard as a young ox, but when the earth will not comply, your work comes to nothing. So we came."

Ruth twisted the wool and pulled. "Would you ever go back?"

"Not unless the Lord placed His foot on my backside and pushed. I loved Bethlehem, but moving was hard. I wouldn't want to go through that upheaval again.

"Some years ago, one of my back teeth festered. I've borne two sons; I know pain. And yet the torment of that little tooth made childbirth seem like a mild fever. It had to be pulled, of course. Such relief, to be rid of that throbbing agony! Would you believe, I still miss that tooth? Moving from Bethlehem felt like that. A great relief to walk away from the threat of starvation, and at the same time, a gaping hole, which nothing will fill. We are strangers in this land, and always will be."

The sound of heavy sandals announced the arrival of the men. Before long they had washed hands and feet and gathered to eat. Naomi had cooked barley stew, flavored with wild onion, garlic, and capers. They prayed before breaking bread. Ruth liked the sound of their prayers, full of thanksgiving and peace.

That night, as they walked back, Mahlon said under his breath so that only Ruth could hear, "I wish you didn't have to leave ever again. I wish you could live with us. With me."

Ruth gulped and sent him a searching look from under her lashes. She was not in love with him the way her sisters spoke of love. Her heart didn't race in his company, nor did she daydream of him every spare moment. But he drew her like a shepherd's fire on a freezing desert night. It wasn't Mahlon alone. It was the whole family. Naomi and her caring ways, the considerations she offered without a second thought. The way the brothers looked out for each other. The lack of jealousy. The presence of easy affection that washed over the walls of the little house like scented oil.

Being with Naomi's family was like an antidote to the bitterness of her own relations.

"You are silent. Do you not feel the same?" Mahlon asked, his voice hushed with strain.

"I beg your pardon. I didn't mean to ignore you. I'm not good with words."

"I think you are. True, you are parsimonious with your speech. But when you say something, it's always worth hearing. I like that about you. No needless chatter that would exhaust a man to death."

Ruth adjusted her veil, which had slipped to the back of her head. "Now I'm sure to keep my mouth closed in fear of exhausting you."

Mahlon laughed. "And here I thought I had given you high praise."

They walked a few more steps. He said, head bent, "May I send my mother to your parents? To ask for your hand?"

Ruth's mouth fell open. She thought of Grandfather—the only person in her family who had truly cared for her, gone from her forever. What had she left in her house? What tethered her to the family that bore her? Without a word, she nodded.

"A small dowry and one less mouth to feed. What more do you want, woman?" Ruth's father screamed. The sisters had been sent out of the house to allow their parents privacy. They hadn't gone far. Finding a spot as close to the open windows as possible, all the girls, including Ruth, strained to hear the conversation.

The fact that Ruth had a suitor had thrown the whole household into chaos. Her unmarried older sisters found it incomprehensible that anyone should want to marry their pole of a sister. Her mother found the identity of the prospective bridegroom an affront to her dignity and ambition. To Ruth's relief, her father seemed quite happy at the arrangement.

"A man worthy of our name," her mother said loud enough for everyone to hear. Ruth winced. She knew that her mother's greed for better connections would put an end to her hope of becoming Mahlon's bride.

"The last time we had one of those for your eldest daughter, I had to mortgage everything but my beard to pay the dowry. This one suits me well. He doesn't ask for much and he says he loves her."

"Love! He may not expect a large dowry, but what manner of bridal price will he give you?"

"He has agreed to serve in my fields one whole day each week for five years. With no sons of my own, I can use his help. Sufficient bride price, if you ask me."

"He is from the backwaters of Israel! No connections. No money. No advantage. We shall lose our standing with such a man for a son-in-law."

"The first one you chose will make up for it. That one has enough high and mighty relations to please your requirements. He preens about like he owns half of Moab. I have yet to see much good come of it. It's been a hard year, woman. If we are not careful, we will lose this bit of roof over our heads and my father's land besides. Perhaps we can find another fine husband when it comes to your other daughters. Chemosh has blessed us with enough of them."

Ruth's betrothal lasted nine months, long enough for her grandfather's mourning year to be completed. Mahlon and Chilion used the time to build two tiny additions to their home—more alcoves than rooms—where they could bring their brides, for Orpah had also pledged to marry Chilion.

Ruth's excitement at the prospect of living with her new family grew with every hour. At home, she only encountered criticism. Everyone seemed quick to point out her faults. At the house of her betrothed, she found extravagant, undeserving approval.

"You are so beautiful," Mahlon told her the night he held her hand for the first time.

"I am not." Ruth knotted her brows, wanting to reassure him that she needed no empty praise. Mahlon looked at her as if she had six toes and fingers.

"I have never seen a more beautiful woman. Hair the color of chestnuts, eyes like ripe wheat, like gold, like a lioness."

Ruth giggled.

"I mean it. You are more graceful than Chemosh's dancers."

"How would you know? You never worship at his temple."

He pressed her hand tighter. "I may have caught a glimpse here or there. Anyway, that is not the point."

"The point is that you exaggerate."

Naomi proved no better. She praised Ruth's figure. She praised her ruddy, clear skin. She praised her gardening skills. She praised her weaving. She even praised her handling of the goat.

One evening, before the men returned from the field, Ruth told Naomi, "When Grandfather died, my heart broke. I had truly thought there would be a miracle and he would be healed. He seemed so much better toward the end. But do you know, I would never have agreed to marry Mahlon if Grandfather had lingered with us. I would have wanted to stay at home and take care of him. It's as if he knew that, and by leaving this world, he gave me the gift of a new family. A family that loves me."

Naomi enfolded Ruth in a warm embrace, before drawing back and patting her cheek. "If God spared us from the piercing shaft of every sorrow," she said, "we could never fulfill His best plans for our lives. Sometimes the sweetest things in life rise up out of the worst things in life."

During the nine months of her betrothal, Ruth felt like she lived half on top of a mountain and half at the bottom of a pit. She would be lifted high to the heavens in Naomi's household and plunged to the depths when she returned to her family. It only served to show how blessed she was to have found this woman and her sons. To have been chosen by them. When she thought of marriage, Ruth didn't dream of time alone with Mahlon. She dreamt of being with all her new family.

On her wedding day, she prayed to the Lord for the first time.

She felt she owed Him for the gift of this family from Bethlehem in Judah. She owed Him for allowing her to have one of His sons. She promised Him, even though He wasn't *her* Lord, never to let them down, no matter what life brought to their door. For the unstinting love they had shown her, they deserved unbroken loyalty. With a brimming heart, she pledged that loyalty for all the days of her life.

Alone at last in the bridal bower, Mahlon removed the garland of pink and white lilies from Ruth's head and slipped off the heavy veil that covered her face. "I have married a queen," he breathed, and kissed her for the first time.

She tensed until her body ached. Now she would have to face Mahlon's horrified disappointment. He didn't understand. Other women had proper curves; she just had hints. If one tried really hard, one might see the slight suggestion of a curve here and there. But she didn't possess the cushiony softness so valued in women.

"I've wanted you like this, in my arms, since the first moment I saw you," he said, and said nothing more as kisses took the place of words. To her surprise, he seemed far from disappointed. He acted as though someone had handed him the throne of a wealthy nation.

Ruth lay awake in her bridegroom's arms until the sun rose the next morning. For the first time in eighteen years, she knew bone deep that she belonged. She belonged to this family. The desire of her heart had come to pass.

With a hurried hand, Ruth dashed away tears. Her time of the month was upon her. Again. For the fifty-first time since her marriage. No baby for her and Mahlon. Although happy with her husband, the blight of barrenness diminished her joy. The grief of it twisted in her heart like a knife whose edge never grew dull.

Not one word of blame passed Mahlon's lips to torment her for the emptiness of her womb. Month after month of disappointment, and he loved her with the same tenderness he had shown the first night she came to him.

Nor had Naomi condemned her for her failure by look or gesture.

She soothed Ruth's worries as if she were her true mother and not a disappointed mother-in-law.

It was a sorrow she shared with Orpah, who also had not conceived. Some nights, after the men were fed and the dishes cleaned, the two young women drew into the yard and wept together.

On the first anniversary of her marriage, Ruth visited the temple of Chemosh to ask the god of her people for the gift of fertility. She went alone without telling Naomi or Mahlon, knowing they would disapprove. But desperation had already set in, making her willing to face their displeasure, if only it meant that she could have a child.

She found it hard to even enter the temple, for crowds swelled all the way down the hill where the temple was built. Young men had climbed the trees for a better view.

"What's happening?" Ruth asked one of them. "Why are there so many people here?"

"Haven't you heard? The king is sacrificing one of his younger sons to Chemosh. Last year, a debilitating disease afflicted him, and he feared death would come for him. He promised the life of the prince to Chemosh if he spared the king's life. The king recovered his health, so they are going to throw the prince into the fire today as an offering."

Ruth knew of such sacrifices. Of course she knew. They happened, though not with everyday frequency. But she had never been present at one. Since living with an Israelite family and being exposed to their horror of human sacrifice, she had unconsciously begun to absorb their deep-rooted disgust at the idea. What kind of god demanded the death of a human being in order to be appeased? Could mercy be bought with murder? A better life with death?

"You've come on a good day," the young man sitting on the branch of an acacia tree informed her. "After the sacrifice of the young prince, Chemosh will be in a generous mood."

Ruth pressed a hand against her heart. Even if Chemosh would condescend to give her a child, would she be able to look upon her baby's face without the constant reminder of this fire? Ruth turned around and went home.

She never returned to Chemosh's temple. To her surprise, the cessation of the worship she had known since childhood was no loss. In a house constantly filled with references to a merciful God whose love endured, Ruth had no lack of worship.

Now, dabbing away the last of her tears, Ruth took in a shaking breath. "Lord, for Mahlon and Naomi's sake, please bless my womb."

A week passed. Life went on; Ruth's disappointed hopes made no difference to the rising of the moon and the setting of the sun. One evening, while busy building up the fire, Ruth heard the sound of muffled voices on the path outside. Mahlon and Chilion came in, their steps dragging. Ruth rushed to greet her husband. Even the waning light could not hide the pallor of his face. The hollows beneath his eyes looked as dark as fat grapes.

For over four years he had worked without ceasing every single day of the week—six days to support his family, and one free day on her father's property to pay off her bride price. Exhaustion coiled about him like a serpent intent on swallowing him whole.

Ruth washed his hands and feet, her hands tender as she dried each calloused finger. "Come and rest on the cushion. Lean against the wall and close your eyes for a moment. I will fetch your supper."

Mahlon smiled and did as she bid him. The smile sat like a shadow on his wide mouth, a ghost of his former brightness. Everything about Mahlon had dimmed. Everything but love.

"Have you been practicing your Hebrew today?" he asked when she returned. He had been teaching her to read and write. The Moabite and Hebrew languages shared the same root and had many words in common. But Ruth had never learned to read. With wild extravagance, when Mahlon perceived how much his wife enjoyed learning, he bought parchment so that she could practice her writing.

"I am so well-versed, Naomi says I speak better Hebrew than you."

Mahlon's smile deepened. "She is probably right."

"She is definitely right."

Ruth placed a bowl of stew before him, but he waved a hand. "I have no appetite. Bed, for me." He tried to rise, then doubled over, a hand to his belly, gasping.

"Mahlon!" Rushing to his side, Ruth reached out to support him. His forehead felt clammy under her fingertips. "You are feverish."

He shook his head, sinking back to the floor. "Nothing to worry about. It's the hard rains. A few of the workers plowing have come down with fever and cramps. Chilion has it too."

"Then you must stay home tomorrow and rest until it passes."

"Tomorrow is your father's day, Ruth. He counts on me. I will not go back on my word."

"You can make it up later, husband. You need to regain your strength."

Mahlon waved a hand and laid his head back against the wall. Ruth let out an exasperated breath. Naomi came in from the garden and cast a worried glance in her son's direction.

"He is sick," Ruth said, hoping to enlist her mother-in-law's help. "Chilion too."

Naomi clucked her tongue and knelt by her son. "This comes of not keeping the Sabbath holy for four years."

"We would go hungry if I did. You know that, Mother."

"You have too much of your father in you, my son. You're such a good man, but you take the responsibility of the world upon your shoulders. You think it's all up to you. The Lord would provide. But you take it upon yourself, and give no room to faith."

They gave Mahlon and Chilion honey and an infusion of herbs to help with the pain, and tucked them into their sleeping mats. The remedy did not help. Mahlon spent half the night vomiting with such force, the small vessels beneath his eyes burst, leaving red, pinprick bruises.

By morning both men were breathless from unceasing cramps; fever raged through them. Mahlon lost his ability to control his bowels. Any liquid they poured into him seemed to pour out faster. Ruth turned ashen when she found the mattress beneath her husband scarlet with blood.

As Ruth wiped Mahlon's dry skin with an infusion of rosemary to try and lower his body temperature, he opened unfocused eyes. "My beautiful queen."

Ruth shook her head, trying to summon a smile. "You are delirious."

He tried to lift a hand, but it flopped back to his side. "You have been the joy of my life, Ruth. The Lord blessed me the day I met you."

Instead of making her happy, his words spread fear through Ruth. They sounded like a tender man's final farewell.

Ruth's father, indignant with anger, came to inquire why Mahlon had not shown up at the field. "He still owes me several months of work. I hope he isn't growing forgetful of his debts."

It was the first time he had visited his daughter's home. Ruth resisted the urge to slam the door in his face. "He is too sick to work."

Her father rolled his eyes. "It had to happen on *my* day."

Chapter Four

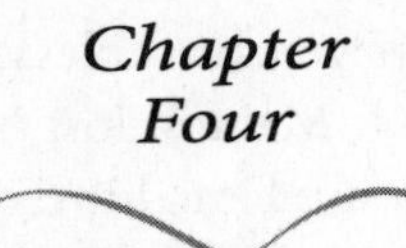

And he went out, not knowing where he was going.
HEBREWS 11:8

Chilion died after battling the fever for five days. They laid him in the ground while still nursing his brother. Mahlon lasted a week.

Ruth reeled, stunned into a grief too deep for tears. In the span of one week, her world had shattered.

All I have left is an empty womb and a full grave. She knew that was bitterness and grief talking, but right then, she didn't have the strength to hold on to hope.

Naomi could not even help in the burial arrangements. She sat in a dark corner, staring at nothing, silent for endless days. It was as if grief had burned through her words, leaving behind ashes. Ruth and Orpah forced her to eat and drink enough to stay alive. But the woman they loved disappeared into the pit of her sorrow.

Dreams plagued Ruth. Beautiful dreams. Dreams of Mahlon alive and laughing, holding her, speaking to her. When she awakened from these false joys and remembered that her husband was under the earth, rotting, it made her mourning even more wrenching. His warm mouth would never whisper against her skin again. It made her want to scream until her voice, like all her dreams for children, died with Mahlon. Then she would remember Naomi and force herself to go on. Her mother-in-law needed her.

One morning Ruth awoke to find Naomi folded into herself on the ground, staring at nothing. In the course of mere weeks, her vibrant face had creased with lines, shrunken and aged with incomprehensible grief. Ruth whispered her name, but she made no response, unaware of her daughter-in-law's presence. Desperate with fear, Ruth shouted the older woman's name. Would she lose this woman who had become her mother? She could not survive another such loss!

Out of desperation, she cried out to Naomi's God. *Lord, help her! Help Your daughter Naomi.*

The dark eyes blinked and came into focus. "Ruth?"

The younger woman dissolved into loud tears and held on to the only person who anchored her to the world of men and sanity. Naomi joined her tears to hers. She said no more, but she did not sink back into the pit that had almost taken her from the realm of the living.

After that, Ruth prayed to the Lord with increasing frequency. It wasn't a calculated, well-examined decision. She gave it no thought. She made no conscious change of allegiance in her faith. She just clung blindly to the One who seemed to bring her a strange kind of relief.

On the sixth week after the burials, they started to run out of provisions, and the young women had to go into the fields to work. The owner of the field knew them because their husbands had labored for him many years. Out of pity, he hired them to work alongside his other female workers. He wanted to clear a new field for the next season of planting, and add irrigation canals, which would allow his land to get the most out of the seasonal rains. Laborious and unending, the work of removing stones, pulling out brush, and digging canals stretched their strength to its limit.

At the conclusion of their first day, when they returned home, they found that Naomi had roused herself to cook them barley stew. It was watery, lacking salt and the herbs that the older woman normally used with expertise. No bread accompanied the modest meal. But this tasteless stew came as an offering of love from a woman whose grief had paralyzed every impulse toward activity.

Ruth and Orpah ate their meal, knowing it had taken a valiant effort for their mother-in-law to rise above so much pain and perform the mundane tasks of every day.

"When Elimelech made us leave Bethlehem, it was to give us a better life," Naomi said after they finished eating.

Ruth's mouth opened slightly. It was the first time Naomi had spoken a full sentence since the loss of her two sons. She gave a nod of encouragement, hoping the older woman would continue.

"He came to Moab to save our lives. He came to protect us from starvation and death. And what has happened? My husband is dead. My sons are dead. And we stand on the brink of starvation, for how are three lonely women to make a way in this world? He brought us to Moab to save us. Instead, we have met our doom here."

Ruth leaned forward and caressed Naomi's arm. "We'll take care of each other. You aren't alone. You have Orpah and me."

Naomi turned her face away and sank back into silence.

Ruth pondered her mother-in-law's words. The irony of it cut like a sharpened scythe through heads of young wheat. The irony of a man who had made a hard decision in order to keep his family safe, only to lead them into death. Would they have lived safer lives if they had remained in Bethlehem?

For her part, Ruth could not regret Elimelech's decision. If not for the man's choice to abandon his home and his people, Ruth would not have met Naomi and her family. She would not have known the happiest years of her life, or experienced genuine love and acceptance.

Week followed week. Orpah and Ruth worked hard, but at the end of each day, they brought home barely enough to see them through the day. They needed more savings to provide for the approaching months between harvest and plowing, when there would be little opportunity for work. They used their meager spare time to plant their own garden with vegetables and herbs that would augment their table. Harvest season approached. Perhaps they would be able to increase their income then.

Naomi walked to the well to fetch water. With the girls gone most of the day, she had to force herself to do the urgent chores that could not be left undone. Most of the time, she wanted to remain on her pallet, buried under her cloak. She wanted to forget. What did food matter, or water? Her sons were gone. Why should she stay alive? But the Lord had left her to live while her children lay under the earth.

Ruth and Orpah were her only reason for living now. As the elder of the family, she was responsible for them. Sometimes she resented them for that unwanted responsibility. At other times, she clung to them not only for their own sakes but also because they were the only legacy left behind from her sons.

For the first time that morning, she noticed the fresh green leaves on the trees. It was as though she had slept through the waning winter months and missed the start of spring. Once home, she went through their stores and became aware that they would not survive long-term. Not with just two women working. She needed to join Ruth and Orpah in the field.

The next morning she rose and prepared herself before the young women were awake. Ruth came to a halt when she noticed her waiting by the door. "Naomi! Where are you going so early in the morning?"

Naomi took a calming breath. "I am coming with you to the field. You need my help."

"You are most welcome," Orpah, her practical daughter-in-law, said. "We can use an extra pair of hands."

Ruth bit her lip. Although she made no objection, Naomi could sense her concern. As they walked to the farm, she lingered near Naomi, her long-legged steps moving with the grace she did not realize she possessed, her hand waving insects away from Naomi's face.

In the field, Naomi worked alongside the girls. They had not gone far when she felt a stitch in her side. Sweat dripped from her brow. She moved slower than the other workers and found it impossible to keep up.

"Come, Mother," Ruth said. "Sit under the shade of this palm and rest. This is no work for you."

At first, Naomi resisted Ruth's pleas. Then she realized that she would collapse and be more trouble than help, and gave in. She felt useless. Why did God leave her on this earth? She was of no benefit to anyone, more bother than blessing.

By midday, the other workers joined her. Some had brought a modest repast, which they enjoyed while speaking to one another companionably.

"I beg your pardon," Naomi whispered as she knocked against someone's arm by accident.

A portly woman with carefully plucked eyebrows turned to her. "You are Mahlon and Chilion's mother, aren't you? I heard of their deaths. I am sorry."

Naomi nodded, not trusting her voice.

"Will you go back to Bethlehem now that they expect such a rich harvest?"

"Do they? I had not heard."

"My cousin traveled through there last week. He said Bethlehem is enjoying unusual abundance this year. Grain is bursting out of the ground like weed. He walked through field after field of maturing barley and wheat. Better than anything he has ever seen in Moab, he said."

Naomi frowned. "The Lord must have visited His people," she said under her breath.

With sudden clarity, an image of Bethlehem came to her, the city peaceful when the dew descended, people preparing somnolently to go to work. She remembered the sound of prayer in the assembly, the smell of roasted grain picked fresh from the fields, the feel of friends' arms wrapped about her as they laughed at the day's absurdities. She remembered feeling at home. Feeling safe.

For the first time since losing her sons, something like a shaft of longing pierced her heart.

Ruth shook the mat before wiping it with a wet cloth. She was returning it to the chamber when Naomi said, "I think we should return to Bethlehem."

Ruth stumbled. "Pardon?"

"The Lord has blessed Judah with an abundant harvest. Why linger in Moab? Perhaps in Bethlehem He will see us through the winter. We leased this house and its land; it doesn't belong to our family. We can walk away and go back to my home."

Ruth sank to the floor. Her mouth turned so dry she could not swallow. Leave Moab. Abandon the only place she had ever known and go to Judah where she was an unwelcome stranger. The Israelites were not fond of Moabites, and Moabite women had a terrible reputation among them. Other than Naomi and Orpah, she would probably find herself ostracized.

"Whatever you wish, Naomi. We'll go to Judah." She forced her tongue to form the words for Naomi's sake.

Orpah, who had been a silent witness to the exchange, threw Ruth a horrified glance. Ruth gave her a reassuring nod. She could think of nothing to say that might bring her sister-in-law a measure of comfort.

After selling what they could, the three women piled their belongings into a dilapidated cart. Not much to show for three lifetimes. A few clothes, several clay jars of pickled capers, olive oil, salt, lentils and chickpeas, dates, three squares of sheep cheese, a reed basket filled with dried herbs, two flint knives, several skins of water and new wine. A handful of woven mats, frayed at the edges. A two-handled bronze saucepan, chipped bowls, rough wooden spoons, a small hand mill, a few odds and ends.

They had used the last of the wheat and barley to make bread for the journey. They didn't even have an extra pair of sandals between them. Ruth tied her headdress more securely around her head and tapped the old donkey on its skinny side. They would be fortunate if the beast did not keel over halfway to Judah.

Naomi had decided to travel on the road to Moab, a secondary highway that would take them through the southern tip of the Salt Sea, before bending northward toward Israel. For Ruth, who had never left Kir-hareseth's borders, the journey loomed like a threatening thundercloud, though it would likely last less than a week.

Naomi had told her that they would descend through the high hills of Moab, into the lowlands surrounding the Salt Sea. "It's a hard journey," she said. "We'll pass through some cities. But much of the road is barren and harsh."

The sun had yet to rise when the three women began their journey toward Bethlehem. Ruth and Orpah had taken leave of their families the day before. Ruth's goodbye had been brief; none of her sisters had even embraced her. Her parents had patted her shoulder with as much affection as they showed the family goat. They had kept their distance in the past four years, and now that she was a poor widow, they had even less interest in her.

Orpah had red-rimmed eyes that continued to shed fat tears as the donkey began to pull the cart. Leaving came harder to her. She loved Moab.

They would begin by traveling northwest to Bab edh-Dhra, in the opposite direction of their destination. The road to Moab bent in the shape of a horseshoe here, going first the wrong way, and then turning back downward, which made the descent through the hills easier. They intended to stop and rest at Bab edh-Dhra over the noonday hour, before journeying south to Numeira.

They had only traveled until the third hour of the day when Naomi came to a stop. Ruth halted the donkey's progress. Before she could ask Naomi why she had interrupted their journey, the older woman lifted up her hand.

"This is not right. You must return, both of you, to your mothers' house. Why come to Bethlehem with me where nothing good awaits you? No husband, no security, no certainty, no old friends. Stay in the land of your fathers."

Ruth's heart skipped a beat. With dumb incomprehension, she beheld her mother-in-law, nausea roiling in her belly.

If Naomi had any idea how Ruth felt, she gave no sign of it. Instead, she went on, her tone hard, brooking no argument.

"You girls are the most precious things I have left in this world. You have treated me well since the day I met you. May the Lord deal kindly with you, as you have dealt with my dear sons, and with me. Go, knowing that I do not take that kindness lightly. I'll cherish it as long as I have breath.

"But now you must return to your homes. May the Lord grant that you find rest, each of you, in the house of a new husband. May He give you men worthy of your sweetness."

She kissed Orpah on both cheeks and then turned to Ruth. Taking her face in calloused hands, she kissed her forehead, her cheeks, her hair. Her lips were dry, scratching where they touched. "My sweet daughters."

Ruth could no longer hold in her tears. She tried to swallow the sound of sobs, but they burst out of her with the bitterness of new grief. Naomi was casting her out. Naomi did not want her. Orpah, already grieved, added the sound of her own cries to Ruth. The donkey looked up at the women wailing on the side of the road and shook its head until the cords of its bridle swayed on either side of him.

"No!" Ruth cried. "This is wrong, Mother. We will return with you to your people. I would never abandon you."

Orpah nodded. "It is true. We owe you that duty."

Naomi shook her head. "You must turn back, my daughters. Why would you go with me? Can I provide for you? Give you new husbands? Do you think this old womb of mine could birth other sons who would grow up and take you to wife?"

Ruth gulped at the bitterness in Naomi's voice. "I don't want another husband."

"Don't be foolish, Ruth. How will you make your way in the world? You need a husband to provide for you. I am too old to marry again. And even if that were possible, and by some miracle I were to marry this very night and bear sons, then what? Would you wait for them to grow up and refuse to marry someone else until then?" Her voice had turned sour with sarcasm. "You can see how preposterous the idea of your coming with me is. I cannot care for you! You must part company with me, and go your own way."

"I would never part from you," Ruth cried. "You are the only good thing left to me."

Naomi sank to the side of the road as if her legs were too weak to support her. "It is bitter for me for your sakes that the Lord has raised His hand against me. I do not wish you to partake of *my* misfortune. You are both young. You can have a new life. A chance to have a future with children and families of your own. Why should you have to bear the weight of my hardships as well as your own?"

Orpah stepped forward. "This is what you want?"

Naomi nodded. "It is."

Orpah hesitated for just one moment. Then she leaned forward and kissed her mother-in-law the kiss of farewell. She turned to Ruth and embraced her in a similar fashion, saying in a hushed voice, "Goodbye, Ruth. I shall miss you every day." It took her only a moment to grab her meager belongings out of the cart. Then she began to walk, her steps rapid, moving her back toward Moab.

Ruth choked on her tears. Horrified, she turned to Naomi. Her beloved family had disintegrated. Only two of them left on a road that stretched in opposite directions. And Naomi did not want her.

Chapter Five

You brought me up from the grave, O Lord.
You kept me from falling into the pit of death.
PSALM 30:3

Ruth clung to Naomi, the way a tree clings to its root. Something pierced her heart when Naomi untangled herself from her grasp and stepped away. The donkey brayed and shook its head.

"Look," Naomi said. "Orpah is being sensible. She has made the right decision; she returns to her people and her gods. You do the same. Go back. Go back to your land and your gods. Go to what you know, Ruth. Be practical." At Ruth's silence she threw up her hands. "What do you want me to do? Hail a chariot to drive you back to Moab? Be sensible. Think of your gods. They cannot come with you."

Naomi's words had a strange effect on Ruth. Instead of convincing her, they cut her free from every doubt. Fear melted away as she considered what Naomi pressed upon her.

Her gods?

For over three years she had not stepped into the temple of Chemosh, nor worshiped any of the other gods of Canaan. For months now, her heart had been full of the Lord alone. Naomi raged against Him with the bitterness of one who felt betrayed. But Ruth saw Him as a source of kindness. Had He not brought her, a Moabite, to taste of goodness at the hands of Naomi and her family? Had He not given her the desire of her heart? To belong? Surely He had called her out of Moab. Surely, He had given her a new family. A new name. A new home. She belonged to Naomi now. And the Lord.

The road stretched before her, a mystery marked in sand. It held two different futures, two opposing destinies. Ruth knew which direction to face.

She took a deep breath and asked for wisdom to put these new feelings into words. Words that would penetrate Naomi's doubts. Words that would not fade through the passing of years.

"Dear Naomi, don't urge me to leave you. Don't press me to stop following you. For where you go, I will go. Where you stay, I will stay. Your people will be my people. Your God will be my God. I have chosen Him and I have chosen you. To you both, I belong.

"Where you die, I will die, and no one will return even my bones to Moab, for I belong to Israel now, and there I will be buried. May the Lord do so to me and more also if anything but death parts me from you, my dear mother."

Naomi took a deep breath and turned away. Ruth saw that rather than being pleased by her declaration of steadfast love, she had grown vexed. She feared too much for Ruth's future to enjoy her loyalty. That would change, Ruth promised herself.

The Lord God will help me. I will not be disgraced as Naomi fears. She set her face like flint and put one foot in front of another, heading toward Bethlehem.

By the fourth hour of the day, the temperature grew sweltering. The women pulled their veils over their faces to protect them against the dust that arose from the rutted terrain in an unending cloud. With determination, they pressed forward and pushed themselves beyond the point of exhaustion. They could not afford to be on the open road when night descended and had to arrive at a city in time to find shelter. Even though they traveled upon a busy thoroughfare, no roads were safe for two solitary women past nightfall.

Just before dusk they arrived at the walled settlement of Numeira, where they intended to spend the night at an inn. Until this point in their journey, as they had descended down the high cliffs of Kir-hareseth, they had traversed through bustling roads. But after leaving Numeira, they could no longer travel alone and would need to join a caravan for the sake of safety. Thieves abounded the lonely stretches of the Moab road. Many fell victim to the iron dagger of unscrupulous robbers.

Most of the money they had set aside from the sale of their goods and few livestock went to the owner of the private caravan they hired. They could only afford a tiny outfit. Altogether, there were twelve in their company including the two women. The majority were passengers.

There were two men who acted as guards—one, the owner, plump and taciturn, ran out of breath when ambling up one set of stairs; the other, a skinny man with frog eyes that darted to and fro, seemed more interested in his jug of wine than in the world around him. Ruth examined their gear with suspicion. Their daggers were rusty and they carried no swords.

They had two servants, sturdy young boys who cared for the twenty donkeys and the carts that belonged to the caravan. By their accents, Ruth recognized them as Israelites. She thought the boys far more capable than their masters. They had strapped well-made slings at their waist, and she could detect the bulge of round stones tucked into their homespun sashes. Ruth suspected they knew how to put them to good use.

Sunlight had barely caressed the earth when the caravan began its slow descent down the hills surrounding Numeira. Every hour drew them closer to the Salt Sea and the wild terrain that skirted it. Heat, insects, thirst, and the uneven roads made their brisk walk harder than Ruth had expected. Even the donkeys seemed out of sorts and tired. When everyone began to wilt under a remorseless sun, the group took rest under the shadow of a great rock. After a modest lunch and some rest, they resumed their interminable trek.

They crossed the Zered Brook where the land of Moab ended

and the boundaries of the nation of Edom began. For the first time, Ruth's feet left the land of her fathers.

Almost immediately, the terrain changed. It grew desertlike and flat. Sand dunes surrounded the road; the winds often whipped up the sand with sudden fierceness, until the fine granules covered the road so completely that without their guides they might have become lost.

They stopped early that evening. No one had the strength to take another step. Their portly leader explained that this one night they would spend out in the open.

Ruth went to their cart to retrieve cloaks and mats for sleeping when the frog-eyed guide approached her.

"Let me help you," he said, coming too close. Ruth could smell the scent of sour wine and rotten teeth on his breath and shifted away with discomfort.

"I need no help. I thank you." She turned her back to him.

The man took no heed of her assurance. Instead, his body followed hers. "No trouble," he said, and bent forward until his torso came into intimate contact with Ruth's back, trapping her between him and the cart.

She felt rage rise up in her, followed by a sharp bite of nausea as he groped her with invasive hands. Without thinking, she raised an elbow and crashed it into his middle. Too drunk to avoid the sharp blow, the man heaved over, a hiss of air trickling out of his mouth.

"Keep away from me, you filth," Ruth whispered, her cheeks crimson.

She said nothing about the incident to Naomi, concerned that the older woman would tell her that it proved her point. With only her mother-in-law for protection, a young woman was easy prey. She lay wakeful on her mat, pulling Mahlon's cloak closer about her.

It was close to the third watch of the night. The stars blazed like fiery torches in the black sky. A strange sound ruptured the stillness of the evening. Ruth sat up and peered about her, seeking the source of the noise. It came again, more distinctly. Horses' hooves. Ruth ran to one of the servant boys and found him awake and ready with his sling. The hooves approached closer. Now Ruth could see three riders in the moonlight, coming straight for the caravan.

They held aloft drawn swords.

"Wake up!" she cried. "Thieves! Wake up!"

With sudden confusion, the little caravan burst into life. Wails of fear rent the silence of the midnight hour. From a corner of her eye, Ruth saw their two leaders scavenge for their weapons. She recalled their dull-looking daggers and despaired. The portly one hastily lit a torch from the fire pit; instead of helping them in their plight, its light served to make them easier targets.

Falling on her knees next to Naomi, Ruth held the older woman in a trembling embrace. "Lord, help us," she whispered.

Naomi caressed her back as if she were soothing a child after a nightmare. But this was not a dream. Naomi's words were indistinguishable, lost in the midst of the horrified cries that surrounded them.

The first horseman, a wide-shouldered giant of a man, arrived a few moments before his companions. He went straight for the frog-eyed caravan leader, his aim brutally accurate. The wine-soaked Moabite stood no chance. There wasn't even a fight. He folded over, like one of Pharaoh's traveling stools, and collapsed with a strangled groan.

One of the young Israelite servants had a stone in his sling and began to whirl it. He was a short boy, barely more than a child, facing a giant. And yet he seemed filled with an eerie assurance. The thief saw him and turned his horse in his direction. The round stone flew before the horse had a chance to take one leap. It landed on the thief's forehead. Wide shoulders quivered, pitched forward, and the man crumbled over his horse and lay still on the sandy ground.

"Well done," one of the guests shouted.

The other two bandits were now almost upon them. They had tucked the flowing fabric of their turbans against their necks, and only theirs eyes were visible. One pair of black eyes turned on Ruth and he shifted his horse toward her.

Her skin grew cold in spite of the heat. She looked around, seeking a weapon with which she could defend Naomi and herself. Besides her frayed sandals, her dead husband's threadbare cloak, and a handful of dates, she saw nothing. The Hebrew boy stood in the wrong spot; Ruth and Naomi's position presented an impossible angle for the sling to work effectively. In the span of a heartbeat, Ruth saw her own death riding toward her. Even if the thief's sword did not cut her and Naomi down, his horse's hooves would crush them.

Had the Lord brought her this far only for her to be slaughtered by bandits, before ever setting foot on Israel's soil? Had the Lord raised His fist against them as Naomi claimed?

Just then, a sight even more frightful than the bandits met her eye. A male lion with an enormous mane appeared out of the darkness, prowling with a powerful grace that made Ruth's hair stand on end. For a breathless moment, the beast turned its head, and it seemed to Ruth to look straight at her. It roared, a sound so horrifying that Ruth would happily have run into the arms of one of the thieves to find shelter.

Then the lion turned and with a running leap jumped toward the highwayman who had targeted Ruth. The beast flew across the back of the thief's horse to sink its teeth into the man's throat and drag him to the ground. Unharmed, the horse reared, screaming in terror, and began to run in the opposite direction. The bandit had no chance. Death came for him swiftly.

The lion shook its full, golden mane and straightened. Again came that strange, fierce gaze, half wild, half focused. It turned and beheld the last thief who had been thrown off his terrified horse. A wet streak marked the front of the man's tunic where he had lost control of his bladder. With a strangled yelp, he ran in the same direction as his horse.

The golden lion did not give chase. He roared loud enough to shake the foundations of every heart in the small gathering before bounding gracefully away and melting into the night.

No one dared even breathe for a long time. No one uttered a word. All thoughts of sleep were abandoned. At least an hour passed before people began to whisper amongst themselves, their words hushed, their hands, as they gesticulated with dark emotion, shaking.

Saved by a lion.

The Lord used very odd instruments to fulfill His will. And it seemed that He intended to get Ruth to Israel against all odds.

Ruth was not sure whether to be reassured or terrified by God's determination. Why did it matter to Him so much if she should arrive on the soil of Judah? What did the life of one Moabite widow matter to the Lord of heaven and earth?

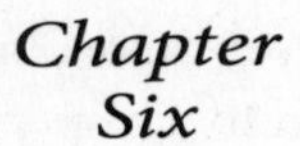

Chapter Six

I am sick with despair.

PSALM 35:12

The next day, after hastily burying the dead, the caravan traveled west and then northward, hoping to make Ain Boqeq before nightfall. Ruth saw the Salt Sea for the first time. Blue green and narrow, it stretched with an eerie stillness.

"It's beautiful," Ruth said, who had never seen a body of water grander than a stream.

"Nothing lives in it," Naomi said. "Not even a single fish. Nothing survives the salt. It would be like living inside a tear drop." She twirled a pebble she had been turning between her thumb and forefinger as she walked. With a sudden movement, she cast the pebble aside. "Barren, like my life. I've turned into that sea."

For their noonday break, they sat by the water's rocky shores.

"If you have any cuts on your skin, don't go inside the water. It will sting like a firebrand," said the young man whose sling had saved them from the sword of the bandit the night before. "And don't take your shoes off. The rocks are sharp, even in the sea, and can hurt your feet so badly you'll need to be sewn up."

"And if you have no wish to die, don't drink the water. Besides the salt, it has poison," the other young man added.

The first young man began to walk along the shore, head bent, examining the ground. "It offers up good things too." He straightened, holding a shiny black rock. "Bitumen. Helps to waterproof baskets and can be used as a seal or even for fuel." He handed the block to Ruth. It reflected the light like a jewel and had sharp edges.

Ruth smiled and pressed the bitumen into Naomi's hand. "So, even a dead sea has good things to offer. Gifts that bring life and help others."

Naomi dropped the bitumen and turned her back.

The rest of their journey to Bethlehem proved unremarkable, for which Ruth gave hourly thanks. There were only so many lions and bandits that she could stomach in a given week.

They spent one night in Ain Boqeq and another in Engedi before pushing northwest to Bethlehem. Other than the sharp sting of mosquitos, they encountered no other instruments bent on piercing their flesh. They bore with the ignominies of travel: heat rash, insects, exhaustion, small rations, never-ending dust, the grumbling of other guests. But Ruth felt too grateful to complain. They had been spared a horrible death. Perhaps worse.

When they arrived near Bethlehem, they parted ways with the caravan, which continued its travel north. Enough light lingered in the sky to see the fields belonging to Bethlehem, overflowing with wheat and barley. Row after row of healthy grain, grown tall and strong, appeared close to harvest. The fields were bursting with bounty.

"When we left Judah, these fields were empty, but I was full," Naomi said, dry-eyed. "I held two vigorous boys in my arms, and my husband bore my burdens." She leaned against a palm tree that stood bent on the side of the road. "Now these farms are full to overflowing, but I return empty. So empty."

Ruth held the callused hand of her mother-in-law, withered before its time, withered with loss. "Let's go home, Mother. Where your husband took you as a bride and you birthed your sons. You will feel better once we are settled there."

Naomi's house sat just inside the southern gate of Bethlehem. Her lands stretched beyond the gate, but they had gone wild in the years since the family left for Moab.

Ruth's first glimpse of the house came as a pleasant surprise. In the outdoor enclosure, where one day they would grow their garden and keep their livestock, God willing, a solitary almond tree survived, clinging to life with a tenacity that made Ruth smile. No sign of Naomi's original garden remained except for a few clumps of mint and rosemary. But that was to be expected after so many years of neglect.

Rough sandstones of varying sizes made up the walls of the house. As they pushed the door open, it became evident that this house was larger than their home in Moab, with two rooms on the ground floor, a small upper room, and a flat roof that would serve well during the sweltering nights of summer. Ruth imagined spreading their mattresses there, and sleeping under the stars, with the gentle night breeze fanning them into sleep.

She fetched a lamp from their cart and grimaced when she lit it. Various critters had made a comfortable home for themselves in the rooms and would have to be expelled. In the roof she detected several substantial holes.

When she attempted to climb the ladder to examine the damage up close, she found several rungs had rotted through, rendering the ladder useless. Carpentry was not one of her talents. She set the ladder aside. Fortunately, they had passed the rainy season, so the repairs to the roof could wait for a few weeks.

Naomi gasped as she beheld the extent of the damage. Instead of feeling comforted by the sight of her old home, by the sight of Bethlehem, she seemed to sink more inward. With swift steps she walked out.

Ruth sighed as she threw open the windows. They would probably be better off sleeping outdoors on this first night. She tied her scarf more securely around her head, fetched her old broom from the cart, and began the hard work of sweeping cobwebs and dust, not to mention some unpleasant gifts from the field mice.

Tired already from their long march that day, Ruth pushed

herself, knowing Naomi would feel better if her home were clean. When the light faded completely, she had to give up. Outside, Naomi sat slumped against the cart. She had ignored the donkey, not bothering to feed it, or rub it down. Ruth frowned. Naomi was usually so thoughtful of others, even a dumb creature like their old donkey.

She forced the older woman to eat and drink before seeing to the beast's needs. The last of their water disappeared inside its cavernous belly.

"We have to go to the well in the morning," she said. "Do you remember where it is?"

"I'm mourning, not stupid."

Ruth swallowed a chuckle. "Shall we sleep outside tonight? I'll set up our mats right here. We should be safe, inside the city gates."

Ruth examined her wrinkled, travel-stained tunic in the pale rays of the early morning sun and sighed. Rummaging through the baskets, she found a fresh tunic, and dampening a cloth with the last few drops of water, she did her best to wash. Unbraiding her hair, she combed it, bringing order back to the thick chestnut mane. Her eyes pricked as she remembered Mahlon running his fingers through her hair, calling it soft like silk.

"How would you know?" she had asked and laughed. "You've never touched silk in your life."

She brushed the tears off and straightened, pulling her scarf over her head. Today, she would meet her Israelite neighbors for the first time. They would judge her deficient, she knew. A barren, widowed, Moabite woman. Was there a greater failure in the sight of Judah? All the combing in the world could not fix that. Tangle-free hair and a clean tunic could not help her avoid their harsh judgment.

She would just have to change their minds one day at a time. And if she couldn't, she would learn to live with their rejection.

As she walked outside, she spied a clump of several plants, growing knee length in what used to be the garden. Gasping, she strode forward to examine them. They were wheat. The plants were healthy, bearing fat kernels, which were several weeks from maturity. They would not yield enough grain for two suppers. Still, their incongruent presence seemed strangely reassuring. Like a sign. No one had planted the wheat. The wind must have blown the seeds from nearby fields, and they had taken root in Naomi's desolate garden just in time to welcome her back to Bethlehem. They sat there waving in the breeze like a welcome flag, like a reassuring promise. Ruth drew a caressing hand over the stalks and turned to fetch Naomi for their walk into town.

Many women had gathered by the city well. As Naomi and Ruth approached, they felt the weight of curious gazes. Then a few audible gasps came from the crowd.

"That's Naomi!" one woman exclaimed.

Another cried, "It looks like her!"

A third woman said, "Is it really Naomi? She's been gone ten years, if not more. Could this be the same Naomi who lived among us?"

Naomi, silent since the night before, turned on them, her lips thin, her jaw clenched. "Don't call me Naomi!" Her voice came out husky, as if she had a cold. "That woman is gone. Lost. Buried in Moab. Call me Mara. That's who I am now. *Bitter*."

Ruth winced. It was one thing to witness Naomi slide down into an abyss of desolation, but to hear her describe her life with such bleak hopelessness tore at Ruth.

A short, curvaceous woman about the same age as Naomi approached and laid a hand on her shoulder. "But, Naomi, why? What has happened to you?"

"The Almighty has dealt bitterly with me. I went from this place full. But the Lord has brought me back empty. My husband is gone. My sons are buried beside him in Moab. Why call me *Naomi*? What is *pleasant* about my life? The Lord has spoken against me. Look at the calamity He has sent upon me."

Ruth could not bite back the gasp that escaped her mouth. Never had she heard her mother-in-law speak so resentfully against God. She had come to see Him as her enemy, the one who sentenced her to irredeemable pain. His hand was the hammer that crushed her with no mercy. No hope. She had lost her sons. But worse, she had lost her Lord. The realization appalled Ruth. But she knew she could not talk Naomi out of this conclusion. She could not advise or admonish her. She needed to remain silent and pray. Let God deal with Naomi's heart.

Let Your presence heal what Naomi's disappointments have harmed, Lord.

The curvaceous woman embraced Naomi. "I share your sorrow. May the Lord restore your crushed spirit."

Naomi seemed to notice the woman for the first time. "Are you Miriam?"

"That's me. Have I changed?"

"Not so much as I. A broken heart reflects on a woman's body. I never thought my skin would shrivel with my heart."

"You're still lovely, Naomi. And most welcome in your home and among your people. Now tell us, who is this young woman you have with you?"

"This is Ruth, the wife of my son Mahlon. I told her to stay in Kir-hareseth among her own folk, and to find herself a new husband. See how young and beautiful she is? But she would not leave me."

"A Moabite?" Miriam asked, with a wince. Ruth did not miss the murmurs that rose up around them.

"A loyal daughter. She is kin to me now," Naomi spoke stiffly before hefting her jar and approaching the well. In silence, she and Ruth filled four jars with cool, clear water.

Before heading back to Naomi's house, Ruth turned to Miriam and gave her a sweet smile and a respectful nod—a mute indication that she held no grudges against the woman for her obvious disapproval. The woman's eyes opened wide and she blinked. Ruth's smile grew wider.

"Thank you for defending me," she told her mother-in-law as they ambled home.

"I spoke the truth, child. I am only sorry that you will pay a high price for your decision. You will suffer for loving me."

"I would suffer more without you."

For seven days, Ruth labored in the house, washing everything with lye. She traveled several times each day to the well, for the work of cleaning required much water. She went alone since Naomi had sunk back to her earlier paralysis and seemed incapable of doing much beyond staring into space. The women of Bethlehem left Ruth alone. They gave her curious stares, as if she were a strange animal they had never seen. But no one came close. No one offered polite conversation. No one offered hospitality.

Once, Ruth noticed an older woman struggling to shift her heavy jar, and without thinking, reached forward to lend a hand. The woman scampered away from her touch with such haste that she dropped the jar, spilling the precious water within.

"Stay away from me, Moabite," she screeched. "Don't you dare touch me."

Ruth apologized, her words mumbled in her embarrassment, mindful of the hostile stares trained her way. After that, she tried to visit the well later in the day, when few women came to fetch water.

While Ruth worked on bringing order to the house, Miriam came to visit Naomi several times. At least her care for Naomi was greater than her disapproval of the Moabite in her house.

"The Lord has given me the bread of adversity and the water of affliction," Naomi told her old friend. "I trusted Him. Why did He turn His back on me?"

Naomi's bitterness lay heavy on Ruth's heart though she could do nothing to allay her suffering. Ruth tried to show her love through the ordinary things of life—cooking, cleaning, fetching water, combing Naomi's tangled hair. Sometimes she feared Naomi had disappeared so far down the dark, cavernous pits of despair that she wasn't even aware of Ruth. At other times, Naomi seemed to rise up and see a tiny glimpse of her.

Once, when Miriam had come to visit, Ruth served both women bean stew with fresh rosemary, a welcome change from the stale bread, cheese, dried fruit, and nuts that had sustained them for two weeks. She had only made enough for two, not expecting a visitor, and made an excuse for not partaking of the food. She did not wish the women to realize that she had given up her share. As she cleaned the pot, she overheard Naomi singing her praises to Miriam, speaking of her kindness to Mahlon and her steadfastness after he was gone from them.

"She gave you her own share of stew, did you notice? She is always generous like that," Naomi said to her friend.

Miriam dipped her bread into the bowl. "You are worthy of great kindness, Naomi."

No one had ever taken Naomi's plaintive demand to call her *Mara* seriously. The residents of Bethlehem continued to call her by her given name. They refused to make *bitterness* her new identity, and Naomi did not insist that they heed her demand. In truth, she insisted on little. She showed no interest in the world around her, except, on occasion, to rise up in her daughter-in-law's defense.

Ruth smiled, her heart lifting, not because of Naomi's praise of her negligible sacrifice but because Naomi's words showed that she had been alive enough to notice. She doubted that Naomi's efforts to make her acceptable in Miriam's eyes would go far. But she appreciated her mother-in-law's care. Even in her broken state, she was trying to carve out a chance for Ruth to settle peacefully in this new land.

By the seventh day, the house shone, and their meager belongings had been arranged neatly, giving the once abandoned place a welcoming aspect. Ruth had managed to build a fire in the hearth and was busy making a lentil stew. After a week of traveling and another spent restoring Naomi's house, they would finally eat something besides stale bread, old cheese, and dried fruit.

As she went through their stores, she could no longer deny how desperate they were for food and income. They would starve if she could not earn a living. How had they become so destitute in the seven months since the death of Naomi's sons? They had never been wealthy. But they had been frugal and hardworking. And still it wasn't enough.

They hovered on the edge of starvation.

That evening, as they shared the meal she had cooked in the hearth, Ruth said, "I saw workers in the fields today. The barley harvest has begun."

"Yes."

"There were some men and women in the field, following the harvesters and gatherers. They were picking the leftovers from the ground. No one seemed distressed by their actions."

"Those are the gleaners," Naomi said. "According to our law, the widow, the orphan, and all who are struck down with poverty can have a share of every field. That's God's provision for them, though they work hard for it. But it is an act of His protection."

"How does it work?"

"The Lord says that no one should reap his land to the very border, nor should his workers pick up the leftover grain after the reapers have gone through. If a laborer forgets a sheaf and leaves it in the field, he is forbidden to go back for it. So the gleaners gather what they can. Not every landowner is generous. Even the most liberal of masters cannot provide more than a meager share. Gleaning is for the truly desperate."

Truly desperate. That's what they were. They could not afford pride.

At long last, here was a glimmer of hope. Hope that they would not starve. Instead of sitting at home and worrying, she could *do* something.

"Let me go to the field and glean, Mother. I will pray that the Lord may give me favor. Perhaps someone will be kind enough to allow me to glean, even though I am a Moabite."

Naomi waved a distracted hand in assent. "Go, my daughter."

Ruth lingered, hoping Naomi would suggest a particular field. A special landowner whose honesty and generosity could be relied upon. But other than her consent, Naomi gave no other information. Ruth had never gleaned and did not know the rules. What if she offended the foreman of the field out of ignorance? Would she anger the others with her mistakes? Would she be in their way? The questions kept her wakeful late into the night.

Early the next morning Ruth arose, drained and bleary-eyed, her muscles already aching with fatigue. She changed into her oldest tunic and covered her hair in a light veil, which she knotted at the nape of her neck in order to have more freedom of movement. She set out for the fields outside the walls of the city, not knowing which one she should approach. *Please Lord, help me find favor with the right master. Guide my steps to the field of Your choosing.*

Unbidden, the memory of the frog-eyed caravan leader's unwelcome groping sprang to mind. Would she have to contend with others like him in the field? She was a foreigner, without a father or husband's protection. If a man set his mind on violating her, who would gainsay him? Anxiety made the contents of her stomach curdle like sour goat's milk.

Almighty God, please keep me safe from evil men and evil intentions.

Fear rose up like a mighty storm until her steps faltered. How could she do this? Face this danger? Bear this burden?

How could she not? Would Naomi not starve if she refused to glean? She must harden herself to these fears and go. She must trust the Lord to be her Father and her Husband. She was not alone. He watched over her. With determination, she put one foot in front of the other and walked.

Chapter Seven

In times of trouble, may the LORD answer your cry.
May the name of the God of Jacob keep you safe from all harm.
May he send you help from his sanctuary
And strengthen you from Jerusalem . . .
May he grant your heart's desires
And make all your plans succeed.

PSALM 20:1–2, 4

Boaz shed his light linen mantle and hitched up his tunic without taking his eyes off the ram. It needed to be moved to a new pen away from the ewes, but the animal seemed unusually reluctant to cooperate. Boaz's head shepherd had already gone for a short flight in the air and landed flat on his back thanks to the ram's curled horns. Boaz swallowed a smile. It had been hard not to laugh at Zabdiel tumbling in the air, a comical look of disbelief on his face.

Boaz would handle the matter himself, although he did not need to. Plenty of men worked for him. Men young enough not to mind a few unintended flying leaps. But this was his prize ram, and Boaz had a soft spot for it. This same ram had sired a number of the strong, healthy lambs ambling in the nearby green pastures. Although during mating season the beast could prove irritable, it was not an ill-humored creature as a rule. Boaz could not understand its sudden quarrelsome attitude.

He maintained his distance from the riled animal for a long while, patiently waiting for it to calm down.

Boaz was good at patience.

The ram stood motionless, keeping Boaz in its sight. Deciding that the man daring to stand in his dominion required no special effort, it turned its head to examine something in the far horizon.

With the experience of long years, Boaz grasped his opportunity and took a running leap. The ram saw him coming too late. Boaz grabbed its horns before it could knock him down and twisted the proud head to one side, then down. In brute strength, the animal stood far superior to the man. But Boaz had a few tricks up his sleeve and wrestled the animal to the ground, unharmed. Zabdiel helped him transfer the now tired beast to its new, commodious pasture.

Fetching Boaz's mantle, Zabdiel held it open for him. "The wealthiest man in Bethlehem, respected throughout Judah, and you have to wrestle your own ram. Why not let the rest of us do the work? That's why you pay us, my lord."

Boaz bent down to straighten the ties of his leather sandals, which had grown twisted in the tussle. In spite of Zabdiel's teasing remark, Boaz knew he had earned his admiration by the way he had dealt with the animal. His men appreciated working for a master who shared in the rigors of their labor.

"Every once in a while I like to show you young ones how it's done," he said, his eyes twinkling. "Besides, I can't let you have all the fun. Nothing like a good challenge to make a man feel alive."

Folding his arms against his chest, he leaned against a majestic palm tree—Melekh's tree. Against all odds, Melekh had lived a few more years after Judith's death. Boaz had never known a dog to live so long. Where Boaz went, the aging dog followed, limping after him with single-minded persistence. When Boaz wept, the dog put a paw on his lap and whimpered softly. When he could not sleep, Melekh stayed awake, thumping its tail softly, biding through the hard night hours with Boaz. Following the hardest years after the death of his wife and children, Melekh stayed by Boaz's side, like a wizened champion sent to keep him company. When finally the dog took its last breath, full of years and almost blind, Boaz buried it here, in its favorite field, and planted a palm over the spot as a memorial.

"A good dog, that Melekh," Zabdiel said.

"The best."

The unexpected voice of a woman cut into Boaz's memories. "What a spectacle, cousin. I hope you haven't broken any bones."

Boaz stifled a groan. Miriam. He had a tender spot for his wife's cousin, as long as she stayed far away. Up close, she could prove trying. "My bones are still in right order. Welcome, Miriam."

"I went to the house and Mahalath said I could find you here."

"Zabdiel, please fetch Miriam a cup of sweet wine."

He led the way toward the shade of a barn. A couple of simple wooden stools rested against the wall and he motioned for her to sit. "What brings you to me today, Miriam?"

"Does a woman need a reason to visit her cousin? Speaking of cousins, have you heard that yours has returned to Bethlehem?" Miriam's face shone like a lampstand.

In many ways Boaz found her an amiable woman. Except for her more than common interest in gossip. "You speak of Naomi, I presume?"

Miriam's brightness dimmed. "You've heard?"

"The day she arrived. She has been burdened with unimaginable sorrow. May the Lord help her to bear her affliction."

Miriam took a sip of her wine. "You understand, better than most."

Boaz said nothing, his face growing blank. Noticing his cold reaction, Miriam went on quickly. "Elimelech was a good man. And her precious sons! Who can believe they are gone? But at least she is not completely alone."

"She returns with a Moabite daughter-in-law, I understand."

Miriam nodded. For once, she did not rush into speech, which Boaz found curious. He had been certain she would jump into a long discourse on the horrors of becoming kin to an untrustworthy foreigner.

"Her name is Ruth. She's not what you might expect from a Moabite."

"No?"

"She left her family and her home to accompany Naomi here. Naomi released her from the duty, but she would not be dissuaded, not even when Naomi made it clear to her that she had no prospects for a future in Bethlehem. You should see the way she cares for Naomi—better than a real daughter."

In spite of himself, Boaz found his interest sparked. "She abandoned her home for Naomi's sake? But I heard Naomi was poor."

"Close to starving, I'd say. Ruth clings to her for love. She's given up her whole life, I fear. The women of Bethlehem cannot overlook her heritage."

"Perhaps she will win them over with her affection for Naomi."

Miriam made a face. "Criticism is rarely won over by love, Boaz. Putting her down makes them feel important. Superior. It's not a pleasure to be given up easily."

Boaz thought over her words; though they were harsh, he knew that often they proved true. Compassion washed through him at the plight of this woman he had never met. What courage it must have required to leave behind her home for an unknown destiny. He couldn't help but admire her for it.

Miriam stayed awhile longer to chat about a small piece of land with which she needed help. When she left, Boaz looked toward the sun, narrowing brown eyes against its bright light.

"It must be close to noon," he said to Zabdiel.

The head shepherd looked up. "It is, my lord. Running late?"

"Very late." Boaz frowned in annoyance. The delay threw the whole day out of order. Harvest required close supervision. Thanks to his rambunctious animal and Miriam's unexpected visit, he would now be unable to maintain his planned schedule. With a quick recalculation, he decided to ride to the closest barley field, which he had not intended to visit that day.

He signaled the servant to prepare his horse and swung on the beast's back before it had come to a full stop. He found the ride exhilarating as he galloped through uneven roads, with the wind blowing his mantle like ship sails behind his back.

He was no longer young, nor was he old, but in the middle years when a man has the advantage of experience and still enjoys the vigor of youth. A fast ride had the power to thrill him as much as it had the first time he had climbed on the back of a horse. He noticed a hawk as it soared above him and Boaz forgot his annoyance and grinned for the joy of being alive, when all the sweet blessings of nature conspired to make the world beautiful.

He could see the barley in his fields, full and bursting with goodness, waiting to be cut down. Waiting to feed his many servants and their dependents. He planned to store a good portion of this harvest. The rains were fickle in his part of the world. With wisdom and judicious planning, he could ride out the famine years, like Joseph in Egypt.

The reapers came into view, and Boaz slowed his horse and turned in their direction. "The Lord be with you!" he cried, as he jumped to the ground and handed the reins to a waiting servant.

"The Lord bless you!" his harvesters replied.

It had become a familiar refrain, this prayerful greeting between master and servants. It would have been enough for Boaz to wish his workers *shalom*—the peace of God. Polite enough. Gracious enough. But Boaz liked to bless them with more. And the workers had learned to respond in kind.

His foreman, Abel, came to greet him. Young and brown-skinned, Abel had a long, handsome face with faint laugh lines around narrow eyes.

"How goes it, Abel?"

"See how far they have come?" He pointed to the eastern border of the field. "All this in half a day."

Boaz examined the progress in the field with satisfaction before turning his attention to the laborers. Some of the men and women were his servants. Others were only hired for the harvest season, though he had come to know them through the years. Using sharp sickles, the men cut the grain in bunches and carried them until the weight became too great to carry. Then they simply dropped the armloads to the ground. From behind them, the women came, bundling the cut barley into sheaves, which would later be carried to a barn. Last came the gleaners.

Though he had never tasted of poverty, Boaz had a soft spot for the gleaners who had no way of feeding themselves other than the bounty of God and the generosity of landowners. He recognized a few widows, and one man who had lost his hand years ago in an accident when his cart had overturned on a rainy day. His infirmity rendered him unable to work for wages since he could not keep up with other men. Instead, he gleaned and depended on the additional largess of neighbors and family.

There were several new gleaners. Among them, Boaz noticed a young woman, tall and willowy, bent over to her work. He could tell she was unfamiliar with the task, though she seemed to give her full strength and focus to it. The angle of her head prevented him from seeing her face. Then she straightened her back to stretch for a short moment. Boaz felt an unfamiliar tightening in his chest.

Her forehead was damp with perspiration, and a streak of dirt where she must have rubbed her face ran down the side of one cheek. Hair the color of dark honey peeked from under her scarf, framing golden skin brightened with ruddy patches on each cheek. Her eyes, which she raised toward him for a moment, were an unusual tawny color. She was young and striking. Yet he knew instinctively that this woman had seen much in life. Sorrow clung like a seal to the lines of her mouth and filled her eyes. Sorrow and something elusive he could not name. But it drew him to look longer and still not be satisfied.

He turned his gaze away, turning red at his own unusual lingering inspection of an unknown female. "Who is that young woman?" he asked, pointing to her with his chin, hoping Abel could not sense his intense interest. "Who does she belong to?"

The foreman shaded his eyes against the piercing light. "She is the one who came from Moab with Naomi, my lord."

"Naomi's daughter-in-law? What is she doing in my field?"

"She asked me this morning if she could gather grain behind the harvesters. Polite as a princess of Egypt, with humble manners and a soft voice—I couldn't refuse her. She is a hard worker and except for a few minutes' rest in the shelter, has continued gleaning since early this morning."

So this was Naomi's Ruth. This tall, golden-eyed girl whose beautiful face was marred with dirt and sweat and suffering. Moabite or not, she had managed to win over Abel. "You did well, allowing her to gather barley here," he said to his foreman.

Boaz thought of her gleaning in unfamiliar fields, exposed to the dangers that an unprotected woman might face, and winced. He found himself unable to bear the thought of her being hurt. It was like standing by and watching a helpless dove tortured by cruel boys.

"Abel, I want you to go and warn the young men away from her. Tell them anyone who dares to lay an improper hand on the Moabite will have to contend with me. Tell them I'll punish them personally before I dismiss them."

Chapter Eight

The heart of man plans his way,
But the LORD establishes his steps.
PROVERBS 16:9

Boaz knew he sounded fierce, but could not keep the intensity of his feelings from spilling into his voice. The thought of this woman hurt, violated, besmirched in any way made his stomach turn.

Abel's black eyebrows rose to the middle of his forehead. "Yes, my lord."

It occurred to Boaz that Ruth's gleaning would be the only source of income for her and Naomi. Why else would Naomi have sent her into the fields without protection?

He determined to provide for both women as best he could, seeing that Naomi was kin to him by marriage. Surely the widow of Elimelech deserved additional provision from his hand.

His mind whirled as he considered their situation. He would have to speak to Ruth in person. The thought filled him with unexpected pleasure. He frowned, disconcerted by his own eagerness to address her, but resisted the urge to examine his careening emotions too closely. His stride purposeful, he approached her where she bent to her task at the edge of the field. Rather than addressing her like a servant as befit her rank, he decided to use warmer language, conveying both his respect and his welcome. "My daughter," he said, trying to put her at ease, and to extend to her the civility that the rest of Bethlehem had presumably withheld from her.

She lifted her face, eyes widening a fraction. The assurance in his words had obviously slipped by her. Something like fear flickered in the back of those extraordinary eyes, and he realized that she expected harsh words from him. She expected him to cast her off his land. Worse even.

Rushing to alleviate her anxiety, he said, "I am Boaz, master of this field. I wished to speak to you in person, because I want you to stay here with us, on my land when you gather grain. Not only today. Do this throughout the harvest season and don't go to anyone else's land. Stay right behind these young women. They all work for me. See which part of the field they are harvesting, and then follow to glean after them so that you are not alone."

Her lips fell open. She rubbed her temple but remained speechless.

"I have charged the young men not to lay a hand on you. You shall remain safe on my property." She still said nothing. He cast about, seeking some way of putting her at ease. Adjusting his light mantle over his tunic, he said, "It's hot today. We have vessels of water sitting on the edge of the field. The young men keep them replenished from the well. Help yourself whenever you are thirsty."

He was taken aback when Ruth fell at his feet with movements as graceful as a doe. She abased herself until her face rested on the ground. With the wave of a hand, he signaled for her to rise up. Instead of standing, she sat on her knees before him.

"What have I done to deserve this great kindness, my lord?" Her voice was sweet and feminine, with just a hint of tears, pushed down. She hesitated, as if trying to decide if she should say more. Taking a gulping breath, she added, "Why have I found such favor in your eyes? Why should you take notice of *me*? I'm not even an Israelite. I'm a foreigner in your land."

"I know where you are from," Boaz assured her gently. "But I also know what you have done for your mother-in-law since the death of your husband. I am aware that you left your father and mother and your native land and chose to come to a people who were complete strangers to you."

He studied her kneeling form, her lowered head, her drooping shoulders and decided to say more. She deserved a little encouragement after what she had been through. "You chose to be an outsider for the sake of a hurting widow. You accepted loneliness so that she could have companionship. You did all this because you refused to abandon Naomi. I know."

Ruth wiped a hand against her girdle. He noticed her nails were ragged and encrusted with dirt. Yet even the dirt could not hide the fact that her slender fingers were long and alluring. They were also shaking violently. "You know about me?"

What she really meant was: *you know about me and still you show me kindness?* He sensed her astonishment.

He felt a strange catch in his breath as he thought of her vulnerability. Other than Naomi, she had no one. She had even abandoned her gods, who reigned in Moab and had no part of Israel.

She had come to take shelter with the Lord, though the Lord's people showed her little welcome. Without meaning to do so, he stretched his arms toward her. "May the Lord repay you for what you have done. May the God of Israel, under whose wings you have come to take refuge, give you a full reward." He said the blessing loud enough for everyone around them to hear, like a sort of public declaration of his approval. And of God's mercy.

She blinked away the sheen of tears that had gathered in her eyes. He fisted his hands to keep himself from reaching out and gently wiping them away. The ram must have hit him harder than he realized when he wrestled with it. This unusual interest in a woman he had just met was the result of a head injury. Insanity brought on by too much sun. Perhaps he had ridden too fast and his brains had turned into stew.

He would make arrangements for her continued safety. That much was his duty. But from this moment on, he would stay away from her.

"I hope I continue to please you, my lord. Before coming, I prayed that I would find someone who would show me favor. Now I know the Lord led me to this field." For a moment the heavy eyelids lifted and she gave him a look that he felt down to his toes.

"You have comforted me by speaking so kindly to me, even though I am not one of your servants." Then she rose up with more regal dignity than the daughter of a king and returned to glean in the field.

Boaz gulped air as if he had been drowning. He forced himself to turn in the opposite direction. It occurred to him that he never meant to come to this field today. He meant to be on the other side of Bethlehem. But for the obstinate capriciousness of a brute animal, which delayed his leaving long enough for Miriam to catch him on her unannounced visit, and delay him further in her turn, he would not be here. He would not have met her or helped her. The very things that had seemed like unwelcome interruptions earlier rose up before him like the most important parts of his day now.

Would she have been harmed without his hand of protection? Cold sweat covered him in a thin film at that thought.

What had she said? The Lord had led her to this field. Perhaps the Lord had led him to this field also, so that he could act on her behalf. The annoying interruption to his day might turn out to be God Himself interceding for Ruth.

But he would now avoid all further contact with her. She had a strange effect on him, and the sooner he evaded her presence, the sooner he would recover his usual unwavering calm.

As mealtime approached, Boaz forgot about that decision. He worried that Ruth had nothing to eat. Gleaning in the brutal heat of the sun was hard work. She could not maintain her strength by water alone. He ought to see to her. After all, she was Elimelech's daughter-in-law, and Elimelech was his own kin. Family duty demanded that he care for her needs.

When the workers took their break, he called to Ruth. It did not occur to him until later that he could just as easily have asked Abel to fetch her and see to her needs.

He caught her attention and bid her to come to the meal.

"Come over here and help yourself to some food. You can sit with my workers."

His servants had spread a clean cloth on the ground and set it with plates heaped with freshly made bread and earthenware bowls of wine. Boaz spoke a blessing over the meal. The laborers who belonged to him were joining the spread, though as a gleaner, she had no right to his table.

Ruth sat at the edge of the cloth, her feet modestly tucked up against her. Boaz seated across from her to ensure that she would not be too shy to eat in the company of so many strangers. He glared at the young woman near her who grabbed a piece of bread without offering Ruth any.

He handed her bread from the plate before him. "You can dip it in the wine."

She took the bread. "Thank you, my lord." He noticed that she had washed her hands before sitting down to eat, and her hair was now tucked neatly behind its veil.

One of his servants brought Boaz a bowl heaped with roasted fresh grain, a delicacy for which he had a weakness. He took two large measures and placed them on a piece of bread before her. Startled, she lowered her head. He could see how hungry she was by the large mouthfuls she took. Still, she rolled half the grain in the thin, flat bread and tucked it inside her sash. For Naomi, he realized.

If it weren't for the wagging tongues that would cause her more harm, he would have given her the whole bowl. Already, he had paid her too much attention. Yet he found himself lingering to ensure that she ate until she was satisfied.

Ruth returned to work before the harvesters had finished eating. Boaz realized that she could never gather enough grain, in spite of the bounty of the harvest, to see her through the rest of the year. A lone woman, unfamiliar with the work, would not be able to feed two mouths.

He turned to his laborers before they returned to the field. "I want you to let Ruth gather grain even among the sheaves. In fact, pull out some heads of barley from the bundles and drop them on purpose for her so that she can gather more. Let her pick them up and on no account are any of you to give her trouble."

He addressed the women next. "You too. I expect you to be kind to her. Don't shame her, any of you. She is unfamiliar with our ways. If she makes mistakes, be gentle in correcting her."

He knew that for the sake of the respect they bore him, they would obey his instructions. He could not force them to like her. To welcome her. But he could demand that they refrain from mistreating her.

He had done all this for the sake of his conscience, he told himself, and for the sake of his kinswoman, Naomi. But long into the lengthening shadows of the afternoon, his gaze sought the Moabite beauty in the fields. He could not stop thinking about the way she had tucked the roasted grain into her girdle for Naomi.

Abel, noticing his regard, said, "She is a fast learner. Look at how much she has gleaned already."

"Has anyone besides you and me talked to her since she arrived?"

"Not that I have seen. In Judah, we do not warm up to Canaanite women."

"She is kin to one of us."

"Which only raises their ire more. She had no business marrying a son of Bethlehem."

"She didn't bind his hands and feet and carry him captive into the wedding bower. He went seeking after her."

Abel held up two lean hands. "I don't agree with them."

Boaz grinned, dragging a rueful hand across his forehead. "Nor I. Do you think she will ever find acceptance among our folk?"

"It would take a miracle, my lord. A man's heart is no easy thing to change. Stones are softer, sometimes."

"But that same heart breaks easily, Abel. It breaks and shatters and no one can put it together again this side of heaven." He thought for a moment and added, "No one but the Lord."

Abel rubbed his hands together. "That's good enough for me, master Boaz."

Chapter Nine

Be strong and courageous. Do not be frightened, and do not be dismayed, for the LORD your God is with you wherever you go.

JOSHUA 1:9

Evening had begun to descend when Ruth stopped gleaning. She beat out the grain that she had managed to gather. With disbelief, she examined the heap before her. She had gathered about an ephah of barley! Two weeks' worth of wages for one day of honest labor.

She wrapped the barley in her spare veil, which she had tied around her waist that morning, and hefted it against her hip. It was heavy, but such a pleasant weight to hold against one's side. The weight of provision. Of security.

As she began to walk back to Bethlehem, her thoughts lingered on Boaz.

He was a landowner—a wealthy man—judging by his fine clothes, his fancy horse, and the number of his servants. Clearly, he enjoyed the respect of his people. And something more. They *liked* him. They were drawn to him. The smallest sign of his attention brought on smiles, as if they enjoyed being in his presence. He had an inner light that drew every man and woman under his care to him. They were bound to him not just by wages but by something intangible though no less real. They were bound to him by his goodness.

And yet he had stooped to take note of a disheveled foreigner.

He had provided for her needs. He had protected her from harm. And most curiously, he had praised her, as though he perceived her to be a woman deserving of admiration instead of a complete failure.

While the rest of Bethlehem looked at her askance and judged her deficient, Boaz proclaimed her worthy.

Ruth shifted the large bundle at her side and hastened her steps. She could not wait to show Naomi her bounty. Boaz's generosity had multiplied the fruit of her work tenfold. His servants had practically thrown the grain at her in the field.

She still could feel the intense beating of her heart, the rush of heat to her face as he lifted sun-browned hands and blessed her. *May the God of Israel, under whose wings you have come to take refuge, give you a full reward.*

He was an ordinary-looking man of middle years, with a touch of white at his temples, brown eyes neither too dark nor too light, lashes neither sparse nor full, a prominent nose, a firm mouth, neither thin nor full. But when he prayed, a light came into those ordinary features, a light so filled at once with power and compassion that his whole countenance was transformed. He became extraordinary.

Ruth felt an incomprehensible conviction that he saw through her, into her. Into her deepest heart. Into her secret longings and ancient hurts. He saw *her*. And he approved. She grew entranced. It was the prayer, she told herself.

She would tell Naomi of Boaz's benevolence, and pray to God that Naomi would crawl out of the abyss of despair that paralyzed her. Ruth carried hope. Hope wrapped in a bundle provided by the unexpected generosity of a stranger.

She found Naomi sitting in the gloomy darkness of the house. She had forgotten to light a lamp and allowed the fire to go out. Not bothering to chide her, Ruth kissed Naomi on both cheeks before lighting the lamp. "Look, Mother. Look what I have brought you."

She dropped the bulging bundle before the older woman and

untied the corners of her shawl. "Here is an ephah of barley, just for you!"

Naomi straightened her slumped back. She stared, her brows drawn together in disbelief. With the slow motions of a sleepwalker, she sifted through the grain. "So much?"

Ruth flashed a grin. "You approve? How about some dinner to celebrate?"

Naomi bit her lip. "I'm sorry. I forgot about food. There is nothing left to eat but a little lentil and chickpea. If you wait, I can make a stew."

"No need." Ruth pulled Naomi up and twirled with her around the room. "I brought dinner too." She pulled out the bread and roasted grain that she had saved from the midday meal.

Naomi sank to the ground, missing the cushion without noticing. "Where did you glean today? Which field?" She tasted a single grain of barley, plump and freshly roasted. "Someone must have taken special notice of you. Who was it? May the Lord bless the man who helped you."

Ruth set a fresh mat between them and brought a skin of water to share. As they ate, she recounted the adventures of her first day as a gleaner.

"I had no idea where to go when I left Bethlehem this morning. I walked by one field busy with harvesters. I noticed the laborers seemed silent. I thought, *there is no joy in this place*, and moved on. The field stretched over a long distance, and I began to wonder if I had made the wrong decision. Then I came upon a new field, also large and well maintained. Men and women worked together, and I heard voices speaking, and snatches of song. Someone laughed and I told myself this is where I should work.

"The foreman, a young man with a pleasant manner, is called Abel. I asked his permission to gather grain in the field behind the laborers. He asked who I was, and I told him I belonged to you. He seemed to have heard of our story and gave me leave to pick the leftover barley. I watched the other gleaners, and followed them, hoping I would not unknowingly blunder and irritate them. At first, I made little headway, for I was behind everyone and most of the grain had been gathered by the time it came to me.

"Then a man arrived on horseback, well garbed and neatly groomed. He greeted everyone with a blessing from the Lord, and I could see from the laborers' response that they held him in high regard. As he spoke to Abel, I realized this must be the owner of the field. The others told me his name is Boaz."

"Boaz! That man is one of our closest relatives, first cousin to my husband, Elimelech, and one of our kinsman-redeemers. He is an honorable and worthy man, known throughout Judah for his wealth and influence."

"What is a *kinsman-redeemer*?"

"A *goel* is a close kinsman who is expected to help a family member in times of exceptional trouble. When a relative has to sell himself into slavery because of dire financial need, a *goel* buys him back from his master and restores him to freedom. He also redeems mortgaged or lost property. In special cases, they are expected to marry the widow of a brother and have children in the name of that brother in order for his line not to perish. Some believe that responsibility should extend beyond a brother to other family members. But it is not written so in the law. Boaz is such a man to us."

"Perhaps that explains his kindness, for you will never imagine what he did, Mother." Ruth told Naomi everything that Boaz had undertaken on her behalf. "When he first approached me, I thought I had committed an embarrassing error, somehow, and he wished to chastise me. Then I thought perhaps he did not wish a Moabite to glean in his fields.

"But instead of casting me out, he showered me with kindness. As if all this were not enough, he insisted that I remain in his fields until the end of the harvest season! He told me not to glean anywhere else but remain with the women who work for him."

For the first time in seven months, Naomi smiled. It softened the lines of her drawn face and washed her expression of the ravages of bitterness. "The Lord has not neglected to show kindness to the living or the dead."

Ruth felt the breath leave her breast, and with it, a weight she had not known she carried. It had been many days since Naomi had prayed. More still since she had spoken of the Lord with trust. She reached out and grasped her hand.

"He has not, Mother."

A tear ran down Naomi's cheek. She pulled her hand free from Ruth's and wiped at it. "Daughter, you should do as Boaz suggested. Remain in his fields and stay close to his young women. They will keep you safe. Besides, they'll be company for you. On someone else's land, you might be harassed. Boaz will shield you from harm."

That night, Ruth slept more soundly than she had since Mahlon became sick. She woke up refreshed, ready for the demanding labor that awaited her. Instead of dreading the day, anticipation brought a new lightness to her steps.

Naomi walked part of the way with her. "I'm going to fetch water. Tonight, we will have warm barley bread with stew for dinner."

Ruth clasped Naomi in a long embrace, delighted to see the older woman showing an interest in life again. "I will bring you so much grain tonight, you'll be able to bathe in it."

Naomi patted her cheek. "I think I shall stick to water for my bath. Have a care. It will be hot today."

Not far from Boaz's field, Ruth heard the sound of hoofbeats, too fast to belong to a donkey. She moved to the edge of the road and turned to see who rode in such haste.

Boaz.

He slowed the beast as he came near her, and to her surprise, dismounted.

"Shalom, Ruth."

"Shalom, my lord."

He led the horse by the bridle and walked alongside her. "You are on the road early. The sun has just risen. Did you walk in the dark?"

"For a little while."

He frowned. "You must take care. It can be dangerous for a woman alone. A couple of the women who work for me live near Naomi. I'll arrange for you to come with them from now on."

"Yes, my lord."

They walked in silence for some minutes. A badger ran through a clump of bushes bordering the side of a narrow field, and the horse neighed, shaking its head with agitation. Boaz whispered to the beast and caressed its smooth, black pelt until it calmed.

"He is magnificent," Ruth said. "What do you call him?"

"Shakhor. He was as black as the darkest hour of the night when he was born, and the name seemed appropriate. Do you know much about horses?"

"Everything I need to know. Dangerous on both ends and uncomfortable in the middle."

Boaz laughed. Ruth couldn't tear her eyes away for a moment. He was a hand taller than she, and Ruth had to look up to see him clearly. His face had transformed with the laugh; straight teeth, white as shorn ewes flashed through his trim mustache and beard, making him appear younger.

"I hadn't thought of it like that," he said, his mouth still softened with a smile.

His deep voice had a warm timbre, which sent a shiver down her spine. She lowered her lashes, annoyed at her own foolishness. Just because the man had been kind did not give her leave to turn into a clumsy young girl. Still, she could not deny the feeling of accomplishment that stole over her when she managed to make him laugh.

Naomi's prediction proved right. The day grew unseasonably hot, more like high summer than midspring. The women Ruth followed in the field paid her little attention. No one spoke to her. Boaz might find her decision to come to Bethlehem admirable, but his laborers were not as easily persuaded. The heat made everyone testy and a few verbal skirmishes broke out among the workers.

Distracted by a fierce argument, Ruth missed the sudden halt of one of the girls and plowed into her. "I beg your pardon!"

"Why don't you watch your step, you stupid Moabite?" the girl snapped.

Ruth nodded and took a step back. Another woman bent to pick up several heads of barley, which Ruth had dropped when she had collided with the other girl, and handed them to her.

"Thank you," Ruth said, surprised at the unexpected kindness.

"Pay no mind to Dinah. She's mean to everyone. It's just her way. She is twenty-five and still unmarried; it has soured her disposition."

Ruth shrugged. "There are worse fates."

"Like what?"

Ruth bent to pick up a stalk of grain. "Like being twenty-six and still unmarried."

The woman laughed. She was younger than Ruth, and pretty, with long dimples that peeped at the slightest excuse. "I'm Hannah. And you are Ruth. The whole of Bethlehem has heard of you, and how you came from Moab with Naomi."

"Do you know my mother-in-law?"

"I was a child when she left; I don't remember her. But we live near her house. Before we began work today, the master asked that I walk with you to the field so you won't have to come alone." Hannah gave Ruth a curious glance.

Ruth allowed her veil to fall forward, covering the reddening of her cheeks. "I am sorry for the trouble. He was kin to my husband's father; I suppose he feels he must watch over Naomi and me."

Hannah shrugged. "No trouble. As long as you don't mind Dinah's sharp tongue, for I travel with her."

That evening Ruth took home an even bigger armful of barley. At this rate, she and Naomi would have more than a year's provision by the end of the harvest season, with sufficient surplus to allow them to barter for olive oil and dried fruit and nuts. Perhaps she might even be able to have the roof repaired. She felt like skipping.

In the distance, she noticed a black horse tethered to a bush at the side of the road. There was no sign of its rider. By the time she reached the animal, Boaz had still not returned. Ruth reached a cautious hand and caressed Shakhor's soft pelt. It stopped lazily grazing on the grass and lifted its regal head to give her a disinterested look before returning to its meal. Ruth wondered at Boaz's absence. Why had he abandoned the horse? Should she linger to find if he needed help?

She heard a sound in the bushes and tensed. A moment later, Boaz emerged, a lamb cradled in his arms.

"Ruth!" He came to an abrupt halt.

"I saw your horse and wondered if you might need assistance, my lord."

He approached her, soothing the trembling lamb as he did. "That was thoughtful. My thanks. I saw this little fellow in trouble and stopped to rescue him. It's one of mine."

Ruth reached a shy hand to caress the lamb. It let out a weak cry. "What's wrong with him?"

"He got caught in brambles and in his struggle to get free, got badly cut. As if that weren't bad enough, somewhere in the process, he broke a leg. Must have become separated from the flock, and the shepherd overlooked it." His tone grew hard as he mentioned the shepherd's oversight.

"Is he suffering?"

Boaz's eyelids drooped. "Yes."

"Can he be healed?"

"Perhaps. My head shepherd has a gentle hand and a great deal of knowledge. He might be able to help the poor creature."

Ruth noticed the tender way Boaz caressed the lamb. He owned thousands of sheep. One more or less could not make a material difference to him. And yet he treated the helpless animal with singular care, as though he were the only one Boaz owned. As though the pain of this little lamb made his heart ache.

She thought of Naomi. Of how wounded she was, and broken. It came to her that the Lord held Naomi with the same tenderness that Boaz held his lamb. With the same care, He caressed His child, bleeding and hurt from the sorrows of life.

"What is it?" Boaz asked. "You have a strange look in your eyes."

"I was thinking of Naomi, my lord. How she is so much like this lamb, bruised and bleeding from the brambles of life. We can become lame in the spirit the same way this creature is lame in his body." She did not tell him of her picture of the Lord, anxious that she might appear presumptuous. Worse. He might think her silly.

Boaz's chest expanded as he took air into his lungs. "That is a good description for how Naomi must feel. Grief is as sharp as thorns. Heavy like a gravestone. It can crush you to the bone." He spoke with the passion of one who had tasted personally the bitter brew of mourning.

Ruth wanted to tell him she knew exactly what he meant. But it was inappropriate for a gleaner in his field to speak so boldly to the master.

He extended the lamb toward her. "Would you hold him while I mount? Then you can hand him back to me. He will suffer less that way."

Ruth cradled the lamb, her heart beating fast, though she could not understand why. Her fingers grazed against Boaz's hand as she handed the animal back to him after he had mounted his horse. Her mouth ran dry.

"Shalom, Ruth," he said, and galloped so fast she lost sight of him before she had a chance to blink twice.

Chapter Ten

Surely the LORD *is in this place, and I did not know it.*

GENESIS 28:16

Boaz handed the lamb to Zabdiel with care. "Can you do anything for him?"

The head shepherd clucked his tongue as he examined the animal. "It's bad."

"Find out the name of the fool who left him in that condition. A shepherd ought to have more wits about him."

Zabdiel removed his turban and wrapped it around the lamb. His wild hair waved about his head in the evening breeze as he strode to the sheepfold, his forehead furrowed in concentration, no doubt planning strategies for saving the lamb.

Boaz went inside the house. He needed a hot meal and a cold drink. The memory of Ruth's face haunted him. *We can become lame in the spirit the same way this creature is lame in his body,* she had said. Rich wisdom from lips too young to have learned it.

The servant brought him new wine, chilly from the stone cellar. It tasted sweet on his tongue, and he tipped the cup again. Shedding his mantle, he seated himself on an overstuffed cushion, blind to the rich colors embroidered on the sturdy wool. All the things that he wished to undertake before retiring for the night paraded before his mind: the household accounts, the report from the merchants who worked for him, the latest tally from the shepherds. He made no move to address any of it, and sat, instead, tipping his cup, wondering about Ruth.

What was it about her that played such havoc with his mind? He recalled the sheen of tears in her eyes the first time he met her, and the powerful impulse to wipe them away. Was he short of women that this foreign widow with her wrinkled garb should affect him so? Had he not had an abundance of young girls and widows shoved under his nose since the death of his wife? Not once had he been tempted to wipe *their* tears away.

No woman had affected him like this since Judith.

More than ten years had passed since he lost Judith. In spite of the needs of his body, not once had Boaz been tempted to unite his life with another woman in all that time. Judith had taken his heart. He had nothing more to give. To risk.

We can become lame in the spirit the same way this creature is lame in his body. It was as though she had seen into him when she had spoken those words. He had a good notion how Naomi felt. Like that lamb, bruised and torn to shreds by the long, sharp thorns of the Judean hills.

Old memories, which he kept locked tight inside himself, sprung loose because of a young woman's unknowing pronouncement. The Moabite who had wormed her way into his mind and refused to leave. He thought of Judith's final days, her life ebbing away as he watched helplessly. The memory faded quickly, replaced instead by an image of Ruth smiling. Ruth eating. Ruth gleaning.

He shoved aside the untouched meal that the servant had served him and forced himself to rise up and attend his work. This overindulgence with thoughts of Ruth had to end. There could be no future in it. He was too old. Too worn. Too spent. She deserved a younger man. One with a whole heart who could give her a future. But even as he pulled the rolls of parchment toward him, the image of a golden-eyed girl with bow-curved lips and the grace of a gazelle disturbed his concentration.

Without warning, understanding dawned. He realized what

had drawn him so irresistibly to her the first day he had met her. Heartache and disappointment might shadow her eyes, but Ruth had a strength that made her go on. Persist. Fight. There was a strange sweetness in her perseverance. She hadn't become bitter and hard from grief. She had grown soft and strong.

Ruth hurt. He could sense that in every expression, every gesture. But there was no hint of self-pity in her. The hardship of her life did not rule her. She bore the pain and made peace with it, and pushed on to grasp at hope.

Boaz knew the worth of such a spirit.

He started as Mahalath came in, her shy steps so quiet, he almost missed her. "May I clean up, my lord?"

He swept an arm. "Yes, Mahalath. I have finished."

As the young woman knelt, her face turned white. "You did not like the meal, my lord?"

Boaz flinched, annoyed at his oversight. "The meal tasted wonderful. It's not the fault of the food that I did not eat; I'm simply not hungry."

Her pallor did not lift. Her hands shook as she gathered the bowl and the uneaten bread. Mahalath had once served Jaala, a man with cruel habits, and even though she had now been in Boaz's employ for eight months, she still startled at every imagined shortcoming, expecting a harsh reaction.

"Did you cook tonight?" he asked, gentling his voice.

"Yes, master."

"You know I enjoy your cooking. Worry no more about my shrinking appetite. You've done no wrong. Take yourself to bed, and I promise to eat heartily whatever you put before me tomorrow."

Mahalath gave a tremulous smile. He expelled a relieved breath as the shadow of dread left her face. For Mahalath's sake, if nothing else, he would like to knock Jaala out with a well-placed blow to the man's straight nose. It was the only straight thing about him; Jaala was as crooked as the horn of a goat.

For three days, Boaz avoided the field in which Ruth worked. On the fourth day, he could no longer resist returning. He told himself his concern for her well-being motivated this visit. Although he had warned his workers to treat her well, he needed to make certain they followed through with his command and that she fared well. He undertook this scrutiny for Elimelech's sake, he assured himself.

He studied her from afar, not wishing to approach her in front of others, knowing such special attention would arouse curiosity. Satisfied that the laborers were treating her with the generosity he had demanded, he spent his time with Abel, discussing the barley harvest and the good progress of the wheat crop in nearby fields. They resolved a few minor problems and made necessary decisions regarding a fight between two laborers, and a dispute over one woman's wages.

Boaz lingered far longer than necessary in his conversation with Abel until the workers stopped for the day and began to disband. Not until everyone headed for home did Boaz mount his horse and with a plodding gait unlike his usual enthusiastic gallop made his way back to Bethlehem.

He came upon Ruth near the city gate as he knew he would. She walked alone, her bundle hefty, held with a protective arm to her side.

Boaz dismounted. "Let my horse carry that for you the rest of the way, Ruth."

Ruth's eyes widened. "That is most of kind of you, my lord."

He secured her veil, bulging with grain, to his saddle and walked by her side, leading the horse by its leather bridle. "How fares Naomi?"

"She recovers slowly. Your generosity has restored a glimmer of hope. I think she despaired of life before I brought her that first bundle of barley. At least, now she believes we won't starve."

A fat fly buzzed near Boaz's face and he swatted it away. "This magnitude of loss requires more than human kindness. It needs God's own hand."

"The trouble is, she . . . cannot draw near to God now."

Boaz considered her words. "That's to be expected, I suppose. She reminds me of Jacob. Have you heard of him?"

"One of the ancestors of your people? Is he the one who cheated his brother of his firstborn blessing?"

"That's Jacob. When he ran from home in fear of his brother's vengeance, he passed through a forsaken wilderness, all alone, not knowing his future, not knowing if he could ever return home. That night as he lay down to sleep, it must have seemed to him that he had nothing, not even a cushion for his head. He had to use a stone on the ground. Can you imagine how solitary and afraid he felt?"

Without a word, Ruth nodded. The merest hint of irony touched the slant of her lips, and he remembered that she had herself, not long ago, set out on a similar journey. "Of course you can imagine," he said, feeling sheepish. "Well, that night, Jacob had a dream—a God-touched vision that brought him hope.

"He dreamt of a ladder. Its base touched the earth and the top of it reached into the heavens. The angels of the Lord ascended and descended on the rungs, coming to earth to do His bidding among us, and returning from the world of men after completing their missions in our midst. In this forsaken wilderness, the angels of the Lord descended to do the work of Him who had sent them. The Lord Himself stood at the top of the ladder."

"Jacob saw Him?"

"In his dream. Yes. And heard from Him too. When he awoke, he said, 'Surely the Lord is in this place, and I did not know it.' Jacob glimpsed one of the great truths of our faith that day."

"What truth, my lord?"

"We travel through many wildernesses in life, be they real like Jacob's Bethel, or wildernesses of the soul. Broken dreams, loss, grief. Sometimes there is nothing to comfort us but the hard stones of a lonely path. In those places, God seems so far away and distant.

The way He does to Naomi right now. Yet, there is a ladder that touches down into the soil of our loneliest wilderness. The angels of the Lord ascend and descend upon it, and He is Himself watchful to give us aid.

"Like Jacob, Naomi has lost her family. She is in a wilderness beyond comprehension. But she is not alone in it. Jacob's ladder reaches into that forsaken place and the Lord is with her."

The young woman at his side came to an arrested stop. Abandoning her usual modest manner, she looked him straight in the eye. The golden irises reflected a stunned wonder. Boaz's chest tightened. She understood. She understood the glory of a God who would reach into the ravaged places of life, like Naomi's shadowlands of death. She understood Boaz and his loyalty to such a God. He could sense the pull the Lord had on her, the mighty pull of a God who was a steadfast helper and a rock of security. Boaz found himself fascinated by that quality of clinging faith that seemed to seep out of her every action.

"I never thought the Lord could be so close. Close enough to be present in the midst of our troubles." There was a catch in her voice.

Boaz twirled a hand in the air. "Jacob's ladder could be touching the soil of this very road. Where you are walking, angels might be ascending and descending. The problem is that like Jacob, most of us spend our days not knowing. The Lord is never far. It is our blindness that makes Him seem so. The veil between heaven and earth is parchment thin."

She said nothing and he liked that silence. It was a silence filled with intelligent thought, with compassionate understanding.

At the gate of the city, she asked, "Does Naomi know the lesson of Jacob's ladder?"

"She is sure to know the story. But not the lesson, I think. Not yet."

"Thank you, my lord," she said as he handed her the barley. "You have given me a great gift."

He knew she didn't mean the barley. "It was a lesson I had to learn myself once, when I walked through a barren land like Naomi. And like you."

"Did you ever come out to the other side of that wilderness?"

He frowned and wondered what answer to give. In truth, he did not know. "In some ways I have. And in some ways, I will always carry a little of it with me, no matter what green pastures I might travel in."

She lowered her lids. To his amazement, he noted that she hid tears. Instinct told him that her tears were for him, not Naomi or herself. It shocked him that she would be so moved on his behalf. He knew she was grateful to him for his protection and benevolence. But gratitude had not produced these tears.

He cleared his throat. Part of him wished to take her home there and then. Forget sense. Forget the past. Forget her grieving heart. Forget Moab. He fisted his hands, feeling nauseous at the strength of this wanting. Had he dropped his brain in a ditch somewhere?

He cleared his throat again, sounding like a sick rooster. "You best head home now, Ruth. It's growing late and Naomi will worry."

Was it his imagination or did her shoulders droop as she thanked him with polite formality?

Chapter Eleven

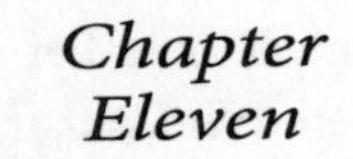

The Lord *upholds all who are falling*
and raises up all who are bowed down.
PSALM 145:14

Ruth fell into a familiar routine, walking with Naomi partway to the well before sunrise, then meeting Hannah and Dinah for the trek to the field outside Jerusalem. Her days passed in a haze, melting one into another. The hard physical labor of constant bending, straightening, carrying, walking, bending, straightening, carrying, walking had a soothing effect on her spirit. At nights she dreamt less. Mahlon stopped haunting her sleep.

One evening, just after concluding her gleaning for the day, the strap on her sandal broke, and she stayed a few extra moments to fix the damage, waving her companions to start ahead of her. It took longer to fix the leather than she expected, so she could not catch up with her friends and had to walk home alone. Around the sharp bend in the road, she came upon Boaz. Ruth gave him a respectful nod, intending to walk on, when he motioned her to wait as he dismounted. The black horse plodded with a sedate pace next to him as he joined her.

"Alone tonight?"

"Yes, my lord."

"I'll walk with you the rest of the way. I need to check on an orchard, which is close to Naomi's house."

"You grow fruit, as well?"

"Figs. Have a weakness for them when they are fresh. So does my horse."

"Shakhor?"

Boaz grinned. "I have to muzzle him when I go there. Gives himself colic if I don't watch his every move."

Ruth shook her head, too embarrassed to admit his horse probably ate better than she did. As they approached the orchard, they noticed a group of children playing. Boaz did not seem put out by their intrusion on his land. He smiled as he watched them. A boy, no older than nine, standing on the sidelines, approached the others. Ruth noticed the crutch under his left arm. He limped badly, and a thick bandage covered his foot. The bandage could not hide the fact that the foot was malformed, more a stump than a proper appendage.

"Let me play," he said.

The biggest child in the group, a sturdy boy a head taller than the rest of the children, shoved him hard so that he lost control of the crutch and fell. "We don't need cripples. Leave us alone."

Boaz's smile faded. Without hesitation he strode into the midst of the children. "Shalom, children." His voice remained pleasant. If he was angry, it did not show.

The children gathered around him. "Shalom, master!"

"You're playing, I see. And Eli?"

The bigger boy who obviously acted as leader stepped forward. "He can't play. He can't keep up."

"I'll fix that, Yair." Boaz lifted the boy named Eli high over his shoulders and settled him there. The child had beautiful green eyes, which lit up with delight as he dangled over Boaz's tall form. "I'll be Eli's feet. He'll be the guide. He'll tell me where to run, and I will be his obedient servant."

"That's not right, master Boaz!" Yair made his opinion clear without the slightest hint of bashfulness. "You'll win. You're much bigger than the rest of us."

"And you are much bigger than the rest of *them*. I didn't see anyone holding that against you. Why do you hold it against me? You choose to use your strength for your glory, Yair. I choose to use mine to help Eli. You see? We are equal. We are both allowed to choose freely."

Of course the outcome of the game was a foregone conclusion. The children who allied themselves with Boaz and Eli did well. The rest lost. But everyone laughed, except perhaps Yair, who grew redder and more recalcitrant with every passing moment.

In the end, he confronted Boaz, his nostrils flaring with annoyance. "I would have won if not for you, master. Why did you help him? He's just a cripple."

Boaz swung Eli down in a slow, careful arc. Ruth could tell that beneath his calm mask, he held back a rising tide of displeasure. He straightened and walked toward one of the fig trees. "Let me show you something, and perhaps then you will understand." He pointed to the pale bark. "What is the weakest part of the tree? Is it the roots?"

"No," the children shouted.

"Is it the trunk?" He wrapped his arms around the trunk and pretended to try to pull the tree up from the ground. The children dissolved in merriment.

"No!"

"Is it the branches?" He tried to snap off a hefty branch where it met the trunk.

"That's strong too," one child yelled. "You can't break that with your hands."

"What about here?" He pointed to a delicate twig farther down the length of a branch. From it hung a fat cluster of green figs. With two careful fingers he snapped off the fragile stem, and the whole cluster of fruit landed in the palm of his hand. "Isn't that stem the weakest? And yet that's what holds the fruit. If you crush it when the blossoms are forming, there won't be any fruit. Do you understand?"

A short girl with two thick braids hanging down her back

stepped forward. "You mean Eli is like that stem? He may be the weakest of us, but he bears sweet fruit?"

"Exactly." Boaz grinned at the girl and gave her a handful of the ripest figs as reward.

"What kind of fruit could someone like Eli provide? He can't dig. He can't reap. He can't do carpentry or build houses," Yair said. "He may be weak. But there is no fruit hanging from his branch that I see."

"That's where you are wrong. Here, Eli. Come sit down and show your friends what you can do." He motioned to a squat stone with a level top. Eli limped over and sat down. He gave Boaz a doubtful look.

Boaz gave him an encouraging nod. "Show them what you showed me last week. Go on."

Eli took a deep breath. He drew out a wooden flute that had been tucked inside his belt, hidden from view. After playing a few sweet notes, he started to tell a story.

"Many years ago, a young shepherd lived in the farthest hills of Judea. He was poor, but he was a good shepherd to his sheep. They never went hungry or thirsty. He knew the land and always found green pastures for them, even if it meant walking a long way."

Ruth was enraptured. In a few words, Eli had been transformed from an ordinary child with a lame foot into a skilled storyteller. The boy clearly had extraordinary talent beyond his years. Ruth bent forward, holding still, waiting for the next words to fall from Eli's lips.

"One night, a stranger approached him," the boy went on. "He was thin and his clothes were ragged. His lips were cracked, his eyes bloodshot, his feet bare and dirty."

The children sat around Eli, spellbound by the tale he was concocting. He was an astoundingly attractive child, with large sea-green eyes and dark blond hair. That beauty came alive as he told his story, his facial expressions reflecting each word. A little girl coughed and several voices hushed her.

Eli went on. "The shepherd knew that the man must be hungry and thirsty. They were a long way from any town or well. He opened his pouch and saw that he had just enough cheese and bread for one meal. This he gave to the ragged man, knowing he would go hungry himself, perhaps for days.

"He fetched his skin of water and washed the man's hands and feet, and let him drink as much as he needed. After the man was full, the shepherd pulled out his flute and played this tune for his poor guest, hoping the song would comfort him."

Eli put his own flute to his lips. The melody that he coaxed out of the simple instrument was new to Ruth. A haunting unforgettable melody, which dipped and soared with such expertise, it pulled the heart with it.

No one even breathed when he finished.

"*That was for you,* the shepherd told the stranger. *My gift to help you in your weariness. I hope it brought you joy.*

"The stranger stood up and allowed his frayed cloak to fall to the ground. The moon was high in the sky and a strange thing happened. His worn-out clothes started to shimmer in the starlight. His face began to glow. The young shepherd realized that this was no ordinary man. He was in the presence of an angel of the Lord. He fell to the ground, his nose buried in the dirt as he shivered with fear.

"But the angel bade him to stand. 'You were kind to me when you thought I was poor and abandoned. You gave me your only food and washed my bruised feet. In your kindness, you played such music for me that even God's messengers would weep to hear. Now I will be kind to you.'

"He took the shepherd by the hand and showed him a hiding place at the base of a twisted olive tree, where the tops of the roots were visible. *There you will find a pearl of great price. It will provide for you for the rest of your life,* he told the young shepherd.

"So the shepherd bade a tearful farewell to his sheep and sold them, every last one, to a sleepy merchant in Bethlehem. With the money he earned, he purchased the land where the pearl was hidden. When he dug out that jewel, he saw that it was as big as a sparrow's egg, fit for a king's crown. He sold the pearl and earned so much money that he was able to build a large house on his new land. He had a well dug right next to the house so his servants never had to walk far to fetch water. Then he returned to the merchant in Bethlehem and bought all his sheep back, and released them into pasture for the rest of their lives.

"Whenever travelers passed by that house, the shepherd made certain to feed them a feast and take care of their needs, for he had learned that a man might entertain angels unaware. This happened countless years ago, and that house has long since turned to dust. But people say that even today, on a star-filled night, if you listen carefully, you will hear the faint strains of the shepherd's tune playing."

Again Eli lifted his flute and played the lilting melody he had played earlier.

When he finished, for a few moments no one stirred. Even the birds seemed utterly still. Then the children rose up and rushed toward Eli, begging him for another story, another tune.

"Are you hungry, Eli? You can have my cinnamon bread," the girl with the braids offered.

Ruth observed the transformation with silent wonder. Boaz, with one clever stroke, had changed the boy's life. Without a single quarrel, without harsh words, he had managed to teach the children to value Eli. To think of him as a gift rather than a cripple. She was struck by Boaz's brilliance in handling the human heart. Ruth had never seen another man so gifted at influencing the way others thought.

"I've not seen anything like that before," she said when they were on the road again.

"Yes. He is a dazzling child."

"That is true enough. But that's not what I meant. What you did, that astounded me even more."

"What I did?" He seemed so baffled that she laughed.

"You turned that boy's life around. With mere words."

"Oh well, they are only children, Ruth."

Ruth realized that he had no true concept of his effect on people. He did not comprehend that he influenced others by words and his mere presence in a way that other men could not. She shook her head. He wasn't a mere landowner. Boaz was what the Israelites called a *gibbor hayil*, an influential man of might and courage, an extraordinary man who shone above others. A man, who in spite of his many responsibilities, took the time to improve the life of a broken child, and to walk a young widow to her door in order to keep her safe.

He stared into the horizon. "I probably won't see you for some time. Harvest season places many demands on me. If you have need of anything, you and Naomi, please send for me. For the sake of Elimelech, my kin, I will do what I can."

Several days later a new girl added to their company. She had dark skin and dark eyes and dark hair and she rarely smiled. Ruth found out her name was Mahalath.

"She works at the master's house, usually. But when he is away from home for long stretches of time, she comes to the field to help," Hannah said. Mahalath herself spoke little.

At first, Ruth assumed she was shy. But when Dinah bumped into Mahalath accidentally, the dark eyes flew open with a startled expression of terror, and the girl raised her arms over her face and head as if bracing for a blow.

"Calm down. No one is trying to kill you, Mahalath," Dinah said sourly. The poor girl bit her lip and slowed down, so that she could walk alone behind the others.

"Should we try to comfort her?" Ruth asked Hannah.

Hannah grimaced, her dimples peeping out. "Best leave her be. She once suffered at the hands of a cruel man, and it makes her wary of people. If not for lord Boaz's intervention, she might not be here today."

"I am sorry for her misfortune."

Ruth did her best throughout that day to show Mahalath kindness and win her trust. She fetched her water, interrupted her own gleaning to give the girl a hand when she struggled with the larger bundles, and even offered her a piece of fig cake, which Naomi had prepared from the dried figs given to her by a neighbor. Mahalath refused, but at the end of the day, when they were leaving the field, she bestowed a shy smile upon Ruth. Ruth felt as elated as Deborah after the victory against Sisera.

Mahalath came again that week since Boaz had traveled to Jerusalem on a matter of business and would remain from home for some days.

"The master doesn't require that I come to the field. But when he is away, I have little to do at home, and feel guilty taking wages from him when I give meagerly in return," Mahalath explained to Ruth as they took their morning rest in the shade. "He did not need me when he hired me. He only did so to help."

"I have tasted of his goodness also," Ruth said.

Speaking of him made her aware of a hollowness that had dogged her steps since the week before, when he had stopped coming to the field. As if he were a dear friend and she missed him. She narrowed her eyes, annoyed with herself. He was a landowner, a man of high repute, with thousands of livestock and a large chunk of Bethlehem for property. Outside the bonds of charity, he had no time for the likes of her. He had as much as said so, when he had taken his leave of her. He would help her *for the sake of Elimelech.* What other reason had he to seek her company? What had she to offer such a man, poor, dependent, widowed, and barren as she was? She might as well try to swim the length of the Dead Sea than bridge the chasm that separated them.

"Best return to work," she said, and Mahalath joined her.

As they walked farther into the field, Ruth's foot caught on a jutting stone and she fell, her face landing in the dirt. The acrid smell of sheep dung and cultivated soil filled her nose.

"Are you hurt?" Mahalath asked, concern coloring her voice.

Ruth pushed herself to her feet and beat the dirt from her clothes. Ignoring the stinging in her hands and knees, she said, "It's nothing." It occurred to her that life had landed her facedown in the dirt. She determined that she would rise up and move on. She would take one step at a time and fret no more about tomorrow or about Boaz.

Chapter Twelve

Wait for the Lord;
be strong, and let your heart take courage;
wait for the Lord!
PSALM 27:14

The heat wave did not break. It intensified with each passing day, making gleaning more difficult. One morning, Mahalath did not come to work in the field and Ruth wondered if Boaz had returned from his journey. She missed the girl's company. Mahalath never treated Ruth as an outsider. Instead, she acted as if Ruth's presence were a precious gift. For her part, although she did not know Mahalath's story, Ruth admired the girl's sweetness, which had survived whatever horrors she had tasted in life.

The laborers were almost finished in the field; they had reaped and gathered row after row of plump barley until the lush land had been reduced to stubble. In a few days, they would move on to harvest a vast wheat field that had ripened and sat ready to be gathered.

Ruth felt tired. She had worked every day from sunup until late into the afternoon for four weeks except on the Sabbath, which Boaz insisted everyone should keep holy by resting.

The day after Mahalath did not come to work, Ruth awoke late. Weariness had leached her strength and she barely forced herself to leave her bed.

"Why did you not wake me?" she asked Naomi, as she rushed to get dressed.

"You seemed so tired, I did not have the heart. Here, take this bread and eat it on the way."

Ruth took Naomi's offering and thanked her. She put it on a stool while she wrapped her hair in a light covering and rushed out, forgetting to fetch the thin bread. When she remembered, it was too late to return. She would just have to work on an empty stomach until the midday break, when Boaz provided a repast for his workers.

Ruth was gleaning more slowly than usual. The heat sapped her energy. She looked longingly at the jugs of freshwater, drawn by the men. But they were far from her, and she felt she could not spare the time for a drink, having already stopped to rest once. She would wait until mealtime.

A nagging headache had dogged her every step for several hours and it was growing worse. Sweat trickled down her back. She wiped an arm against her damp forehead and straightened. The world tilted and Ruth gasped. She realized with sudden useless insight that she had been foolish not to drink water on such a day. Dizziness and nausea made her sit hastily on the ground. She gulped, putting her head on her raised knees, hoping the weakness would pass soon.

"Drink this," a voice said close to her ear. She knew that voice, the deep, warm timbre of it. Swiveling her head, she came face-to-face with Boaz. He had knelt at her side, his face close enough to touch.

Without a word, he put a cup to her mouth. "Drink. It's the sun. You have had too much of the heat."

Ruth drank until she had to stop to take a deep breath. She felt foolish, half-collapsed on the ground, still unable to rise.

"Drink the rest."

Ruth obeyed until she drained the cup. "Where did you come from?" she blurted, too sick to sort through her words.

"I returned from Jerusalem yesterday and decided to inspect the field today. It's good that I did. I noticed you seemed unwell before you collapsed. When was the last time you ate?"

Ruth remained mute.

"When?" he insisted.

"Last night."

He frowned. "What were you thinking? You can't do this work on an empty belly. I suppose you've had no water all day, either."

Ruth reddened and pulled her veil forward.

"A hedgehog has more sense," he muttered. Behind him, other workers had gathered, gawping.

Boaz rose. "Nothing of interest here. Everyone back to work."

In spite of their curiosity, his laborers were quick to obey. He knelt back by her side. "I'll take you home."

With a gasp, Ruth raised her head. "No need, my lord. I am well now." She forced her body into obedience and pushed herself to stand. To her mortification, her legs wobbled and she collapsed back on the ground.

Boaz put a steadying arm on her back. "Home," he said, his tone brooking no argument, and Ruth did not dare protest again. He called for Abel to fetch his horse.

A wave of nausea almost proved her undoing; she felt hot and cold at once, and only willpower kept her from collapsing altogether. Boaz slid an arm beneath her knees and lifted her up. He swung her into the horse's saddle. Dizzily, she grabbed what was in front of her to keep herself from slipping, and found herself clutching a fistful of Shakhor's black mane. The unhappy animal pawed the ground and shook its head up and down. Ruth hastily loosened her hold and would have toppled over if Boaz hadn't swung behind her and held her securely to him.

He quieted the horse and brought it under control. "Ready?"

"If you only allow me to rest in the shade for a while, I—"

"No." He signaled Shakhor to start walking.

Ruth felt too weak to sit straight. When she tried, the pain in her head became unbearable, triggering more nausea. Giving up, she subsided against him. His arm tightened protectively, preventing her from falling.

"I'm sorry to be so much trouble, my lord."

She felt him shift as he shrugged. "I've had worse troubles. Now close your eyes and try to sleep. You are still shaking."

Sleep! As if she could, held in his arms, bouncing atop his big horse, the world careening around her. How could she have been so witless? A child knew better than to allow herself to get into such a state by not drinking and eating, or taking appropriate shelter from the sun.

Boaz shifted in the saddle and drew her up a little. As if reading her restless thoughts, he said, "It has happened to me too. I suffered from heatstroke once."

"You, my lord?" she managed to say.

"I was ten years old. But yes, I became very sick and almost died for lack of water. I can still remember how miserable I felt."

Ruth's lips felt dry and chapped. They stung as she licked them and she winced. He was trying to make her feel better, and succeeding. "Well, I am not going to die, unless embarrassment can kill you."

He laughed. The sound washed over her like a balm, and even though she still felt sick and her head hurt as if someone had hit it with the sharp end of a plow, she wanted to smile.

Naomi saw them coming from where she sat in the yard, grinding flour, and ran into the road to meet them, her mouth trembling with anxiety.

"Fear not, Naomi," Boaz said as he dismounted. "She stayed in the sun too long and was overcome. A couple of days in bed, and she will be ready to glean my fields until they are bare." He lifted Ruth up in gentle arms and brought her inside.

"Oh, my poor girl. My poor girl. She seemed so tired this morning, I ought to have kept her home."

"Don't fret yourself, Naomi," Ruth said. "I'm well."

Naomi rushed to set up a mat with extra bedding and a pillow for her head. Boaz laid her down. For a moment he lingered, looking at her. "I don't want to see you in my fields until after the Sabbath."

"Yes, my lord."

"Come to the new field when you are better. You can glean wheat there."

Naomi thanked him, but he waved away her words and spoke a reassurance that Ruth did not catch. She lay back weakly against the pillow when he left and wondered why the room felt empty and bereft without him. Naomi stood at the door, a thoughtful look on her face. But as she fell asleep, it wasn't Naomi's face Ruth saw. The image of a man with brown eyes and a bright smile claimed her last waking thought.

Naomi pressed another glass of barley water, sweetened with honey into Ruth's hand. "Where did you find honey?" Ruth asked, sipping the delicious concoction.

"Bartered for it yesterday morning. A woman who lives close to the city gate found a hive. You've brought home so much grain that I have been able to trade some of it for fresh supplies. How do you feel?"

"Recovered, thanks to your care." Ruth had slept through the afternoon and into the night, and woken up ravenous. Naomi had filled her with bread and cheese and barley water in the hours since. "I'm as stuffed as the geese in Pharaoh's kitchens. If I'd had all this food and drink inside me when I fell ill, lord Boaz would not have been able to lift me."

"I wonder why Boaz did not summon a cart and have one of his men convey you here, instead? He would have saved himself an uncomfortable journey." That strange, thoughtful expression settled on Naomi's face again.

"Because I am Elimelech's daughter-in-law. If not for that, I think he might have forbidden me to return to his fields."

"Why do you believe that?"

"He was so angry when he first found me, his hands shook. He said I had the sense of a hedgehog."

A hint of a smile touched Naomi's lips. "Men sometimes hide their fear with anger. He must have been concerned when he saw you collapse."

"Why would he be concerned for me? What am I to him but the poor widow of a long-lost relative?"

Naomi rose to fetch wool. She had taken to spinning again, which she had not done since Moab. "He watched his wife die, they tell me. So he is probably deeply moved by the sight of a sick woman."

Ruth felt her throat close. "His wife?"

"When Elimelech and I left Bethlehem, Boaz was married. Happily married, though he and his wife had lost their only child, a beautiful girl named Sarah. But Miriam tells me that several months after our departure, his wife died in childbirth. He has shown no interest in taking another wife since, and not for lack of effort on the part of every mother with a young, unmarried daughter from here to the hills of Jerusalem."

"That is why he understands so well."

"Understands what?"

"The pain of grief." Ruth related the lesson of Jacob's ladder as Boaz had taught her. "The Lord has not forgotten you, Mother. He still rules over your coming and going."

Naomi listened, her eyes red, her mouth tight.

"Shalom!" a soft voice called from the open door. The women turned to find Mahalath waiting respectfully outside, a large basket balanced on her head. "My master sends me with greetings. May I come in?"

"Come, child. How nice of Boaz to remember us." Naomi offered Mahalath a cushion.

"The master bid me to bring you a few gifts, mistress." She lowered her basket and drew out a goatskin.

"Wine!" Naomi tasted a little and smacked her lips. "It's wonderful."

"He had guests last night and they slaughtered a lamb. He sent you some of the leftover meat."

Naomi examined the salted lamb and wrapped it back in the linen. "If this is the leftover, I wonder what the first portion might look like. He has sent us the best cut."

Mahalath gave a shy smile. "And here are a few cakes of figs and raisins. He thought you might enjoy them."

"To what do we owe so much kindness?"

Mahalath shrugged. "My lord thought with Ruth sick, you might be able to use extra provisions."

Naomi nodded. "Please tell your lord that we are thankful. Tell him I pray I shall be able to return his kindness one day."

Ruth nodded. "I am his grateful servant." She would have preferred Boaz himself to all the lambs and figs and raisins of Judah. That thought made her blush and she sank abruptly on a cushion.

Mahalath rose to take her leave, empty basket swinging by her side. "Can't you stay?" Ruth asked. "Your company would be a blessing."

The dark-eyed girl hesitated. "For a little while. It's quiet at home today. The master won't mind, I know."

"You are very faithful to Boaz, aren't you?"

"He helped me when no one would. I was under the yoke of a cruel master. My father had many debts and had mortgaged our home to a man named Jaala. Unable to repay the mortgage, my father gave me to Jaala as a slave in exchange for the money he owed. We knew he was reputed to be a hard man and a fox in business. But what could my father do?

"I never knew why, but Jaala took a special dislike to me. He enjoyed punishing me for every small mistake. His threats were so cruel, I began to fear my own shadow. He was hard with all his workers. But toward me, he showed unbearable brutality."

Naomi, who had been listening to the story with quiet intensity, gasped. Ruth wondered what made her mother-in-law so pale and still, as if she were personally affected by the details of Mahalath's account.

"I am pained to hear of your suffering, Mahalath. Why did no one interfere? Bring him to answer for his malice?" Ruth asked.

"Jaala is a crafty man. He never broke the law, but rode the edges of it over and over. What could anyone do? I was a slave and he a rich landowner.

"My mother worked for lord Boaz. One day, afraid that I would do myself harm, she approached him and begged for his help. Lord Boaz is kin to Jaala, you see. I don't know what he had to do to persuade the man to let me go. But I expect it wasn't cheap, though he has never mentioned the price to me. I am no longer a slave thanks to lord Boaz. May the Lord bless him all his days. And may He preserve others from being under Jaala's power."

Inexplicably, Naomi reached a hand and pulled Ruth to her in a tight embrace. Ruth could not help noticing that the older woman's lips had turned white with distress.

Chapter Thirteen

Hope deferred makes the heart sick.
PROVERBS 13:12

The heat wave broke the day Ruth returned to glean in the new field. Row after row of ripe wheat waved in the breeze, like jubilant hands lifted up in a dance of praise. The color of the plants had changed from green to a bright gold that carried with it the promise of a bounteous year, a year free of hunger.

Three days at home had restored Ruth's health. She worked with nimble fingers, her body satisfyingly strong and obedient to her demands once more.

There was no sign of Boaz. For days, Ruth had eaten his meat and drunk his wine, and finally had to admit to herself that she missed the man: his astute wisdom, his quiet kindness, his God-soaked prayers, his warm voice.

She missed Boaz and resented him for it.

Why had he stolen his way into her heart when he could never be anything to her? He was too high and she was too low. He owned the land and she gleaned it. She was lower even than a day laborer.

She let out an exasperated breath and picked up a few abandoned stalks of wheat with more force than necessary.

"What's pestering you, Moabite?" Dinah asked, bending to gather a large clump of wheat with slow, lazy movements. "It's like there's a storm blowing through your insides."

"My name is Ruth."

"That's what I said. *Moabite*. Poor as dirt and barren too. As if

Bethlehem needs Moab's leftovers."

Ruth went cold. She clenched her teeth to keep from returning Dinah's comments with sour words of her own. She knew that would gain her nothing.

When she had turned thirteen, Ruth had gone through a season of rebellion. Tired of her sisters' baiting, she baited them back, returning anger for meanness. Her harsh words won her nothing but misery. Her sisters grew sharper and more unkind. Ruth lost the little peace she had known among her kin. After several anguished months, Ruth learned to control her tongue. She stopped trying to repay her sisters' torment. Sometimes, she even managed to return kindness for their evil. She was amazed by the change in her siblings. They never learned to love or appreciate her. But to her surprise, they stopped baiting her as often. They sheathed their claws and began to ignore Ruth instead of tormenting her. She had learned her lesson. Dinah would not push her back into the helpless wrath of a thirteen-year-old. She knew how to contend with women like her.

Just beyond them, a man straightened and turned toward them. Ruth recognized Adin, Abel's younger brother. His wife had died recently of a wasting disease, leaving him the care of two young sons, which had kept him from work for several weeks. Ruth barely knew him as a result of his absence. She was surprised when he took a large handful of the wheat he had just cut down with his sickle and dropped it in front of her.

She picked up the sheaves and gave him a grateful smile. To her shock, Dinah grabbed the cluster of wheat out of her hold. "That's not yours."

Adin gave Dinah a measuring look. "Give it back. Now, Dinah."

The young woman bit her lip, her skin turning a dark shade of red. She threw the sheaves at Ruth's feet and stalked away.

"Pay her no mind. She can be tiresome."

"My thanks, Adin."

She noticed Adin gazing at Dinah where she slumped in the

shade of a twisted olive tree, her feet kicking the dirt. To Ruth's surprise, it wasn't annoyance or disapproval that marked his features. If she didn't know any better, she would have said it was longing. Before she could be certain, he turned away and put his sickle to use again.

Ruth returned to her work. Hannah walked over and bestowed a dimpled smile. The girl had a talent for bringing sunshine into dark places and Ruth smiled back.

"What is the matter with Dinah today?" Ruth asked. "Her tongue is especially venomous."

"It's Adin."

"Adin? Why should he cause her grief?"

"Dinah loved Adin when they were young. She was a sweet girl, then. Full of life and charm. It seemed to all that Adin returned her affection. But his father disapproved of Dinah's family. They had an old feud between them. So his parents arranged a different marriage for Adin. He obeyed them, of course. Dinah never recovered.

"Now he is a widower. I think Dinah hoped that after the passing of his wife, he would turn to her again. But he has ignored her completely."

Ruth rubbed her cheek. "Poor Dinah."

"You might not feel the same by the end of the week. She won't take kindly to Adin defending you."

Ruth snorted. "It seems to me she doesn't take kindly to anyone on principle."

Boaz knew Ruth would return to glean, and kept away from the harvest for two whole days before succumbing to his need to be near her. He found her resting in the shade with some of the women. Her skin, ruddy with good health and activity, was smooth as polished marble. Long legs were bent, her arms wrapped around her shins, as she smiled at someone.

Adin.

Boaz swallowed convulsively as he studied the young man. Handsome, with no touch of white in his thick, black hair and beard, a blade of a nose as straight as the shaft of an arrow, and jaws square like the corner of an expertly made building. He had everything a woman like Ruth might want; virility and youth and beauty flowed out of him like a mighty river after the rains.

He noticed Adin laughing at something Ruth said, his head thrown back, his chest shaking. He wagged a finger at Ruth and she shrugged one shoulder. Boaz's mouth grew dry and he turned swiftly, his back to the charged scene. He strode toward his horse, not caring how strange it might appear that he had come for a visit and not spoken a word to anyone before taking leave.

Abel spotted him, and misunderstanding his move toward the horse, said, "I will take care of the beast, my lord. Come and see this wheat we have harvested. It's the best I've ever seen, every grain plump and healthy, bigger than any crop we've had in my recollection."

Boaz could think of no excuse to refuse Abel. He examined his extraordinary harvest, a mark of the blessing of God upon him and his people, and he could not move himself to feel cheerful or even thankful. He went through the motions of saying the right words, nodding at the appropriate moments. But his only desire was to depart. Leave Ruth to her young suitor. Leave her to build a life for herself while his fell apart.

"My lord?"

"Ruth!" His thoughts had engrossed him so deeply that he had missed her approach. Not wanting to give away his feelings, he forced his face into an expressionless mask. It wasn't like her to approach him, and he wondered what gave her the courage to be bold.

"I wished to thank you for your goodness to Naomi and me. You have taken all this trouble for us. We are indebted to you."

Boaz felt his chest tighten. "You owe me no obligation, Ruth." He felt the last slim glimmers of hope dying. She felt *indebted* to him. Even if he were to overcome his own objections—be fool enough to seek her hand in marriage—she could not choose freely now. She would say yes out of gratitude. What use was that to him? Obligation and debts were not what he desired from her.

She bent her head, the curve of her neck long and white. "I don't know what I have done to find such favor in your eyes."

He took a step back and adjusted the linen at his waist. For one insane moment he considered telling her that he longed for so much more than gratitude from her. Then someone called out her name, and, distracted, Boaz remained silent.

Again, the call came. "Adin seeks you, I believe. He doesn't know you are here."

Ruth's hands tightened against the folds of her brown, shapeless tunic. "Yes, my lord." She ran back toward the others, her gait graceful. Boaz rubbed his forehead with a calloused hand before heaving himself up onto the saddle of his horse and galloped away, with no idea where he was headed. Just away from here.

The Sabbath dawned hazy and brought with it a ferocious wind, which whipped up waves of dry, sandy dust. Ruth felt shut in and restless. Even the wind seemed more welcoming than the four walls of the house. Late in the afternoon when the wind finally quieted its howling rage, she pulled her old scarf low over her forehead and went for a short walk.

Not far from home, someone owned a diminutive olive grove. On the Sabbath, when work was forbidden and Ruth had to lay aside the responsibilities of survival for herself and Naomi, she sometimes came to the place. Here, she found a strange peace in the shade of the ancient, twisted trees and their dainty, silver leaves. The world appeared to come to a standstill there. It would be a long time before the trees would be ready for harvest, yet they seemed to harbor a promise of life. Life to come. Ruth trailed her fingers through a fanning branch of twinkling leaves and smiled.

"*The Lord suckled Jacob with honey out of the rock, and oil out of the flinty rock*," a husky voice spoke out of the shadows.

Ruth turned so fast, her scarf caught on a branch and pulled off her head. "My lord Boaz!"

"I see you've found my olives, Ruth."

"I did not know they belonged to you. Forgive my trespass."

"I count it no trespass to find you here."

Ruth sighed in relief at that reassurance. His unexpected presence in a grove she had come to think of as her private hiding place shook her equilibrium. "Thank you, my lord. There is something restful in this place," she said, although what she really meant to say was *what are you doing here? Of all the land that belongs to you, how came you to be at this spot at the very moment when I arrived?* She swallowed her curiosity and studied her sandals.

"I'm glad you think so. I own many parcels of land, some lush and rich. Yet none is as dear to me as this one. I find a strange peace among these gnarly trees."

Ruth gave a half smile. She wasn't surprised to discover that he found the same unusual sense of tranquility in this grove that she herself did. It was as if some precious part of heaven dwelt here. "What was it you quoted when you first saw me?"

"The Song of Moses. He spoke of these trees, of their roots insinuating themselves into the flinty stones of our homeland, and finding life, feeding our people with their rich oil. I am always encouraged by the sight of them."

"Because they survive?"

Boaz lowered himself on a stump, stretching a leg. "Because they thrive. Because they turn the hardness of this unyielding ground into a treasure. They turn stones into life." He pointed toward a single row of fig trees, barely visible on the eastern edge of the land. "Fig trees are the same. They root themselves into this harsh, rocky bed, and produce from it the sweetness of honey. These trees give much more freely than they receive. It's hard not to admire them."

Ruth leaned against a scratchy trunk. "Some people say the olive tree is ugly because it isn't as stately as an oak, and it twists and turns and never grows very tall. But I think they are splendid. They manage to live such long lives and stand firm against storms and winds and time itself. They endure. Long before I was born, these trees stood here, and they will still be here, bearing fruit, long after I am gone."

"That's a sad thought."

"What?"

"You being gone."

Ruth tipped her head up and studied the sky through the shade of narrow, silvery leaves. "I wasn't planning on an immediate departure, God willing."

Boaz smiled. "I'm glad to hear it." He plucked a leaf from behind him and twirled it this way and that. "Are you settling in? Does Bethlehem feel like home yet?"

Ruth wondered if an olive ever felt at home in an olive press. It belonged there. But it probably didn't feel like home once it had been plucked from its tree, and shoved between two heavy stones to be crushed over and over again in order to produce its precious oil. She smiled at the thought.

"What puts that smile on your face?"

Without calculation, the truth sprang to her lips. He had that effect on her, causing her to open her hidden thoughts without any intention of doing so. "After Naomi's sons died, it felt like my life became an unending night. Everything I knew and cared for was taken from me. When we came here, I had no one left but Naomi. I suppose after so much loss, I feel more like a ripe olive plucked at harvest, than I do this tree, with its tenacious roots in the ground of Judah."

A small, inarticulate exclamation escaped him. "So Bethlehem feels like the olive press?"

"Not so much Bethlehem as this season in my life. I know how blessed I am. I do not take God's many mercies for granted. Still, I feel like I am being pressed on all sides."

"I know how that feels. When first my daughter and then my

wife and newborn son died, I thought myself crushed beyond hope."

Ruth wrapped her arms around her middle and leaned harder into the tree trunk. "How did you rise above it?"

"One day, a distant relative and his wife came to visit. She was great with child, very near her time. That night, I could not sleep. I kept thinking of this woman, her belly swollen with her child. At first I thought she reminded me of Judith and our unborn son. Then a conviction filled me that this image was more than a mere longing for my wife. There was something of God in it.

"As I prayed, I felt a powerful urging to speak to the child in this woman's womb. To describe to him the world outside into which he would be born. I felt foolish at first. How do you speak to an unborn babe who isn't even there? But the urge seemed so strong that I could not resist. I began to speak to the babe, doing my best to describe the beauty of our world. I told him that he would breathe air instead of the waters of the womb. I told him he would taste milk and as he grew older, his tongue would burst with the flavors of wheat and cheese and cinnamon and honey. I told him about the joy of a fast ride on the back of a horse, and the scratchy wool of a little lamb. I told him about cuddles and kisses and being loved. I told him about hope.

"Then the Lord asked me, '*Do you think he understands? Do you think he knows what your world is like now?*'

" '*No, Lord,*' I replied. '*How could he? He only knows his mother's womb. His world is too small. I could use every word the world has to offer and he would still not perceive our world. He has to be in it to understand.*'

" '*No more can you understand My kingdom,*' He said to me. '*No more can you perceive where your wife and daughter and newborn son reside now. Yet that world is no less real than your own.*' "

Ruth inhaled, the air a sharp punch in her lungs. "They are with Him, now?"

Boaz nodded. "I do not pretend to understand what this means. Like the babe in the womb, I haven't the capacity for comprehension. I only know that they are safe with Him. This knowledge helped me rise out of my grief. I realized that God had left me in this world for His own purpose. He was not finished with me here, and so I could not be finished with the world. It did not happen overnight. But day after day, I gained ground. I learned how to live without them."

"You always help me to understand the Lord better."

Boaz's smile flashed, sweet and generous. "It is because I am so much older than you."

Ruth frowned. "I had not noticed."

Boaz laughed. "I had. And I can tell you that if you are in the olive press now, then like the olive, you produce nothing but goodness for those who are near you. I noticed this about you weeks ago." With an abrupt motion he rose. "I had best return home and let you enjoy your solitude."

If she could, Ruth would have told him that she enjoyed his company more. Without him, her favorite grove seemed shrunken and empty.

"I can see the way you look at her, Adin. You are not indifferent."

"That shrew? I would not expose my sons to her tongue. A snake is more tenderhearted." Adin waved his sickle in the air for emphasis. They were in a corner of the field by themselves. Ruth knew him as a righteous young man and felt safe in his company. She had allowed herself to grow separated from the other women so that she could converse with him in private.

"Why are you so concerned for Dinah, anyway? She vents her spleen on you more than anyone."

Ruth sighed. "Bitterness and jealousy have left their mark on her; it's true. For years she's had to bear a burden of loneliness and rejection. How long did she have to watch you with your wife and your children while she had no husband of her own? You can't keep company with so much disappointment without being shaped by it.

But she can be restored. She wasn't always angry, I'm told. Do you not recall her sweetness?"

"Those times are gone, Ruth. You can't recapture your youth."

"No. But you can't run from it either. Sometimes you can't move into the future without contending with what you left behind in the past."

"What do you want from me? I will not woo her. I don't even want her."

Ruth gave a rueful shake of her head. "Be kind to her. I ask for no more, to start with. Show her some attention. Stop ignoring her. Stop avoiding and chiding her."

"She deserves it."

"If we all received only what we deserved, this would be a bitter world. What if under her angry bite, the sweet girl still lingers, too afraid to come out? Wouldn't you be sad to miss that?"

Adin gave a particularly forceful blow from his sickle. He crouched low, cutting the wheat as near the ground as possible so that none of the straw would be wasted. "You dream, Ruth. Some people are plain mean. There is no goodness to be uncovered."

"Perhaps. But I think you are wrong about her."

"Wrong about who?" Dinah asked, pushing herself in the middle of Adin and Ruth.

Ruth gave Adin a warning glance. He made a growling noise in his throat. Ignoring Dinah's nosy intrusion, he said, "You look very nice today, Dinah."

For a moment the girl stood, arrested, her mouth wide-open. Then she waved in the air, as if wiping away his comment. "More than can be said about you," she said with a sour expression, pointing at his dusty tunic. "You might consider washing your clothes once a year."

Adin rolled his eyes heavenward, kicked at the wheat stalks, and stormed away.

"What are you staring at, you stupid Moabite?" Dinah said to Ruth and flounced off in the opposite direction.

Chapter Fourteen

Do not be like a senseless horse or mule
That needs a bit and bridle to keep it under control.
PSALM 32:9

Mahalath came to visit in the evening and stayed for supper. More and more Ruth felt a kinship with the young woman. Gentle as a spring shower, Mahalath soothed those around her with her easy company. She judged no one, having herself suffered under harsh judgment once. Ruth was willing to stand on her head if it would make the girl's dark eyes light up with joy for a short moment.

Naomi insisted on making the meal, leaving the younger women to chat in private. She refused their help, saying, "You've both worked hard already. Let me take care of you now."

Mahalath chewed on a date between stories. "The master bought a new horse yesterday. It's brown. I can say that much for it. Far be it from me to censure a creature of God, but that horse is ugly. When it runs, it hits its back leg with its front hoof. It's short and fat, and as bad-tempered a creature as I've ever seen. Lazy too. Zabdiel chided the lord for wasting his money. But the master insists that with the right treatment this horse will be a champion. The beast has heart, he says. What use is heart in a horse, I say, when what you need is a broad back and willingness to work? But the master sees the best in everything, even a horse. Well, especially a horse. He has a soft spot for the beasts and can't resist them."

"I've noticed him riding Shakhor. I think he likes to race the wind. Sometimes, I even think he wins."

"Did he ride fast the day he brought you home after you became sick?"

"No. He plodded like an old turtle. He must have feared I would be sick over his linen mantle. He was probably right. I'd never felt such misery."

Mahalath smiled. "You have recovered well. He worried for you after he brought you home. He told me you were as white as the first snow and weak like a kitten. I had to assure him that you were too strong to keel over and die from too much sun. At sunrise, I found him sitting on his bed, praying. He looked like he hadn't slept all night."

"He was probably praying for his horse to survive my intrusion upon its fine back."

After Mahalath left that night, Ruth withdrew into a lonely patch in the garden to pray.

"*I am full of praises and tears,*" she told the Lord. "*Tears because I am lonely. You have given me Mahalath and Hannah. They are better friends than I had in Moab. But they aren't bone of my bone. I'm still on the outside of everybody.*"

Mahalath's innocent talk about Boaz had stirred Ruth's heart. An unfathomable longing settled like a stone in her gut that would not dislodge. "*Oh Lord, I feel so passed over and unworthy of notice. Who would want me now? Not Your son, Boaz.*"

She realized that this was the crux of her loneliness, the source of her tears. She was lonely for *him*, whom she could not have.

"*Still, I won't forget that I am blessed, Lord. Blessed to belong to You. Blessed to belong to Naomi. Blessed to receive Boaz's generosity, and to have my strength so that I can provide for our welfare. And for these things, I praise You.*"

"Were you praying?" Naomi asked, as Ruth came back inside.

"Yes."

"You were ever fond of the garden. I remember you spent many hours in the tiny plot behind our house in Moab." Her head drooped as she twined the white wool.

Ruth wrapped her arms around Naomi. "I miss them too."

They sat together in the light of their one lamp, remembering what they had lost, and could never again have.

"I've decided Adin should marry Dinah," Ruth said abruptly into the heavy silence.

Naomi moved away from Ruth's embrace. "Indeed? And what do they have to say about it?"

"Adin thinks my mind was permanently damaged by the sun, and Dinah knows nothing about it."

Naomi laughed. It was the first time Ruth had heard her laughter in months. She felt her heart melt. Sinking on the floor, she laid her head on Naomi's lap and the older woman caressed her unbound hair as if she were a little girl.

"Adin might be right. It's no small matter taking two people's hearts into your hands."

"Wouldn't you do it, if you thought it would bring them happiness?"

"I didn't say that."

Ruth lifted her head from Naomi's lap. A strange rigidity had entered Naomi's expression. The older woman almost looked ferocious.

"Are you hiding a secret from me?" she asked with sudden insight.

"It wouldn't be a secret if I said."

Six days into the wheat harvest, Naomi fell ill with a fever and cough. Ruth stayed home to nurse her. Although Naomi's sickness appeared not to be life threatening, Ruth could not sleep for worry and only left the older woman's side to fetch water from the well. The memory of Mahlon and Chilion's sickness remained too fresh for Ruth to feel calm about Naomi's condition.

They had plenty of food at home after her weeks of labor in the fields. She made Naomi fresh bread every day and covered her chest with a mustard poultice, hoping to ease her coughing. Naomi's old friend Miriam came to lend a hand when she heard of the older woman's illness.

"I'm not dying. Such a fuss this daughter of mine makes over me," Naomi complained.

"You are blessed to have a daughter-in-law who loves you better than any daughter." Miriam's shrewd eyes followed Ruth as she cared for the older woman.

"You need strength to recover," Ruth said, undeterred by Naomi's complaint. "Drink the wine and eat this honeyed bread, and I will leave you be."

After Miriam left, Ruth worked in the garden, watering the newly sprouted plants while Naomi slept. Leeks, cucumbers, and beans had begun to grow and would be a welcome addition to their diet in several weeks' time. She attacked the stubborn weeds that always seemed hardier than the plants themselves. Then she collected mint and rosemary and brought them inside to dry.

She looked in on Naomi and found her still sleeping. Her breathing sounded ragged from a chest filled with congestion. Too warm with fever, Ruth decided, biting her lip. She remembered that a clump of rue had grown large in their garden. Ruth fetched a small handful and mixing it with mint, she added it to boiling water with a touch of honey and let it steep. She hoped the mixture would aid in quieting Naomi's breathing.

That evening, Naomi sat in bed, her chest sounding better, although the fever had yet to leave. To Ruth's delight, Mahalath came to visit them, another full basket clutched at her side.

"Everyone in Bethlehem is speaking of Naomi's illness, and of Ruth's tender care for her," she said, her eyes twinkling.

Ruth, who had shed her veil in the privacy of her home, pulled her thick braid over one shoulder. "How do they know?"

Mahalath folded her legs under her. "When you went to fetch water at the well yesterday, you told the women there that Naomi has a fever. By the noon hour, everyone from Abel to lord Boaz had heard the tale."

"But what makes them think I am taking good care of Naomi?"

"You owe thanks to Miriam for that. To hear her tell it, you are the most tenderhearted daughter-in-law bestowed on womankind since the time of Noah, and no one in all of Judah compares to your goodness."

Naomi patted Ruth's hand. "That much, I can agree with."

Ruth laughed. "One moment I am the scourge of Judah, armed with Moab's wickedness and ready to corrupt every young man in my path. The next, I am cast in the role of the ideal daughter-in-law. The women of Bethlehem need to make up their minds."

Mahalath pulled out a skin of wine and a round of fresh cheese wrapped in clean cloth from her basket. "I don't know about the women of Bethlehem, but lord Boaz has made his opinion clear. It's becoming a full-time chore bringing gifts to your house." She rooted around the basket. "Ah yes. He bade me soak almonds in milk for you, Naomi. To settle your stomach."

"My stomach is fine!"

"Humor him, I beg."

"At this rate, I think Ruth and I should take turns falling ill. It's proving very profitable."

Mahalath and Ruth burst out laughing. "I think you are improving," Ruth said.

Ruth stayed home the next day, worried that Naomi, who still had a mild fever, would push herself too quickly out of bed and suffer a relapse. The day dawned fair, with wisps of clouds dotting a blue sky and a soft breeze that refreshed the soul.

Ruth fetched extra water from the well and washed Naomi's sweat-stained clothes before cleaning the house and cooking them a light stew. There was water left over, and Ruth used it to wash before changing into her clean tunic. She combed through her long, thick hair, leaving it unbound, enjoying the freedom of it hanging loose down her back.

Naomi had fallen asleep after eating and snored gently on her mat. Ruth gave her a fond smile. Her chest was beginning to sound clear, and her breathing seemed easier. Giving in to temptation, Ruth lay down on her own mat and slept in broad daylight, a luxury for which she no longer had time, unless she was unwell.

She woke up refreshed after an hour of deep sleep and found Naomi sitting up, twirling her spindle. "Did you sleep well, daughter?"

"I did, Mother, thank you."

"You work too hard, child. If I could, I would give you an easier life."

"You are my easier life."

A knock came at the door. The women had left it open as was custom during the day, and Ruth had not bothered to close it before she had slept. Just outside, stood Boaz. Startled, Ruth sat frozen to her mat.

"Come in, my lord," Naomi said, her mouth stretched open in a wide smile.

Ruth sprang up, remembering that her hair was uncovered, hanging loose down her back. Boaz stared at her for a moment before looking at his feet. Blood rushed up Ruth's chest and neck, and she could feel the heat of it in the skin of her cheeks. She grabbed her veil and threw it over her head.

"I have come at an inconvenient time, I fear," Boaz said, his voice sounding strained.

Ruth composed herself. "Not at all, my lord. We are honored by your visit. As you see, my mother is improving."

"I am happy to hear it." Boaz's deep voice reminded Ruth of warm honey. "I heard you were sick and I grew concerned, Naomi."

Naomi gestured for him to sit on their plumpest cushion. He folded his long legs with ease and sank on the ground as if sitting on skinny cushions and bare floors was nothing out of the ordinary for him.

"I am much improved, thanks to Ruth's care." Naomi straightened the hem of her green tunic. "The Lord favored me when she joined my household."

In a chipped cup, the best they had, Ruth served Boaz the wine he had sent them the night before. "I think you will find this tastes familiar," she said. "We are serving you your own wine."

"I'm glad I didn't send the vinegar, then."

Boaz reached to take the cup from her. Their fingers brushed. Awareness shot through Ruth like the streak of a wandering star in a dark night, so that she found it difficult to breathe. The cup hovered between them, half in his hand, half in hers. Neither remembered to let it go or claim it. Boaz's gaze shifted to her face and lingered.

Ruth let go of the cup, and Boaz barely caught it in time before it spilled on the floor. "How clumsy of me," he said, as he steadied the wobbling base. Shoving the cup to his mouth, he took a deep draft of his drink before setting it aside.

"I best leave. You need your rest." He took two long strides to the door and was over the threshold and on the back of his horse so quickly, Ruth had no chance to follow him to the door.

"Well," Naomi said, stretching the word. "I didn't think the wine was that bad. What was his hurry, I wonder? You'd think he had a bee stuck under his tunic."

Dinah tried to squat before a large clump of wheat and promptly fell on her behind. She giggled and twirled two long stalks in the air. With a wobbly motion, she tried to rise and fell back again. The fall reduced her to more giggles.

Ruth straightened, shading her forehead, unable to believe her eyes. "Are you well, Dinah?"

"Wooonderful!" The stalks of wheat quivered through the air in a lazy, undulating wave.

"Dinah, perchance, have you been drinking?"

"Why? You waaant some?" Her head weaved as she smiled vacuously.

Ruth hissed out a loud breath. "Abel will dismiss you if he finds you like this. Come. We'll sit in the shade until you are yourself."

"I don't want to go with you. You're trying to steal Adin from me. He likes you better than he likes me."

Ruth squatted near the girl. "That is not true."

"What's the use of denying it? I've seen you talking to him, and laughing and . . . and such." She stuck a thin blade of straw between her teeth. "I care not. He's stupid. You're stupid."

"Be that as it may, please believe me when I tell you that Adin has no interest in me, nor I in him. Now come with me before you are discovered. I need to take you where no one will observe us."

"No."

"You wish to lose your work with lord Boaz? Is that what you want?"

Dinah hung her head. "No. He is a good master."

"Come then. I will help you." Ruth placed her hand around Dinah's waist and pulled up. They both staggered a few steps before coming to a stop. Dinah laughed uproariously.

"Please try to be silent. The rest of the women are looking our way."

A few rows down, Hannah straightened. "Is everything well?"

"Yes. Dinah has just been in the heat too long. I am going to take her to the shade and fetch her some water."

Fortunately, because everyone was wary of Dinah's sharp tongue, no one else offered to help. Ruth pulled the young woman toward the shade of a wooden shelter in the far corner of the field. "Where did you find wine?"

"In a goatskin."

"Yes, but where?"

"Behind that cart. Over there." She pointed to Abel's cart in the distance and stumbled. Ruth had to catch her hard to prevent her from falling.

"That's Abel's aged wine. A gift from the master. How much did you drink?"

"Jussst a sip or two. What kind of Moabite are you? I thought you people were supposed to enjoy lively enter . . . enter . . . feasting."

Perspiration trickled down Ruth's sides as she tried to support Dinah, while hiding her erratic walk from curious eyes. For all Dinah's giggling, this was a serious situation. Stealing and drunkenness would lead to instant dismissal. The shame of it would follow Dinah all the days of her life in Bethlehem. She would not be able to rise above it, or to secure more work. Her family was not so rich that they could afford an idle daughter.

"What possessed you to do this foolish thing?"

"You did. You and Adin and your sweet chatter, sneaking off to lonely spots in the field. Everyone says he wants you." She shook a finger at Ruth. "You . . . You Moabite man thief."

"Lord, give me patience. I told you, I have no designs on Adin."

Weaving, bumping, and staggering with every step, they finally made it to the shelter. Ruth dropped the younger woman until she slumped, leaning against the wooden slats. "Stay here and do not move. Do you understand?"

Dinah pulled her veil back and scratched her curly, ebony hair. "I don't feel well." With a sudden lurch, she bent over and heaved the contents of her stomach onto the brown earth. Ruth winced at the sight.

"I'm going to fetch you water. Lean your head back and close your eyes. You'll feel better."

Dinah moaned, her giggles coming to an abrupt end. "I think I'm going to die."

Ruth, who had seen her father recover from many such bouts, ignored that outburst and sprinted toward the water jugs, which were all the way on the opposite side of the field. By the time she returned, Dinah was moaning.

"Here now. Rinse your mouth and then drink this. You will soon feel better."

"I hate aged wine." The young woman's skin had taken on a greenish hue.

"If we can hold the others at bay long enough for your head to clear, you can say you are sick and go home with no one the wiser."

"I *am* sick."

"What has come to pass?"

Abel!

Chapter Fifteen

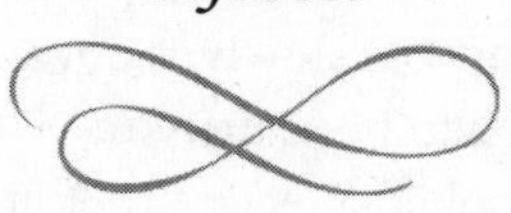

The eternal God is your dwelling place,
and underneath are the everlasting arms.
DEUTERONOMY 33:27

Ruth turned and stood in one fluid motion, hoping to cover Dinah with her body. "Dinah is ill, I fear. Best she return home early today."

"What ails the girl?" Abel's voice was uncharacteristically dry, and unsympathetic.

"I am no physician. But it is clear that she is suffering."

Abel went around Ruth and studied Dinah's hunched over figure. "Go home, then. But you better be the first one here tomorrow and the last to leave."

"Yes, my lord," the girl mumbled.

"And Dinah? If I catch you *sick* again, I'm telling your father before I cast you out." He lifted up a half-empty goatskin, which he had been holding behind him. "And I'm taking this out of your wages."

"Thank you, my lord."

"I'll walk her home," Ruth said, biting her lip.

"You want to lose half a day's gleaning over her? She's made your life a misery from the first day you came. Why would you want to help her?"

"She needs it. May I go?"

Abel shrugged. "I pay you no wages. You can come and go as you please."

Halfway down the road that led them away from Boaz's land, Ruth finally regained the strength for speech. "He knew you were drunk!"

The walk, the water, and even the purging of her stomach had done Dinah good. She was slowly recovering her wits. "And he knew it was *his* wine I had been drinking."

The two women looked at each other and dissolved into helpless laughter.

"Why did he not punish you, do you think?"

"We were friends when we were young, Abel and Adin and I. We lived next door and played in the dirt together as infants. Abel taught me how to use a slingshot. He stopped his instruction when my aim grew better than his. He still recalls those days. For the sake of our old friendship, he covered my trespass."

"You are blessed to have such friends."

"Do you mean it when you say you have no design on Adin?"

"Nor he on me."

"I almost want to believe you."

Ruth chuckled. "You are a hard woman to convince."

They were passing by a vineyard. Through the broad filigreed leaves, Ruth saw the flash of an orange pelt. "A fox," she pointed.

"Where?"

"Under that stretch of vine, see?" The fox, sensing their presence, vanished deeper into the field until he disappeared from their sight. Ruth nudged Dinah in the ribs. "You know, Dinah, left unattended, those little foxes could ruin the vineyard. Are you listening?"

Dinah groaned. "I sense another lecture coming."

"Just a mild one. Remember, it's the little things in life that could wreck your happiness. Like little foxes. They don't seem so powerful or threatening by themselves. But you let them loose, and they'll destroy a vineyard. Don't let that happen to your life, Dinah. Get rid of these little foxes in your heart. Your bitterness. Your despair. And whatever you believe about Adin and me, please do not gorge yourself on wine again, especially someone else's."

Dinah vented a miserable moan. "I wouldn't go near it with a long-handled scythe."

Boaz listened to Abel's story with raised eyebrows. "How much did she drink?"

Abel raised the goatskin he had brought along and showed him. "I had tasted half a cup, if not less. The rest is courtesy of Dinah."

Boaz leaned against the cushion at his back. Abel had come to his home to keep this conversation private, and they sat in the large, airy chamber set aside for entertaining guests. "What has happened to her? She was a sensible girl. Now all I hear is complaint."

"She never accepted Adin marrying another."

"Everyone has bitterness, Abel. Who is exempt from suffering and loss in this life? What matters is that you make peace with what you are given, and with the Lord for allowing it."

"Do you want me to dismiss her?" The young man's mouth pulled down as if he had tasted a morsel of week-old fish.

"She can stay. If she slips one more time, mind, she is gone."

"Agreed."

"How did she make it home? She must have been in a bad state from what you have shown me."

Abel bent a knee and leaned his arm against it. "Ruth took her."

"Ruth?"

"First, she tried to help the girl hide her condition. If I had not kept my eye on Dinah after I suspected she had filched my wine, Ruth might have succeeded. Then, she walked her home."

"Did you ask her to do that?"

"Of course not. I tried to dissuade her, in fact." He shrugged. "She had her mind made up."

Boaz rubbed the back of his neck where he could feel a crook coming on. "I thought you said Dinah had been taunting her. Why would she help?"

Abel threw his hands in the air. "I asked that same question. She said because Dinah needed the help. I tell you, my lord, Ruth either lacks sense or she is an exceptionally good woman. For myself, I would wager on the latter. A good woman, even if she is from Moab."

Boaz did not need convincing. Making his tone casual, he asked, "Is Dinah resentful of Ruth because of Adin's interest? Is he pursuing her?"

Abel shook his head. "I don't know, my lord. He hasn't said so to me. But they spend time together on occasion."

Boaz forced his lips into a smile until his face felt like it would crack. Without his volition, he found himself softened by sympathy for Dinah. Her decision to drink herself into a stupor did not seem completely self-indulgent and childish anymore. In fact, if he were a few years younger, he might be tempted to join her.

The next morning Dinah shocked Ruth by coming to her door to fetch her. Ruth, engaged in putting on her sandals, managed to say, "Shalom, Dinah."

"How you dawdle. Are you leaving, or would you like a servant to carry you? I am supposed to arrive early, before everybody."

"Leaving right away." In the past, Dinah and Hannah had met her partway on the road to the fields. Today, Dinah had actually deviated from her path to fetch Ruth in person.

Ruth did her best to cover her surprise. "You needn't have come for me. You owe me nothing."

The woman shrugged. "It's not safe walking alone in the dark, and I know you're an early riser." She shivered. "I feel like a sick rooster, being up before the sun."

Ruth fell into step beside her. "I've heard you sing. You definitely don't sound like a rooster. More like one of the Lord's singers on a holy festival."

"What next? Are you going to flatter my toenails?"

"Uh no. I've seen those."

Dinah laughed. "You are a strange woman."

"Thank you."

"For what?"

"That's an improvement on *stupid Moabite*, which is what you usually call me."

Dinah dipped her head. "How about I call you Ruth?" She picked up speed before Ruth could think of an answer.

Dawn had spread its pale, grey light over the horizon when they heard the steady beat of hooves behind them.

Dinah glanced over her shoulder. "He's abroad early."

Boaz rode toward them at a more steady speed than his usual wild gallop. "You never know when he will turn up." Ruth was remembering Boaz's unannounced visit at their home. She cradled her cheeks, trying to cool their heat.

"Dinah. Ruth. The Lord be with you!" Boaz said as he drew abreast of them.

"The Lord bless you!" they responded.

He dismounted, and leading his mount by the bridle, began to walk next to them. It was his new, brown horse of which Mahalath had spoken.

"I hear you had some excitement yesterday, Dinah."

Dinah's head snapped up. "I had to go home early, my lord. I didn't feel well."

"So Abel tells me. How unpleasant for you. But then, life is full of twists and curves, isn't it? We have to learn to make do."

Dinah mumbled something under her breath that sounded like an agreement.

"I always say you have to treat life like a pomegranate. You can only enjoy it if you learn to deal with the seeds."

Dinah lifted her bowed head and stiffened her back. Ruth tensed, hoping the girl wasn't about to give vent to one of her sharp diatribes.

"Some pomegranates are all seed and no flesh, my lord," she

said. Ruth let out the breath she had been holding. Dinah's tone had remained respectful, at least.

Boaz slashed an expressive hand in the air, the bridle of his horse following his movements. "That's self-pity speaking. It will ruin your life if you keep giving in to it. You have lost much. No one argues with that. Now, you must contend with the life you have been given and find joy where you may."

The air grew thick with tension. Ruth cleared her throat, deciding she better interrupt Boaz's discourse before Dinah cast off all self-control and said something she might regret. Gesturing toward the horse, she said, "Is she new?"

Boaz gave a faint smile. She had a notion he knew exactly what she was doing. "She is a he. And yes, he is new. His name is Khaymah."

"You have named him *fury*? Sounds ominous."

"His former master named him. He can have a bit of a temper, though he has improved since I acquired him. Do you like him?"

"You know my opinion of horses, my lord. And to be truthful, this one is not even particularly comely. His knees are knobby and he walks with a strange gait."

His smile broadened. "You should see him run. He may not be pretty, but he has the heart of a warrior."

Ruth shrugged. "Still a horse."

"Didn't riding Shakhor change your mind?"

"Only confirmed it."

He seemed about to say something and then closed his mouth. With an abrupt nod, he remounted and, wishing the women shalom, departed down the road.

Dinah groaned. "I thought he would never leave. Do you think he knows? Do you think Abel told him?"

"I fear that's likely. This whole conversation was his gentle warning that you are not to repeat yesterday's adventures."

"No warning needed." She put a hand to her head and gave a moan. "I don't know what makes people drink to excess. It is surely not worth the price."

"I heard what you did for Dinah," Adin said quietly while they took their midday repast with the other laborers. "That was good of you."

"I did nothing. And you best avoid me. She thinks you like me."

"I do like you."

"Not like that!"

Adin grinned. "Fine. I'll avoid you."

"But don't avoid her."

"What? You want me to woo a drunk for the mother of my children?"

"She is not a drunk! She misstepped once, out of misery." Ruth set down the piece of bread she had just picked up. "How did you know, anyway?"

"My brother told me when I asked him why she left early."

"Do the others know?"

"Of course not. Neither Abel nor I would ever shame her like that. She is doing a good enough job of that herself."

"You must be more forgiving, Adin. She stands at a precipice, do you not see it? We must help her choose right. If you judge her harshly now, you might push her over the edge until it's too late."

Adin's jaw clenched. Then, lifting his head, he grinned with a sudden glint of mischief. "The master sure looks your way a lot."

"He does not! And don't you start rumors, or I'll have Dinah beat you with the hard end of a broom."

Adin laughed aloud. "For that matter, there are two or three young men here who show keen interest in you, though you ignore them as if they were puppies under your feet. If you give them a little encouragement, they might even ask for your hand."

Ruth rolled her eyes and rose to her feet. "The ones who already have wives, you mean?"

"So you'd be a second wife." Adin shrugged. "At least you'd have a husband."

"I don't need a husband that badly." But she wondered if she was being selfish. For Naomi's sake shouldn't she consider any kind of marriage if it meant some measure of security in their lives?

Ruth stayed close to Dinah as they worked in the field. The girl moved slower than usual and seemed pale under the sun-touched brown of her skin. A twinge of pain ran through Ruth's knees from crouching too long and she straightened to stretch.

Dinah had been struggling with the same bundle of wheat for some moments, trying to tie them without success. Ruth stepped forward to offer help, but Adin was there before her.

He knelt on one knee next to her. "I don't need your help," Dinah barked at him.

"You're going to get it, anyway." He shoved her ineffectual fingers out of his way and grabbing several long stalks, twined them around the rest of the bundle with deft movements, making a secure knot.

He leaned back, surveying the woman in front of him. "You need to rest. You're the color of whey."

"Leave me alone," Dinah snarled.

"You are going to take a rest, I said." Adin grabbed Dinah's hand and pulled hard until she stood up next to him. "After yesterday's mischief, you're hardly in any shape to work from sunup till sundown without a pause."

Her spine drooped. "You know about yesterday?"

"That you were foolish enough to steal my brother's wine and drink until your brains were addled? I know."

Dinah bit her lip and looked down. Ruth saw a single tear course down her pale cheek. It was the first time she had seen the girl cry.

Adin reached a hand and gently wiped at the tear. "Don't cry."

Dinah stiffened and shook her arm to get free of him. "Let go!"

Adin refused to release her. In the brief struggle, her veil slipped, revealing ebony curls flowing down her back and swirling against her cheek. Adin seemed fascinated. Reaching a finger, he twined a curl. "You are still so pretty."

Dinah stopped struggling. She remained rooted to the spot, her eyes large and dark, focused on Adin like he was the whole world. He leaned in and kissed her once on the lips, then stepped back hastily.

Running a hand over his head, he said, "Pardon. I don't know why I did that."

Ruth groaned inwardly. Not the best words he could have chosen.

Dinah swung around, her body taut. Ruth waited to see if Adin would follow, but the young widower remained where he stood, his Adam's apple bobbing up and down as if he had trouble swallowing.

Ruth joined Dinah and reached for her hand. "Let's fetch some water."

To her relief, Dinah did not shake off her hold. "He is such an idiot," she said.

"Yes. But did you like his kiss?"

Dinah gave her a sideways look. "I didn't like that he stopped."

Ruth bit down on a smile before it escaped. "Give him time. He knows he can't take liberties without first committing himself to you."

"That's why he's an idiot! Why is it such a struggle to commit to me?"

"I cannot understand the mind of a man, Dinah. But you must admit there are many things to give him pause. His wife died not so long ago. Perhaps he feels obligated to her memory. Then there are his parents. I don't suppose they have changed their minds about your family just because he is a widower and no longer under their rule. And then, there is you."

"What about me?" Dinah asked hotly.

"You can't deny that you act like a hornet with its sting out first and the rest flying behind. A man takes his life in his own hands, approaching you."

Dinah stiffened. "I'm not such a shrew as that."

Ruth tilted her head. "Try going for one week without being sharp-tongued and critical toward everyone in your path."

Dinah threw her hands in the air. "Am I as bad as all that?"

"Not really. Sometimes, you are worse."

Dinah burst out laughing and Ruth joined her. "What have I done to deserve so much haranguing in one day? First lord Boaz, and now you."

"I care for you. I don't want you to be consumed by bitterness. I know what it's like to lose your dreams, Dinah. Mine lie buried under the sands of Kir-hareseth. I know the temptation to give up on hope and goodness. To drown in bitterness."

"I'm sorry."

Ruth sighed. "Not long ago, I stood on the road to Moab with a choice before me. To place my life under the wings of the Lord or to stay in Moab with what I knew. I chose the Lord and Naomi's love. I knew there would be no husband for me here, for I am a stranger among you. But I chose to take the good in the life that awaited me here and bear with its heartaches.

"It's not easy. Some days, I want to scream and throw a few things. Then I remember the faithfulness of the Lord in so many things. Naomi's love for me. The provision we have found in our poverty. The new friendships God has provided.

"So what shall I do? Drown in my longing for what I cannot have or anchor my feet to the joy that I do have?"

Dinah sank to the ground and buried her face in her hands. "I could not bear it if Adin rejected me again."

"Yes you could. The Lord helps us bear all our tribulations. He does not remove the sting of them. He does not wipe away their pain. But He helps us forebear. Think of Joseph."

"Joseph who?"

"Joseph Ben Jacob. Who do you think? Do you know his story?"

"Of course I do. I'm not from Moab!"

Ruth laughed. "Sometimes I wonder."

Dinah rolled her eyes. "What about Joseph?"

"Remember how for long years, things went from bad to worse for him? He went from having to contend with jealous brothers to the bottom of a pit. They sold him into slavery and sent him off into Egypt with shackles on his feet and brutal slavers for company. Still, he clung on. He worked hard and was rewarded with success in the house of his master. He did right in every way, but instead of continued success, he suffered the horrors of unjust betrayal and landed in the stinking hole of a foreign prison.

"He was thirty when he was finally released. All those years away from home and family and his father who loved him. His youth gone. The best years of his life stolen. No wife, no children, no land or home of his own to show for it. We all think of the reversal of his life, and how he became a great man. But even great men cannot turn back time. He could never get those years back."

"Are you trying to encourage me?"

"All I'm trying to say is that sometimes God allows bad to slide into worse, because in His hands difficulties have a way of yielding incomprehensible blessing. Joseph suffered unimaginable hours of torment and loneliness. Yet in the end, he saved a nation. Without him, you and I might not be here today. And every moment of his suffering played a role in the future of Israel. He became the man he was in part due to those heartaches. You think the God who used Joseph's burdens for good can't turn the ashes of your pain into beauty? Even if Adin were to reject you, the God of Joseph would see you through. No sorrow is ever wasted in His hands."

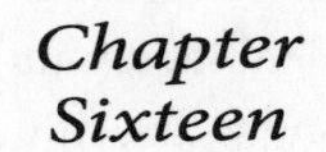

Chapter Sixteen

I have calmed and quieted my soul,
Like a weaned child with its mother;
Like a weaned child is my soul within me.

PSALM 131:2

Ruth noticed a tear in the hem of her tunic. She only owned two and both had grown threadbare. After supper, she sat close to the lamp, doing her best to mend her garment. The dim light made it hard for her to see, and she squinted, bringing the fabric closer.

"How are you progressing with your plans for Dinah and Adin?" Naomi asked as she washed the heap of wild capers she had picked that morning, before the buds had a chance to open. Her pickled capers were the best Ruth had ever tasted; her stomach gave a light rumble at the thought of them.

She tapped her belly to quiet its murmurings. "He kissed her today."

Naomi raised her head. "Is he taking her to wife, then?"

"Not exactly." Ruth stopped her mending and laid her tunic across her lap. "Adin needs a little prodding."

"Some men are like that. I could name one or two, myself. You have to know the right approach, or you will cause more harm than good."

"I didn't force him to kiss her, Mother. He did that on his own."

The corner of Naomi's mouth tipped. "I'm relieved to hear it." She started her preparation of brine, adding her special blend of herbs and spices.

Ruth picked up her needle again and adjusted the wool. "For all that Dinah pretends to be so hard, she has a tender heart. Adin could break it with a harsh word."

"Does he love her?"

"He is not indifferent. I suspect he cares deeply for her, though, of course, he won't admit it to me."

"I hear she has a bad temper."

Pulling the tunic toward her nose, Ruth tried to see her handiwork in the dark. "She has been known to say a few harsh words now and again."

"I've heard she has turned that tongue of hers in your direction more than once. Not that you've ever complained to me."

Ruth gazed up in surprise. "Are there no secrets in Bethlehem?"

"Few. Why did you not tell me that girl was harassing you?"

"And worry you needlessly? You can see for yourself that she has changed toward me."

Naomi shook her head. "What did you do to tame her malice? I couldn't believe my eyes when she came to fetch you this morning, like you were her childhood friend."

Ruth grinned. "I showed her kindness."

"I wonder if it will last."

"My kindness, or her civility?" Ruth asked, her voice wry.

Naomi's brown eyes crinkled on the sides. "Both, I shouldn't wonder. It's hard to be kind to such a girl."

"Some days, it is."

Dinah showed up at Ruth's door again the next morning. She had changed into a clean blue tunic, her face shining from recent washing. A slight scent of almond oil clung to her.

"Shalom, Ruth," she said. Ruth waited for the usual, sarcastic barb to follow. Nothing came as she waited for Ruth to braid her hair, demonstrating unusual patience. Hannah joined them on the road, and together they walked in companionable silence to the field, for once free of tension.

Dinah went immediately to work, positioning herself behind a couple of laborers who hacked at the wheat with high speed. Ruth noticed that she made no complaint, even as the heat of the sun gained strength. She thanked one of the men, who gave her a hand with a particularly unwieldy bundle.

"Did Dinah just express gratitude?" the man asked in a loud voice. "Is the world about to end?" The laborers around them snickered.

Ruth grimaced. Why couldn't they leave Dinah be? But the expected explosion of defensive speech did not come. Dinah merely smiled and continued her work. Ruth was no less astonished than everyone else. Being caught by Abel and realizing that lord Boaz knew about her indiscretion must have shaken her more than Ruth had realized.

Over the midday repast, Dinah sat next to Ruth and handed her the bread before taking some herself.

"You are good with a needle," she said, pointing to Ruth's repair of her tunic. "If I had tried to do that, it would have looked like the gap-toothed smile of a seven-year-old."

Ruth dipped her bread into a bowl of wine. "I get a lot of practice."

"All the practice in the world would not remedy my ignorance. I can outrun and outclimb any man, and I have better aim with a slingshot than most boys in Bethlehem. But I can't sew a straight line."

Ruth remembered the young man, who on their journey from Moab had saved their lives with one well-aimed stone. "I have an offer to make. You teach me how to use a slingshot, and I will do your sewing as long as the lessons last."

"You want to learn how to sling stones? I've never known a grown woman to show interest in such a pastime."

"It can come in handy." She told Dinah about being attacked by thieves.

Dinah slapped the ground next to her. "I wish I had been there. That third bandit would not have escaped if I had been with you. One stone right here," she said, pointing to the middle of her forehead. "That's all it would take."

Ruth laughed. "I never realized what a bloodthirsty girl you were."

Just then, Boaz, who had been striding toward the group of laborers, chose to settle down in the empty spot next to Dinah. After greeting everyone, he turned to Ruth and Dinah. "I overheard a bit of your conversation as I walked by. You were attacked by lions?"

Everyone around them stopped speaking and turned their attention on Ruth. She squirmed where she sat. "Just one, my lord. And he did not attack me. He attacked the bandit that attacked me."

"One seems enough," he said with a smile and raised an eyebrow as an invitation for her to continue.

Again Ruth recounted the story of her journey into Bethlehem and the lion's strange role in her survival. Her listeners seemed spellbound as she described the terror the bandits had inspired. When she told of the lion, even the men gasped.

Boaz shifted his body until he faced Ruth. "You don't believe in living a boring life, it seems."

"I believe it. I just haven't figured out a way to manage it." Everyone laughed.

"Do you think God sent the lion to save Ruth's life, my lord?" Dinah asked him. "Or was it mere chance that he showed up at that moment?"

"Chance?" Boaz dipped his bread into the wine. "Chance is God's way of showing up without making an announcement." He rose with fluid grace. "Here comes Abel. I need to have a word with him."

Adin, who had lingered in the field to finish the patch he worked on, joined them a few moments later. With a casual nod of his head, he sat in the spot left open by lord Boaz's departure.

"You two seem very friendly today," he said, eyes narrowed as he studied the two women.

Dinah smiled serenely. "I have to return to work. I need to make up for the afternoon I missed." Without a backward glance, she ambled to the wheat field, her blue tunic swaying against her hips with every slow step.

Adin swallowed, seeming distracted as he followed her with his gaze. Ruth shook her lap clean of crumbs and rose.

He whipped his face around. "What did I say? Why is everyone leaving?"

"Nothing to do with what you said. We just have to work, Adin."

A few evenings later, Ruth came home with a particularly large bundle of gleaned wheat. After helping Ruth sort through it and eating a modest meal, Naomi hurried out of the house to deliver a clay jar of pickled capers to Miriam.

Ruth decided to tidy up their meager belongings. As she folded her light veil and placed it in an old wooden chest, her eyes caught the old roll of parchment that Mahlon had purchased for her so long ago.

She pulled the delicate rolls out with careful fingers. The parchment was one of the few things she had refused to sell as they left Moab. It had been a long time since she had practiced writing Hebrew. Thanks to Mahlon's and Naomi's tutelage, she spoke Hebrew with a fluidity that would have been uncommon for the average Moabite. She wondered at Mahlon's insistence that she learn the particulars of his language so that she could speak it like a native. Had he always sensed that she would live in his country one day?

She thought of how the Lord had directed her path, drawing her step by implacable step to Bethlehem. She did not comprehend His ways or why He had wanted her here. She only knew that He had never forsaken her.

She decided with sudden determination to write her story. It was a way to practice her writing and keep from forgetting the precious knowledge Mahlon had passed to her. It was also a way of acknowledging the faithfulness of the Lord—of remembering every seemingly inconsequential act of mercy.

Searching in the cracked, wooden box that held her few possessions, she found the stylus and ink and began to tell her story starting with the day she met Naomi. As she wrote, she wondered what Boaz would think of her journey. Would he see Jacob's ladder touching down on her life? Touching down in the wilds of Moab, from the day of her birth?

She stopped writing. *Why, Lord? Why did You bring me here to meet him?* She scratched his name on the parchment. *Boaz.* She thought for a moment and added: *Why did You let my heart get tangled up with a man I can never have?* Writing the words somehow brought a small flood of relief. It took away the sting of keeping a secret so deep no words had ever expressed it.

She missed the sound at first, too deep in thought to be mindful of the noises around her. It wasn't until the second time the knock came that she lifted her head and found Boaz standing at their door.

She stood, clutching the stylus, disbelief etched on her face. "My lord?"

"Shalom, Ruth." He hesitated, appearing confused. "Naomi sent for me."

"Naomi?"

"She sent word that I was to pick up a jar of pickles she had set aside for me. She knows I have a weakness for them. The last time I tasted them was over ten years hence, before she and Elimelech left for your country."

"Please come in, my lord." Ruth could not understand why Naomi would invite Boaz and leave without telling her about it. Nor could she even comprehend the reason behind the invitation. Good manners dictated that Naomi take the pickles to Boaz's house and leave them with a servant. It certainly made no sense to invite a man of Boaz's standing to their home to pick up a jar of pickles. What was Naomi thinking?

"Please forgive me, my lord. Naomi is away from home at present. She took some of the capers you mentioned for Miriam. I am sure she will be back momentarily."

"I hope she didn't take *my* jar," he said with a smile as he came in. "My mouth has been watering since Mahalath told me about them this afternoon."

"She probably saved a bigger container for you."

Boaz lowered his eyebrows. "Is that a stylus in your hand?"

Ruth stared at her fingers as if she had never seen them before. "Yes."

"You can read and write?"

"I can, my lord. Mahlon taught me."

Boaz took a few steps toward her until they stood very close. "You have ink on your cheek. Just there." He pointed his index finger and when she missed the spot, he reached out and touched her softly. "Here."

She felt something like a blaze of fire stain her skin. It wasn't embarrassment or timidity. It was something she had never felt with Mahlon. Boaz removed his finger and stepped back. His gaze fell on the parchment and he bent to it.

"Your work?"

The fire turned into ice in her blood as she remembered the last words she had written. Dry-mouthed, she nodded.

"May I?" Before she had a chance to speak, he unrolled the parchment. It fell on the beginning of her account, and missed by a few fingers, that embarrassing reference to the man himself. If he unrolled half a revolution, his eyes would fall on his own name. Ruth felt like a paralytic, unable to move a limb.

Chapter Seventeen

When you walk through the fire you shall not be burned,
And the flame shall not consume you.
ISAIAH 43:2

"You have neat handwriting," he said, and she realized that he had not read her words but given them a cursory glance that protected her privacy. He let the parchment close. She took a deep breath, dizzy with relief.

"I had not expected you to know how to read. You have many startling talents."

Ruth pulled a trembling hand through the dangling end of her sash. "But I can't make Naomi's pickled capers."

Boaz laughed. "I am deeply disappointed."

Ruth swallowed through a dry mouth. The idea of being alone with Boaz was both agonizing and delightful. She fidgeted with her linen sash, unable to think of anything to say.

His laughter dried up, forgotten as a serious note crept into his voice. "You have one quality that makes up for your lack of skill with capers."

"What quality?"

"You love the Lord. Moses taught us that we must love the Lord our God with all our heart and with all our soul and with all our strength. You love God like that. It's rare in our day, when everyone does what is right in his own eyes, and many pay little heed to the commands of God. You are from Moab, and yet you follow the Living God with all your heart. What made you turn to Him?"

His question knocked her sideways. She had not expected him to see her in such a light. He waited expectantly, not put off by her silence.

"I lost almost everything," she said when she could form sensible words. "My husband, my dreams, my family, my future. Shattered in the course of a week. At my extremity, I became forcibly aware that I could not depend on my own strength or wisdom. But there was One on whom I could rely. If I seem faithful to you, it's because I have no choice. I need the sheer goodness and power of the Lord to make it through every hour."

"That's a good reason." Warm approval colored Boaz's voice. He had a way of giving simple statements a kind of gravity that made them more meaningful.

Flustered, Ruth glanced toward the door. "I can't imagine what is keeping Naomi."

He crossed his arms across his chest and leaned against the wall. "I refuse to leave until I have my pickles."

The sound of steps made Ruth jump.

"I do beg your pardon, my lord," Naomi cried from the door. "It took me longer than I expected to walk from Miriam's house. These old legs of mine don't move as fast as they used to."

Boaz straightened. "I thought you forgot about me."

Naomi went into the back of the chamber near the fire pit, where she did most of her indoor cooking, her feet moving with rapid agility, which belied her earlier assertion that age had slowed her down. She grabbed a stocky clay vessel and lifted it up for Boaz to see.

"I would never forget about you, my lord."

"You are very kind, Naomi. You know my weakness for these."

"You haven't tasted my honey cakes."

Boaz groaned. "Remind me to send you honey. Bushels of it."

Naomi laughed and accompanied him outside, waiting for him to mount his horse.

"Why did you not warn me of his coming?" Ruth asked when she returned.

"Didn't I? How forgetful of me."

"I almost swallowed my tongue when lord Boaz arrived. How odd that you should have invited him to fetch his own jar of pickles. I could have taken it to Mahalath while you went to visit Miriam."

Naomi waved in the air, a vague expression on her face. "It's good for him to see how ordinary people live. Tell me, what did you speak about?"

"Your capers, mostly."

"Oh." Naomi sounded disappointed. "That's all?"

Ruth set her jaw. "What did you want us to talk about, Mother?"

"Me? What have I to do with it? You can talk about anything you please. Or you can act as mute as one of his sheep. Why would I be bothered by such a thing?"

The next morning, Ruth and Dinah drifted to an abandoned corner of the field after Dinah noticed that the women gatherers had overlooked the sheaves of wheat that lay there, uncollected.

"I thought Adin would fall on his head when you behaved with such dignity and ignored his jibe last week." Ruth stopped to retie her veil more securely around her head.

Dinah stooped, concentrating on her task. "Adin falling on his head might be an improvement."

With deft movements, Ruth gathered the abandoned wheat stalks that Dinah left behind. "The less attention you pay him, the more he seems to notice you."

"I've decided that I'm not going to torment myself with thoughts of Adin anymore. If he wants me for a wife, he knows where I live. In the meantime, I am going to do what lord Boaz suggested. I am going to enjoy a lot of pomegranates and spit out the seeds. And if Adin is one of them, so be it."

"That seems a wise . . ." Ruth stopped, forgetting what she meant to say. An acrid, unfamiliar stench made her straighten up with slow movements. "Do you smell that?"

Dinah looked up, distracted. She sniffed the air and dropped the bundle she had been wrapping. "Smells like smoke."

Ruth narrowed her eyes against the sun and turned in a circle. Sweat broke out on her brow when she saw a column of smoke not far from them, rising out of a section of land where the wheat had yet to be harvested. She pointed her arm. "Over there. Fire!"

Dinah sprang to her feet. "Lord, give us aid," she said under her breath. "This could spread in the blink of an eye and destroy the crop."

Ruth ran toward the fire, screaming as loud as her lungs allowed, "Fire! Help! Fire!" No one turned to pay them heed. "It's no good. They can't hear us from here." She ran faster.

"What are you doing?" Dinah grabbed a handful of Ruth's tunic and pulled her back. "Get away! You want to get killed? We'll fetch help."

"There is no time," Ruth called over her shoulder and pulled free from Dinah's restraining hold to sprint toward the rising smoke again. "By the time we fetch the others, it might spread too far."

Dinah pursued her. Within moments she overtook Ruth, running like a gazelle. Before they could see the flame, their eyes began to water from the pungent smoke. It wrapped its way down their throats and irritated every patch of flesh it touched. Ruth bent over, coughing so hard, she had to fight not to wretch, then pushed on, one unsteady step after another. She came to a sudden stop at the sight of flames leaping up from the ground, reaching up as high as her hip. To her relief, she realized that the fire was not as large as they had feared in spite of the billows of smoke it produced.

"We have no water!" Ruth said, and coughed again.

Dinah pulled off her veil and began to beat at the flames. Ruth followed next to her, beating until with a sudden flare, her veil caught and she had to abandon it, releasing it with a gasp. Dinah's veil suffered the same fate.

"It's too strong. We can't beat it," Dinah said, her face streaming with tears from the smoke.

Ruth pointed behind her. "See that?" There was a wide swathe where the laborers had cut the wheat almost to the ground. "Nothing to burn there. It will slow down the fire. If we contain it on this side, we can keep it from spreading."

She unwound the spare veil she wore at her waist, emptying the precious wheat she had gleaned during the morning hours. Untying her sash, she said, "Quick, give me yours. Then go and fetch the men. I'll try to slow it down until they come."

"No, Ruth. It's too dangerous."

"Run! You are much faster than I." Ruth began to beat at the fire again, her eyes burning with soot, her lashes sticking together.

Dinah did not move.

"Go!" Ruth shouted. Throwing her sash and extra veil at Ruth's feet, the girl began to run.

Time stretched endlessly for Ruth. The fire hissed and crackled in front of her, and she beat and beat and beat at the flames until her arms ached, and still she went on beating. Sparks landed on her tunic. She extinguished them with hurried strokes of trembling fingers. Once, she missed a spark that had landed on the fabric resting against her thigh, and it caught, growing to the size of a scorpion before she became aware of it. She scrubbed at it with urgent horror and relief flooded through her as it died, leaving a round hole and a red blotch on her exposed skin. For a small wound, it hurt with a viciousness that made her head swim. She ignored the pain and sent up a prayer of thanks, of desperation, of need, all wrapped in one.

Her second veil was reduced to cinders. She picked up Dinah's spare one. Deep, agonizing coughs throbbed through her body, and at one point she bent over and vomited, unable to control the need. She didn't even take the time to wipe her mouth before she went back to the fire. She forced herself to keep going, gasping for air with every move. Light-headed and weak, she stumbled and almost pitched forward into the fire, barely regaining her balance in time. Without warning, Dinah's spare veil went up in flames and now there were only two sashes left, and still the men did not come.

Ruth could smell the singeing of something other than fabric and plant, and realized it was wisps of her own hair, loosened from their braid, melting in the heat of the blaze. She herself would surely begin to melt soon.

A powerful impulse to run assailed her. To turn back. Give up. Fly away as fast as her wobbly limbs allowed from this destructive wall that was eating everything in its path. Surely the fire had won. People would find a way to make up for the shortfall of grain this winter. She couldn't keep going. Her hands began to droop. She thought of Boaz and his disappointment. His anguish at not being able to provide for his workers and their families the way he hoped. Gulping a quick prayer, she forced the fear down. Swallowed it and picked her hands up again and compelled her body to move. Just one more moment, she thought. One more push.

And then she heard the sweetest sound she had ever heard—the sound of men shouting and running toward her.

"Merciful God, are you hurt?" a deep voice said in her ear. She knew that sweet, deep timbre even though it was shaking.

"No," she said and realized no sound came from her throat, and shook her head instead.

Boaz wrapped a hard arm around her waist and pulled her back. "Enough." He propelled her against his body, and for a short delirious moment she was in his arms, held tight, and then he pushed her away into someone else's hold. "Take her from here."

"Come, Ruth. We'll care for you." Ruth recognized Hannah's face through eyes still streaming from the sting of smoke. She tried to assure the young woman that she was unharmed but found that her voice remained mutinously uncooperative.

She must look a fright, she thought, stained with soot and tears. Behind her, she could hear the men beating at the fire and shouting encouragement at each other. For the first time since detecting the rising smoke, she felt her body release its hard tension. All would be well now. They would save the harvest. The strength left her body in an abrupt shift, and Ruth sank to the ground, unable to take another step.

Hannah cried out and a few of the other woman joined her and helped to lift Ruth up, carrying her with strong hands at her back and waist until she came to a wooden shelter where she could sit. Dinah rushed to her side and enveloped her in a tight, wordless embrace. Tears ran down her face, and they weren't from smoke. Stunned silence surrounded them.

"Are you well, Ruth?"

She nodded, stroking Dinah weakly across an arm, trying to reassure the fear out of her.

"I thought you would surely die," Dinah said, her voice breaking.

"Too stubborn," Ruth croaked, and Dinah laughed.

"You should see yourself. The children of Bethlehem would have seven years of nightmares if they see you now."

"You aren't looking like the Queen of the Nile yourself."

Ruth put her head in her hand. With the excitement of the moment over, she was becoming aware of the discomfort of her body. Her chest burned with every breath; her thigh throbbed with ferocious severity where she had scorched it; and her head ached. She groaned. "I burned both our veils."

Dinah scooted closer. "I think we can spare them."

"I can't. What will I wear tomorrow?"

"Bandages," Dinah said, pointing at her thigh. It was already covered in blisters. For the first time Ruth was hit by the full force of the pain, pain that went bone deep. She had suffered small burns before, an inevitable outcome of cooking over an open fire. But nothing had ever prepared her for the piercing agony of this injury. She bit down on a groan.

Someone was handing her a cup of water. Ruth found that her fingers could not hold it steady enough, and Dinah grabbed the cup and put it to her lips. She coughed, her whole chest burning with the effort, and pushed the water away.

"I was the same when I first left. You'll feel better soon. Here, put your head on my lap and lie down. Rest for a while." With gentle fingers, Dinah covered Ruth with someone's mantle. She wet a piece of soft fabric and began wiping at Ruth's hands and face.

Ruth began to drift into a light sleep, jerking herself awake every now and again when another fit of violent coughing overcame her.

"How is she?" she heard a voice ask from far away and forced her eyes open. Boaz knelt on one knee next to her, his face drawn.

"She is recovering," Ruth said and pushed herself up from Dinah's lap. She felt a wave of dizziness and ground her teeth, determined to overcome her rebellious body.

Boaz's hand fluttered up, as if he were about to touch her face. Then he jerked his fingers away, clenching them.

"You could have died."

With a restrained motion, Ruth shifted the mantle that had slipped to one side back over herself to cover the multitude of small burns and the larger hole in her tunic. "I was careful."

"How can you be careful against a wall of fire?"

A storm of coughing interrupted anything Ruth might have thought of in response. She emerged grey with fatigue and pain to find him staring at her, his face as pale as her own.

"You're not well. I've sent for Naomi," he said. "As soon as she arrives, we'll take you home." He handed her a cup. "Try to drink a little. It will soothe your throat."

She found not water but wine sweetened with honey in the cup, and took a cautious sip. "What happened to the crops?" she asked, wondering at the outcome of the fire.

Boaz's swept a hand through his hair and rubbed the back of his neck. "They are safe, thanks to you and Dinah."

Ruth began to smile. "We saved the harvest?"

"Yes." His answer came short and abrupt.

She chose to ignore his inexplicable brusqueness. "What started it, have you discovered?"

"We found a warm fire pit in the lane that runs behind that

portion of the land. We think a hungry traveler must have built a fire to make roasted grain. Only he was too careless to check that the fire was properly out when he left. Perhaps he heard the workers arriving and feared they would reprimand him for roasting the wheat without permission and departed in a hurry. We don't know. We assume the wind carried a spark from the fire pit into the field."

Ruth could not control a spasm of painful coughs that left her ribs sore. Boaz sprang to his feet. "Abel is bringing a cart. As soon as Naomi arrives, I've decided that we'll take you to my house. Mahalath's mother understands healing herbs. She will treat your burns. You swallowed a lot of smoke. Your voice is still raw from it. She is sure to know how to help you."

"That is kind of you, my lord," Ruth said, her back rigid. "But I prefer to go back to my own home."

"My home is more comfortable. I'm sure Naomi will see the wisdom of it and agree with me."

To Ruth's annoyance, Naomi did, and before long, she found herself ensconced in an upper room in Boaz's house. Nothing could have conveyed the reality of the vast differences between them more than the opulence of her surroundings. Boaz's house was large, built around a courtyard, with a diminutive marble pool in the middle, and the silvery shimmer of olive trees, interspersed by colorful clumps of roses.

A thick, soft carpet decorated the room to which they brought her. The walls were covered with rich hangings, their scarlet, blue, and deep green thread making the room feel like a forest glade. Several large latticed windows were carved into the walls, allowing light to pour in.

For the first time in her life, Ruth was placed on a bed, with a mattress of feathers under her so that she felt as if someone had laid her on a cloud. They covered her not merely with an old mantle but with a proper bedcover, embroidered in beautiful patterns of blue and grey-green.

Instead of feeling comforted, Ruth grew tenser with every

moment. Her clothes were filthy. Soot still covered most of the surface of her body, and her hair stank of old smoke. She feared that if she touched any of Boaz's fine textiles and furniture, she would ruin them.

Mahalath's mother, Sheba, was a rotund woman with a square face and kind hands. She and Naomi fussed over Ruth, stripped her, cleaned her, wiped her with unguents, and poured herbed drinks down her throat. They washed her hair in a massive basin and rubbed it with perfume that carried a faint hint of lilies.

Then came the really enjoyable part. Sheba spread a foul-smelling ointment over her blistered thigh and the smaller burns that had either branded her skin in angry red marks or bubbled up into small blisters. At the first touch of the ointment, Ruth almost jumped out of her skin. It burned worse than the injury, and that was surely something. But after a few moments, the pain faded, leaving her skin numb. Ruth could have cried from the relief. Sheba bandaged her thigh with careful precision. Afterward, no matter how much Ruth insisted that she wished to go home, they ignored her, until exhausted, she fell asleep.

She did not awaken until the sun straddled the middle of the sky the next day. With shock, she realized it must be near the noon hour. She could not recollect ever sleeping so late. What would Boaz think of her? Feeling addled, she moved to rise out of bed, quickly diving under the soft caress of the covers again when she had a look at herself. Except for a loincloth and bandages, she wore no clothes.

Chapter Eighteen

What a man desires is unfailing love.
PROVERBS 19:22

She took stock of her body. Her burns smarted a little, but the piercing agony of yesterday had diminished considerably. Sheba's ointment had done wonders. Her chest was sore, as were her eyes and her throat. She felt well enough to get up, though, if only she could get hold of her clothes.

She remembered the women clucking over her like concerned hens the day before, taking away her tunic, and she looked about anxiously for it. Every article of her clothing had vanished. Nor was there any sign of Naomi. What was she supposed to do now? Wear her blankets?

The door creaked open, and Mahalath came in, balancing a round tray with careful hands.

Ruth sat up, clutching the covers against her. "Mahalath, I beg your pardon for sleeping overlong. I would be up, but I don't seem to have any clothes. Have you seen my tunic?"

Mahalath nodded and set the tray down. "You deserved your sleep after the day you had. How do you feel?"

"Fine."

"Well, you look pale. I've brought you almonds pureed in milk. My mother says you are to have no solid food for two days; you have swallowed a lot of smoke and were sick with it most of the night."

Ruth had a flash of memory, of vomiting with helpless violence into a bowl while someone wiped the back of her neck with a cool cloth. "I had forgotten."

"And you still sound like a sick frog."

"That is not fair to the frog. Is Naomi here?"

"She went to fetch you a few necessities. She should return shortly."

"May I have my tunic?"

Mahalath looked shifty. "Beyond help."

Ruth pulled the covers higher. "I am good with a needle. I can mend it."

"I'll fetch my mother. She'll want to look you over." Ruth did not miss Mahalath's prevarication. A disturbing suspicion began to nag at her. Before she could pester Mahalath, however, her mother came in.

Sheba had a habit of clicking her tongue when she was in deep thought. She listened to Ruth's breathing and examined her eyes and throat, and clicked between every new examination.

"May I have my clothing back?"

Sheba snorted. "There were more holes than there was wool. Besides, the smoke had ruined the fabric beyond repair. Naomi took it home to use for rags. She'll fetch you a new tunic and anything else you might need for the next day or two."

Ruth bolted up, clutching the covers to her rigid shoulders. "No need for that. I will be going home now, surely. You can see I am not injured."

"One more night of rest and care, and you will be ready to leave. Not before. The master bid we take good care of you, and we intend to do that."

"But I don't wish to intrude on his hospitality more than I already have." Ruth's voice rose higher with excitement, and she began to cough. Her throat, she realized too late, was still irritated from the smoke.

A broad hand tapped her back. "No intrusion, child. He feels beholden to you. You saved his largest crop from destruction, you and Dinah. You think he would begrudge you a few days under his roof? Now let me see you eat. I worked hard on that almond broth."

"Thank you." Ruth had no appetite. But she forced the bowl to her lips and took a sip. It was surprisingly refreshing. "It's delicious."

Sheba nodded. "Mahalath will stay with you until Naomi arrives. The master's orders. He doesn't want you alone."

Mahalath sat at the foot of the bed when her mother left. "I doubt if Deborah the Judge received so many callers. You've had twenty visitors and more lining up by the hour."

Ruth turned pale. "What visitors?"

"Dinah, for one. She refuses to leave, so she should really count as two. Abel, Hannah, Adin, and many others from the field. Miriam and a few other women who are Naomi's friends have also stopped by."

"Naomi's friends? They avoid me as if I come bearing the plagues of Egypt when I go to the well."

"No longer. I suspect few will turn their backs on you after this. It's not every day that a lone woman endangers her life to save the property of others."

"It's bad enough Boaz is saddled with me. But having to welcome so many additional guests for my sake is mortifying. How can I get rid of them?"

Mahalath shrugged. "You can't. Besides, the master has made no complaint."

Ruth put her head in her hand and groaned. Peeking through her fingers, she asked, "Must I entertain them?"

"Not today, in any case. Master Boaz keeps sending them away, telling them you are too sick for visiting. He plies them with refreshments and reassurances first, so no one leaves unhappy. If you ask me, he is worse than all the callers put together since he pesters us for news of you every hour. The only one who importunes us nearly as much is Dinah. Seeing as she helped you quench the fire, the master has allowed her to remain."

Ruth remembered Dinah comforting her as she coughed and

heaved. "Would you fetch her here, Mahalath?"

"Are you certain? She has a tongue on her, that girl. You don't need her barbs as you recover."

"She is changing. I haven't heard a bitter word out of her mouth in days. She has been sweet company to me."

Mahalath frowned. "I had not noticed. But now that you mention, she has been strangely polite to me this past week and more."

Ruth nodded. "Please fetch her. She must be worried if she lingers here."

Dinah arrived, head bent and silent. She knelt by Ruth's bed and other than a faint greeting, kept her mouth shut.

"Did you injure your mouth?" Ruth asked finally, after several failed attempts to make Dinah speak. "It's not like you to be so quiet."

"I should have stayed with you." Dinah clenched and unclenched her hands. "Instead, I ran away. I ran, not because I was eager to fetch help but because I was terrified. I shouldn't have abandoned you."

Ruth reached out and grabbed Dinah's hand, stilling her convulsive movements. "Of course you were terrified. No shame in that. I was afraid myself. Running was the right thing to do. You fetched the help that saved the harvest. I could only hold the fire at bay for so long, and would have given up if the men hadn't arrived when they did. You did the right thing, Dinah. You must stop tormenting yourself with guilt."

To Ruth's surprise, Dinah burst into noisy tears. Her nose ran and her eyes turned the color of radishes. Ruth bent forward and hauled Dinah into her arms, patting her back, taken aback by the girl's intense reaction.

"You were the only one who showed me kindness," she said, wiping her nose with a crumpled rag. "Even my parents have given up on me. I couldn't stand to think of you perishing in that fire because I abandoned you."

"Going to fetch help is not the same as abandoning me. I hold no grievance against you, Dinah. In my eyes, you did right. All of Bethlehem respects you for what you did."

"That's the worst of it! I feel like a hypocrite. They keep congratulating me as if I were so brave, when all the while I know what a coward I was."

"Come and sit next to me, here on the bed." Ruth patted the fluffy mattress. "And stop scourging yourself."

Dinah sat gingerly on the feather mattress, her back hunched low, her body rigid as the handle of a shovel.

"Not like that. Put your feet all the way up and rest back against the wall." The girl obeyed and sighed as her back leaned into the cushions.

"Soft, isn't it?" Ruth said.

Dinah ran a tentative hand over the covers. "Too soft. I wouldn't dare pass gas on this mattress in case it tore a hole in the fabric."

Ruth threw her head back and laughed. "You are a scandal, girl."

"I'm glad I made you laugh. You looked so pale and miserable when I came in." She was wearing a new cinnamon-colored tunic that matched her eyes. In the privacy of the guest chamber, she had removed her veil and her clean, tight curls fell down her back.

"That tunic suits you," Ruth said. She touched the edge of the fabric, admiring its fine texture. "Linen?"

"Lord Boaz gave it to me. It belonged to his late wife, I think. I haven't been home since they brought you here, and Mahalath said my begrimed clothes would leave smudges on the carpets. She forced me into a bath and gave me this tunic."

Ruth felt an arrow of pain pierce through her. Boaz had given Dinah one of his wife's tunics, but he had offered her none. Was it because she was a Moabite? A foreigner? A widow? Was she not good enough to wear his wife's old clothes? She pulled the covers higher, feeling cold.

Trying to hide her distress from her friend, she asked, "Did you see Adin while you waited to visit me?"

Dinah nodded. "He didn't say two words to me. Just sat there and stared at me until I got up and left the room."

"Of course he stared at you. You look so pretty."

"You are kind to say so. But you are wrong. He wouldn't avoid me if he cared for me. Everyone in town has stopped to ask how I fare. If I meant anything to him, he would at least ask after my health. Wish me shalom. Anything rather than this distance."

Ruth thought of Boaz's avoidance of her own company and could offer no comfort. She understood how Dinah felt, though she sensed that Adin was far from indifferent to the girl. For his own reasons, he chose to hide his feelings.

The door opened with a quiet burst of fresh air as Naomi came in, her arms full. There were dark smudges under her eyes and her skin had a sallow tint. She lit up as she spied the young women perched on the bed. "Behold, the two most famous women of Bethlehem resting sweetly on lord Boaz's fine bedding. Or should I say *hiding*?"

Ruth and Dinah looked at each other and grinned. "You have caught us out, I fear," Ruth said. "There are too many callers below. But I have a good excuse for hiding. You have stranded me in a stranger's house without a stitch of clothing."

Naomi dumped her handful of articles at the foot of the bed. "I have brought you a tunic and one of my own veils; both of yours were destroyed in the fire."

Ruth thanked Naomi and wriggled into her clothes under the covers. "Can we go home now?"

"Boaz wishes you to stay until tomorrow. It would be rude to leave precipitously. Are you not comfortable? That bed looks very appealing from where I stand."

"It's a cloud," Dinah said. "Not a bed. The problem with it—"

Ruth poked her in the ribs. "Don't dare repeat what you said earlier." She tapped the space to her other side. "Come and join us, Mother."

Naomi nodded and sat next to Ruth's other side, propping her feet up on the bedding. She heaved a sigh of contentment. With the three of them on the feather mattress, it was a cozy fit. Ruth wriggled farther under the covers. "Do you think Boaz will let us take his bed home with us?"

"If he does, I'm coming to live with you," Dinah said on the back of a yawn.

"I think we all need a good nap," Naomi declared. She reached out a thin hand and patted both women on the belly as if they were little children. "Bless you, my dear girls. And shalom to you as you dream."

When Ruth awoke, she found herself alone. Her stomach rumbled with hunger. Leaving the bed, she stretched and straightened her twisted tunic. It was old, threadbare in places, and sleeping in it had not helped. She made a face and pulled on the grey fabric in a futile attempt to diminish the creases. Naomi had brought her a comb, and she sat down to untangle the knots that had worked through the long strands after lying on them for so long. A soft smell of lilies clung to her clean hair, courtesy of the soap Mahalath's mother had applied to her the day before.

With efficient hands, she braided her long hair and covered it with Naomi's scarf. In the brightness of Boaz's luxurious room, it too appeared faded and long past its best. The linen belt grandfather had bought her so many years ago sat amongst the small pile on the bed, and she wrapped it around her narrow waist twice, then allowed the long ends to dangle in the front. Now at least she looked respectable.

She decided she could no longer hide in her chamber, expecting others to fetch and carry for her comfort. It was time for her to carry her share of responsibilities. Although she preferred to remain in the privacy of Boaz's guest room, she realized that she needed to go below stairs. It was her duty to face the company who had come for her sake.

Perhaps going below could even offer an advantage or two;

for one thing, she could sneak some solid food while Mahalath's mother wasn't watching. Most of the afternoon, she had smelled roast lamb and rosemary and frying garlic and wild onions. Sheba only allowed her to drink broth and almond milk. It was cruelty, she decided, to parade such smells right under her nose, but not allow her a single morsel.

A narrow, stone staircase led to the verdant courtyard at the center of the house. Ruth placed her foot on the top step when she realized that a man had begun to climb from below. She froze mid-step. Boaz, glimpsing her, also came to a stop. They looked at each other, their eyes arrested, neither moving. Afternoon sun lit Boaz up from behind so that Ruth could not make out his features clearly. It was as if the length of the stairs disappeared between them, and they were face-to-face, close enough to touch. Ruth tried to swallow and could not. She ran a damp palm down the side of her dress and fidgeted with her scarf.

"My lord." Her voice came out a croak.

"Ruth. Shouldn't you be in bed, resting?"

"I feel well. Thank you. I thought I better come and greet the callers."

Boaz climbed a few steps. Out of the direct path of sunlight, his features came into clear view. There were new lines around his eyes and a sheen of perspiration shone on his forehead. He looked like he had not slept well. *He is beautiful.* Ruth cringed as that extraordinary thought took hold of her. What was wrong with her?

Boaz smiled, the tense lines around his mouth relaxing. "Mahalath says you dread the visitors. No need to brave their company, yet. Everyone understands that you are recovering. Come down, and I will take you outside where you can enjoy the sunshine in peace. You probably long for some fresh air."

Ruth let out a relieved breath. "Yes. Thank you, my lord." She walked down the stairs, self-conscious of the way he gazed at her as she descended. He waited until she reached the step just above him. For a moment he hovered, their bodies separated by the merest whisper of air. He backed down one step with slow, distracted movements, then turned and clattered down, with Ruth following sluggishly.

"I have a small paddock outside the house, and a barn for the horses. No one but my men go there. You should be safe from inquisitive visitors."

"Is that where you keep your new horse?"

"The one you called ugly? Yes."

Ruth bit her lip. "I beg your pardon. That was rude."

"That was honest. He is ugly. But he is no less astounding because of it."

"What makes him astounding?"

"He runs like the wind. Only when he feels like it, I admit. His last owner used the whip too much. It has scarred him inside and out. The outside scars, we have treated with poultices. The inside scars are harder to contend with. At least he has stopped biting. And yesterday, he beat Shakhor in a race. I've never known another horse capable of doing that."

"What made you want him in the first place? Seeing how damaged he was, why did you not walk away? What made you wish to purchase him?"

Boaz waved a hand in the air. He had long, narrow fingers that moved with an odd eloquence. "A damaged horse can be restored. That's part of the challenge. Part of the joy. You need eyes to see beyond the scars, beyond the bad behavior and the temper and the laziness into the real horse. You need to figure out how to draw him out, how to turn him from a terror into a champion."

"How do you do that?"

He shrugged. "Different with every horse. This one needs freedom. When I first found Khaymah, he had been relegated to a cart horse. His old owner saw no value in him." Boaz's voice grew rough. "He had come near to ruining him and blamed the animal for his own ineptitude."

"But how did you know his worth? How could you tell that he

wasn't just an ordinary horse?"

Boaz grinned. "Every horse is unique. Valuable in his own way. But I knew this one as a champion when I looked into his eyes. He had wily, sharp eyes that grabbed my gaze and wouldn't let go, as if challenging me to best him. I knew then he was worth the effort. Worth any cost."

Something inside Ruth twisted and rose up with a roar of longing. If he could see the worth in a scarred horse, why could he not see the worth in her? Why could he not look past her poverty and her background to see that she *loved* him? *She loved him.*

Chapter Nineteen

For I know the plans I have for you, declares the Lord,
Plans for welfare and not for evil, to give you a future and a hope.
JEREMIAH 29:11

Ruth stumbled and almost fell when those words echoed in her mind. Boaz grabbed her arm to steady her. "You are not well. I beg your pardon. I shouldn't have brought you traipsing out here and exhausted you with talk of horses."

Ruth shook her head, beyond words. Fearful that her eyes would give her away, she stared at her sandals, trying to swallow tears.

"Come and sit." Boaz drew her, his touch firm, and she found herself being pushed onto a stool. He crouched down until he was level with her. She kept her face lowered, refusing to look at him. A gentle hand grasped her chin, forcing it up. "Do you feel dizzy?" he asked. "You look a bit grey."

"No." Then to distract him, she asked, "May I see the horse?"

He frowned. "Tomorrow, maybe. You aren't up to it, now."

She felt torn between the desire to escape his presence, and the desperate need to clutch at the rare opportunity to spend a little time alone with him. Her longing to remain with him won. Later, she would hide in a private corner and think through the shocking discovery of her unreasonable attachment to him. She would seek a way to quash her feelings, and overcome what would only cause her useless pain. For now, she would linger close and enjoy the crumbs that she could have of him.

"It would be a welcome distraction, my lord. Truly. I don't feel sick."

Boaz sucked in his cheek, before rising. "Stay here. I'll bring him to you."

She could hear him whispering gently to the horse in the shadows of the barn. He came out leading Khaymah, one hand tapping the side of its neck. "Behave well for our guest, now," he murmured, and the horse nodded its head up and down with comical vigor.

Ruth laughed and rose up to approach him. She stood a few steps away from Boaz, too shy to draw closer. He misunderstood her hesitation.

"He won't hurt you. Would you like to pat his neck? He likes that."

She had no desire to pat any part of the horse, for all his charm. There must be a reason he was called *fury*. But she stepped closer since it offered her an excuse to be near Boaz. With an awkward motion, she tapped the side of the horse's neck and drew away quickly when the horse gazed at her with mild reproach.

"Not like that," Boaz said, and she could tell from his tone that he was trying not to laugh at her incompetence. "Let me show you." He took her hand in his long fingers and drew it lingeringly against the horse's side, neck, and forehead. The horse blew air out of his nostrils and lowered his head.

"He likes you. He likes when you touch him."

"Does he?" Ruth's breath caught; without meaning to, she took a half step toward Boaz.

With abrupt haste, Boaz dropped her hand and stepped away. "I should take him back to his stall." He pulled on the horse's lead without another word of explanation and drew the beast back into the barn.

Ruth's eyes widened. Had he sensed her attraction to him? Had his speedy departure been in response to her unintentional move to stand closer to him? Horrified shame made her stomach roil with nausea. She could not bear the thought that he had recognized her feelings, and been embarrassed by them. What other explanation could there be for his hasty retreat? The horse had been content with their presence. Boaz had run from her, run before she shamed them both more than she already had.

Raising shaking hands to her hot cheeks, Ruth turned and sprinted back to the house. Climbing the stairs two at a time, she hurled herself inside the bedchamber. She had to get away from this place. From him.

Naomi walked in, a steaming bowl in her hand. Ruth threw herself at her mother-in-law in a heedless rush so that she barely avoided a scalding. "I want to go home," she wailed. "I want to go now."

Naomi managed to place the bowl down on a table, while clasping Ruth in one arm. "What's happened? Why are you distressed?"

"Nothing! Nothing has happened. I just want to go home."

Naomi pulled her back by the shoulders. "This isn't like you, Ruth. Tell me what has upset you?"

Ruth turned her back, fearful that Naomi would guess her secret. She could not bear that final humiliation. "*Please*," she said. "I'm homesick."

"Peace, daughter. Sit yourself down while I go and explain to Boaz."

Ruth whirled around. "Must you? Can't we just leave?"

"No, we can't. What has come over you? After his generous hospitality, he deserves a polite farewell."

Ruth wiped the moisture gathering on her upper lip and nodded. She forced her knees to bend until she sat at the edge of the bed, her body as unyielding as a tree trunk.

Naomi found Boaz leaning against the wall of the barn, his arms stiff against his sides, his gaze faraway and unfocused. He had shed his mantle and rolled up the sleeves of his tunic as if the heat of the day had grown too much to bear. His dark hair waved at odd angles, as if agitated fingers had pulled through the curls more than once. Naomi had to wish him shalom twice before he took note of her. He straightened with haste, blowing out a long breath.

"Naomi," he said. He opened his mouth as though he wished to say more, and closed it again abruptly.

"I've come to take leave. It's time we went home."

His brows drew together and the color left his face. "Ruth wants to leave." It wasn't a question, Naomi noticed.

"She misses home."

"Of course."

Naomi's shrewd gaze didn't miss Boaz's discomfort beneath his smooth reply. She shifted her weight from one foot to another. "She is a good woman, my Ruth."

Boaz swallowed convulsively. "You will hear no argument from me, cousin."

Naomi picked up a pebble from the ground and twirled it aimlessly, casting it from one palm into another. "I hope someone in Bethlehem will appreciate her worth and take her for a wife."

Boaz lost the last trace of color in his face until he looked like a stone carving. "No doubt a young man of her own generation." He turned his back to Naomi, for once displaying bad manners.

Naomi narrowed her eyes and studied his stern posture. No wonder he was famed to like stubborn horses. He was as bad as ten of them together. She gathered the hem of her garments and left his presence without the usual polite rituals. Boaz did not even notice.

If the fire that had burned a portion of his field came down and swallowed him up in its grip, Boaz could not feel more dried up and singed. A heavy haze had settled over his mind so that he could not think with clarity.

He had allowed himself to spend time alone with her, to hold her hand at any excuse. To pull her close. Dismay shot through him as he remembered his reaction to the proximity of her body, to the smell of lilies clinging to her skin, to the strong, vibrant feel of her flesh under his fingers. The strength of his own ardor had shocked him. He had known from the first day that she drew him. But his response to her today had been at a different level. He had wanted her to be his. Wholly, completely his. He had wanted to shield her from every danger, to provide for her every need. He had wanted her for his own.

She had leaned into him with such trust, not understanding that all he wanted to do was pull her into his arms and kiss the shy smile off her face. The feelings that drove him had proven so strong that he had had to leave like a boy on the verge of manhood, unable to control the fire in his own blood. She must have been mortified. He knew that was why she had left so abruptly. Why she sent Naomi and did not come herself.

How was he supposed to face her now?

He sank down on the stool she had occupied earlier. Why did this woman have such an unaccountable effect on him? His head drooped. He prayed, asking the Lord for peace. For guidance. For help. For anything! He had not been this wretched since the early days after Judith's death. Was this a death he mourned again? Death of hope? Hope to have her? Hope to be loved by her?

Because, the Lord have mercy on him, he could no longer deny that he loved her.

He sprang up from the stool and took several restless steps until he came to the well at the entrance of the field. He drew up some water and splashed his face. A little water remained at the bottom of the vessel. His reflection gazed up at him from the gentle waves on its surface. White at his temples, lines marring the corners of his eyes and mouth. Ordinary features touched by time and sorrow. She deserved more. Wanted more, if her flight was anything to go by. Even the thought of his interest had unnerved her enough to send her fleeing.

He knew that if he asked for her hand, she would give it. What choice had she? With his wealth and standing, she could not refuse him. She would agree for Naomi's sake, if nothing else. But he did not wish to give her material comfort while leaving her heart cold. He wanted her to have the joys of a loving marriage. Having once known that joy himself, he could not bear to think of her trapped with him, without love. Nor could he live with a wife he loved if she did not feel the same.

Boaz poured the rest of the water over his head. *Lord, wash away these unwanted feelings and restore tranquility to my soul.* It wasn't a prayer. He was begging. He begged some more, beyond pride until the agony that had a hold of him receded a little and he realized that he had not been speaking to God. Not really. He had been running from the pain, like a child crying too hard to hear the comforting murmurs of its mother. He tried to pray again, this time focusing on the truths he knew about God rather than on the raw affliction of his feelings for Ruth. *Lord, my God, You are preparing a future for me that I do not comprehend. This is part of Your plan for my life. Help me trust You in the midst of the pain of it. Help me stand secure in Your steadfast love. Help me remain confident and strong that You will uphold my cause for the sake of Your covenant.*

"Boaz, what is it you're mumbling under your breath? Lost your mind, have you?"

Jaala? Boaz sprang to his feet. "What do you want, Jaala?"

"I want to sell you a piece of land. Unbelievable value. Came into my possession not long ago. But I don't have the resources to cultivate it. With two wives and three sons, I have sufficient responsibilities, unlike a carefree man such as yourself. What do you have but land to occupy your time? No sons. Not even a single wife. Might as well accrue more property, though what good it will do you, I cannot imagine. A man without sons is more pitiful than a poor widow."

Boaz kept his face expressionless. It was not the first time Jaala had tried to bait him for his lack of wife and sons. Nor would it be the last. "What land?"

Jaala described it. "Come, and I will show you."

Boaz almost rolled his eyes. He was familiar with that parcel, which except for a narrow band of tolerably fertile soil, consisted mostly of a useless stony pit, worthless for farming or pasture. He knew the man's dishonest ways well enough to realize that Jaala would lead him straight to the fertile portion and try to hide the pathetic state of the rest.

"How much?" he asked.

Jaala named a price that would have been suitable for a piece of land twice as big and ten times as lush.

"I'll think on it," he said, in no mood to enter a prolonged discussion with the argumentative man.

"Don't think too long. I have many men desperate to get their hands on such a prize."

Boaz's smile did not reach his eyes. "I'll take my chances."

Naomi studied Ruth's silent figure. For a whole day, she had sat in the corner of their modest house, pounding barley into flour in the hand mill. She made excuses not to go out, even to the well, as if she were afraid of facing people. Naomi knew that something had happened between Ruth and Boaz. But since both chose to remain tight-lipped about that afternoon, she could only guess at the content of their thoughts.

By the third day after the fire, Naomi had had enough. "Are you going to tell me what is wrong?"

"Nothing, Mother. What should be wrong?"

"You don't wish to speak about it. I understand. It concerns Boaz, I take it."

Ruth stood up so fast she spilled the flour on the floor. She gasped and dropped to her knees, trying to collect every particle of the grain, without gathering the dirt of the floor with it.

"Tell me this. Do you dislike him?"

Ruth's hands shook so hard that she dropped half the flour on the floor again. "Dislike him? Of course not!"

"Has he said or done something to offend you?"

"He would never do anything offensive to me or any woman! How could you ask that?" She bent down again to try and gather the spilled flour, forgetting the handful she held in her fist, which overflowed afresh on the floor. With uncharacteristic agitation, she threw her hands in the air and groaned before bending down and starting the work again.

Naomi bit her lip but forced herself to push through. "Are you fond of him, daughter?"

Ruth made an inarticulate noise in her throat, dropped the flour she had once again managed to gather into a nearby bowl, and walked out of the house, her gait unsteady. Naomi smiled, her heart lifting. The plan she had been considering with some trepidation now seemed like the very light of God penetrating the darkness of two people she loved dearly.

The next day Mahalath came with an armful of gifts. Two linen veils so fine that light shone through them, one thicker woolen veil for the winter months, a brand-new tunic in green wool, another in delicate blue linen, and even a fresh pair of leather sandals. "The master has had my mother and I set aside every other duty to work on these for you, Ruth. He said you sacrificed your veils and garments in order to save his land. So it was only right that he should replace them."

Ruth sat in stony silence, unable to bring herself to speak one polite word of appreciation. She wanted nothing so much as to grab the bundle and throw every item off a high mountain. He had sent her clothes to soothe his conscience. He could not return her feelings, so he tried to buy her comfort. Rage and humiliation battled like a rising hurricane inside her.

Mahalath, confused by Ruth's lack of warmth, shifted from one hip to another. "These aren't his wife's old clothes, you know. They are brand-new. He brought the fabric from Egypt some years ago when he traveled there with a group of merchants. These are just for you, Ruth."

The mention of Boaz's wife made Ruth's lips narrow in an unconscious attempt to swallow the bitter comments that were at the edge of her tongue. Of course he wouldn't give her his wife's old garments. He would never make such a gesture to her. Better waste valuable fabric on the childless widow from Moab than demean the memory of his beloved wife by allowing it to touch Ruth's skin.

Naomi came over and placed a comforting hand around Ruth's waist, drawing her close. "These are beautiful, Mahalath. You and Sheba have managed to sew better stitches in three days than I could turn out in one month. Tell your master his generosity knows no bounds. Ruth and I are both grateful."

No I'm not, Ruth wanted to scream. The intensity of her anger shocked her. What had he done wrong, after all? He could not force himself to return her feelings.

When Mahalath left, subdued by Ruth's inexplicable coldness, Naomi drew Ruth into her embrace.

"You love him, don't you?"

Ruth gasped and said nothing. She let Naomi pull her even closer in her arms and wept.

Chapter Twenty

The LORD will fight for you: you need only to be still.
EXODUS 14:14

Ruth returned to the field several days before they started winnowing the grain. Rebelliously, she wore her old grey, threadbare tunic, having stored all of Boaz's luxurious gifts in her chest. She tried to bury his memory in the same place, with little success.

Physical labor, she knew from experience, acted as an effective balm for a troubled mind. She worked with fast efficiency next to Dinah and Hannah. Dinah, she was pleased to note, had gained a new measure of popularity since the fire. One young man in particular paid her marked attention. Without being asked, he fetched her water when the sun grew hot, and saved her a warm piece of bread during their midday repast. Dinah smiled, neither encouraging nor dissuading his attentions.

"You have a new suitor," Hannah teased when they returned to the field.

Dinah shrugged. "It means nothing."

But the next day when the young man teased her about her corkscrew curls, which peeked from beneath her veil, she teased him back and they laughed as if they had been dear friends for years. As Ruth turned to pick an abandoned stalk, she caught Adin watching, brows lowered, his mouth a flat line. She moved toward him, following a trail of barley stalks.

"Peace, Adin," she said. She had not seen him since the morning before the fire.

"Peace? What peace? What's wrong with her? Did the fire go to her head? Why is she acting like this?"

"Dinah? How is she acting?"

"Like . . . like Rahab before she repented."

Ruth, who had heard of Rahab, suppressed a bubble of laughter. "I've seen Canaanite girls of that occupation and I can't perceive the similarity."

"True. They are probably too modest for the comparison."

"Adin!" Ruth crossed her arms over her chest. "What do you expect? You don't talk to her. You don't pursue her. She won't sit around waiting for you forever while her youth passes by. If you don't want her, others do."

"Who says I don't want her?"

Ruth drew nearer so that she could stare him in the eye. "*Do* you want her?"

He shuffled like a little boy. "I've always wanted her."

"Do you love her enough to marry her? In spite of your parents' displeasure? In spite of her occasionally sharp manner?"

Adin said nothing. Ruth threw her hands in the air. "Then you must bear the pain of watching her grow fond of another man. Stand by as she marries another man. Bears the children of another man."

A fit of coughing shook Adin. "Are you trying to ruin my day?"

"You are doing a good job of that yourself."

"What do you want me to do?"

"Make up your mind, Adin. Marry her, if you love her. Grow up. Be a man and bear the cost of your love."

Boaz sat atop his black horse, surveying the field. From the height of his seat, he had a clear view of the majority of his land. He had come for a glimpse of her. In spite of the fact that every one of his workers was here today, he picked her out with ease among them. Her tall, long-legged grace as she strode forward, bent, picked, straightened, and repeated the pattern had already become as familiar as his own name. She was dressed in a frayed, grey tunic. She had spurned his gifts, then. Or perhaps they were too fine for working in a field. Perhaps she was saving them for special occasions. And perhaps his goat could speak Egyptian fluently.

He followed Ruth as she turned to approach Adin. He was too far to hear them, but it was clear that emotion ran through their discussion. They stood close and gesticulated with passionate movements.

Adin and Ruth. Ruth and Adin.

He cradled his head in his palms and stifled a groan. Somehow God would give him the strength to watch their relationship blossom. Would he have to attend their wedding? Give a blessing as elder? The thought made him want to vomit.

He trampled on the urge to go near her. She did not wish to see him. All he had of her now were these secret, distant glimpses. His absence had become the best gift he could give her. In time, perhaps he could discipline his affections, rein them in hard until he could stay away from her altogether. For the sake of his own sanity, he hoped so.

Adin had had enough. For three whole days, he watched Dinah flirt with some good-for-nothing field hand as if he were the most captivating male to walk God's earth. She simpered and giggled and blushed like an idiot girl. Not once did she bite off the man's head with a sharp word or a critical comment. Honey couldn't be sweeter.

Evening had almost fallen, and everyone was making their way home when he noticed that instead of walking with Ruth and Hannah as she usually did, Dinah was walking with her new *friend*. In the descending shadows of dusk, he saw the man grab her hand. The gall! He couldn't go around grabbing the hands of unmarried women as if he had a perfect right to them. Not even in Judah, where men acted as they pleased, had they become so outright indecent. Did he mean to marry her, then?

Without thinking, Adin stormed over and ripped her hand out of the man's snug hold and grabbed onto it himself.

"You are coming with me!" he shouted at the top of his voice. Everyone had stopped to stare.

Dinah pulled her hand free. "I am not! Who are you to tell me what I must do?"

Adin grabbed that resistant hand one more time and began pulling her behind him. "I'm your future husband. That's who I am."

Dinah stopped dead in the middle of the road. "Since when?"

"Since I am going to ask your father as soon as I can get you to your house."

"You are going to ask my father?"

"Who else? I'm not going to ask you, that's for certain. I've decided for both of us." Adin pulled harder. Dinah, who was no longer resisting, landed in his arms in a breathless bundle of arms and legs. Her face was too close for him to neglect. He bent and kissed her thoroughly, ignoring the gasps and titters of their growing audience.

"What was that?" she asked, breathless.

"Down payment on your bride price."

"What do you mean Adin is marrying Dinah? How can that be?" Boaz threw both his hands in the air to emphasize his utter stupefaction.

Abel scratched his beard. "You know they have cared for each other since childhood, my lord. Adin just took his time making up his mind. Why are you bewildered?"

"I thought Adin and Ruth . . ." Boaz straightened. "If he has hurt her, I will break every bone in his useless body. I care not if he is your brother, Abel!"

"I don't believe there is any hurt in that quarter, my lord. She was laughing as hard as any of them when he kissed Dinah in front of half the city of Bethlehem. I heard Ruth congratulate him myself.

She sounded as cheerful as a newly crowned queen."

"She is good at hiding her emotions."

"But not at dissembling. There is not a woman alive who could pretend that well. I'm telling you, my lord, there was never anything between Adin and Ruth. If you ask me, Ruth was playing matchmaker. That's why they seemed so friendly."

"Matchmaker?" Boaz thought of all the hours he had tormented himself with thoughts of Ruth and Adin. He had misjudged the situation. He had never been so wrong about anything.

No man had ever been this happy to discover his error. He shoved a fist in front of his mouth as a silly grin bloomed over his lips. He could not stop himself if lightning came down and struck him. Had she been matchmaking between Adin and Dinah? He remembered her growing friendship with the young woman. It would be like her to try and bring happiness to those she loved. Relief flooded him with potent joy. She didn't love Adin. He sat down hard on the dry grass.

Calm yourself, he cautioned. *Just because she does not wish to wed Adin does not mean that she wants you.* Yet for all of his sensible attempts at prudence, his heart rejoiced.

"When is this wedding to take place?" he asked Abel, still needing concrete reassurance that his worst fears had been a delusion.

"After the winnowing of the barley and wheat is over."

Boaz allowed his grin to show. He decided he would give Adin and Dinah the biggest, most ridiculously extravagant wedding present anyone had ever received in Judah.

"Sit down, daughter. I wish to speak to you."

"I thought I would wash the dishes." They had had a simple repast early in the day, and there were not many dishes to speak of. But Ruth would have used any excuse to avoid this particular discourse. She sensed Naomi's intention to talk about Boaz.

"There will always be dirty dishes needing attention. This is more important. Sit near me and let me speak my mind. The dishes won't run away if you make them wait a little."

Ruth would give up a month of wages, if she had any, to be spared this humiliation. What could it accomplish besides adding to her shame? Then again, if Naomi would feel comforted by talking, she did not have the heart to rob her of the opportunity. Taking a deep breath, she sat down on a mat, pulling her knees up against her chest.

"My daughter, shouldn't I seek to see you settled in peace? Shouldn't I want the security of a home of your own for you? I want to see you well provided for."

"I am happy with you, Mother."

"Are you?"

Ruth lifted heated eyes. "I belong to you. That's enough for me."

"Well, it isn't enough for me. Boaz—"

Ruth bent her head over her knees, trying to fold into herself. "Boaz doesn't want me."

"I think you are wrong. I've seen him watch you. That is not the gaze of an indifferent man."

"I'm only a responsibility to him. The widow of a young cousin, dead before his time. His only feelings for me are pity and duty."

"You think so? Boaz is a close relative; that's true enough. And he has been exceptionally kind to allow you to gather grain with his own young women, seeking to protect you from harm since the day you first met him. But there is more to his care of you than the actions of an indifferent relative. If you trust me, Ruth, I will show you I am right."

"Mother, if he wanted me, would he not have said so?"

Naomi's brows knotted in thought. "I cannot with certainty tell you what holds him back. You are much younger. Perhaps he feels you could not want him for a husband. He mentioned to me that you deserved a young man of your own generation."

Ruth snapped upright. "You didn't tell him about how I feel—?"

"Of course I did not, child. Would I reveal such a thing? We were merely speaking in generalities."

"It was his way of telling you to look elsewhere. He is not dim-witted. He must have known your interest. I assure you, he does not want me."

"And I say he does. So we must settle this matter once and for all."

Ruth hunched over again. "How?"

"Tonight he will be winnowing barley on the threshing floor. He won't leave the grain under the watch of servants but will stay with the winnowed barley himself as they did in the old days. You will have your opportunity to speak to him privately, then."

"Privately?"

Naomi ignored her outburst. "Today, I want you to prepare yourself with care. Bathe and perfume yourself. Wear one of the dresses he sent you. Then go down to the threshing floor, but don't let him know you are there. First, give him time to eat and drink. Let him be in good humor when you approach him. Allow the feasting to be done, so that you will not be interrupted by others. Take note of where he lies down. When everyone has fallen asleep, go to him."

Ruth balked. "Go to him? What do you mean, *go to him*?"

"You must be courageous, Ruth. There is a hazard to this plan, I don't deny it. You must risk exposure, perhaps even rejection. But Boaz is worth it. What was it you told Adin? *Bear the cost of your love.* It is your turn to do that for Boaz, for this part is crucial."

Slender arms crossed over her chest until her hands could grasp her stiff shoulders like a shield. "What is it you wish of me?"

"Go and uncover his feet and then lie down. He will tell you what to do next. You start. He will finish."

"Uncover his feet?" Ruth buried her face on her knees. "You mean offer myself to him?"

"It's the chance you must take. You have come to know him. Do you believe he will take advantage of your offer? Take you, without proper provision? Without marriage?"

Ruth shook her head.

"My thoughts exactly. If he loves you, he will offer you marriage. If he does not, he will reject you, as gently as he can. But he won't lay an improper hand on you. For his own reasons, he has chosen not to come to you. So you must go to him. I say he is worth such exposure. Worth the price. What do you say?"

Ruth rose to pace around their cramped room. She felt like she stood at the edge of a high precipice and Naomi was asking her to jump.

"What are you afraid of, Ruth? You know he would never willingly expose you to contempt. Is it your pride that means so much to you?"

Put in those terms, Ruth felt her hesitation must seem petty. But to her, the idea of going to Boaz, offering herself to him, asking for his protection, all seemed untenable.

"Trust me, Ruth. I would not expose you to his rejection if I had not a strong inkling that he cares for you. Your future hangs in the balance of your decision. Pray on it for a while. Seek the Lord. Be guided by Him as Deborah was when she went into what appeared an impossible battle. Boaz's heart cannot be as hard as nine hundred chariots of iron. If it is God's will that you be his, surely He can overcome every obstacle."

Ruth flopped against the wall, her legs too weak to keep her upright. Never in her life—not when she had decided to marry Mahlon, not when she had chosen to leave Moab and come to live in Bethlehem, not even when she had faced a ferocious lion and marauding bandits in the wilds of Edom—had she experienced such terror. It was easy for Naomi to contend that she only had her pride to lose. Naomi could not understand that the thought of throwing herself at Boaz and being spurned by him was as bitter as the idea of drinking the waters of the Salt Sea. How would she continue to live in Bethlehem and look him in the eye year after year if he turned her away this evening?

Once, in the early days of her marriage to Mahlon when they had faced a particularly harsh winter and worried about their future, Mahlon had reminded them of God's promise to Israel when the people had been running from the threat of Pharaoh's chariots. Ruth had never forgotten those words. *Fear not, stand firm, and see the salvation of the Lord, which He will work for you today.* Those words came to her now, with an incomprehensible reassurance.

If she resisted Naomi's suggestion, she might miss out on seeing the salvation of the Lord. She drew in a shaking breath. "I will do everything you say."

Her responsibility would be to resist fear and to stand firm. God's responsibility would be to deliver her. Provide her with His salvation. Ruth hoped she would not get the two mixed up.

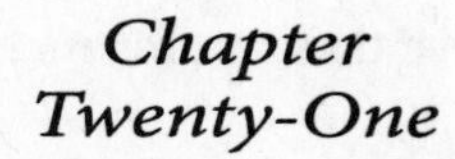

Chapter Twenty-One

I lay down and slept,
Yet I woke up in safety,
For the LORD was watching over me.
PSALM 3:5

Ruth spent several hours preparing for the approaching evening. While most of Bethlehem celebrated a bountiful harvest and winnowed the barley stored in its barns, she bathed and washed her hair with a sliver of Sheba's lily soap. She rubbed scented oil into her skin and painted her eyes with kohl, which Naomi had borrowed from one of her friends.

Carefully, she pulled out the blue linen dress that she had never worn, and never even unfolded, from her cracked and dented chest. As she shook out the folds, she heard the metallic clink of something falling to the ground. Curious, she bent down and searched the floor. After a moment, she spied a pair of earrings made of delicate gold, with round, tiny lapis lazuli beads, and a single pearl in the shape of a teardrop dangling in the center. She picked them up, enchanted with their beauty. Even a cursory glance revealed that they were old, and foreign. She guessed Egyptian.

"What do you have there?" Naomi asked as she worked on her spindle.

"These were tucked in the middle of the dress. I think Mahalath must have placed them there by mistake."

Naomi examined the earrings. "How enchanting." She gave them back. "It's not likely that Mahalath would have given those to you by mistake. They are part of your gift from Boaz. Wear them tonight."

"I really don't believe they are for me! Why would Boaz give me jewels?"

Naomi chuckled. "I'll wear them if you prefer."

Ruth threaded the gold through her pierced ears. "Thank you. I shall spare you that sacrifice. If I am going to make a fool of myself tonight, I might as well go all the way and wear jewels that don't belong to me."

"Come over here and I will comb your hair for you." Naomi twined Ruth's long tresses into dainty braids and wrapped them into an elaborate knot at the back of her neck. "Now put on your new tunic and let us see. I thought I saw an embroidered girdle in that bundle he sent. Try it with the dress. And the white veil for your hair."

Ruth dressed layer by layer, trying not to think of her coming interview with Boaz. When she finished, she stood before Naomi, awaiting her response. Naomi rose slowly. Her eyes brimmed with tears.

"You are beautiful, my daughter. The most beautiful woman belonging to Judah."

Only Naomi would consider her a true daughter of Judah. Ruth could feel Naomi's genuine admiration wrap around her like a loving touch. For once, she actually felt beautiful, seeing herself through Naomi's affectionate regard.

My mother. My true mother.

Naomi would never lead her astray. She would not expose her to needless pain. If she believed Boaz cared for her, then perhaps he did, just a little.

"Do you remember that day, on the road to Moab, what you said to me?"

"On the road to Moab?" Ruth, disconcerted by the new turn in their conversation, had a difficult time focusing.

"You said to me, *where you go, I will go; where you stay, I will stay.*"

"You remember?" Warmth filled Ruth at that realization. At the time, Naomi had acted as though her promise was an annoyance. Yet she had hidden every word in her mind, as though precious.

"I will never forget it. I want you to do something for me, Ruth. I want you to pray those words to the Lord tonight."

"The Lord? I don't understand."

"Tell Him, *where You go, I will go*. Tell Him that you will follow Him, even to the threshing floor. Even if it means the pain of rejection. Tell Him, *where You stay, I will stay*. Even at the feet of Boaz, where every fear may rise up to swallow you whole. Tell Him that you will stay there and face those fears if He leads the way.

"Tell Him, *Your people will be my people*. He has given me to you as your mother. He has given you Mahalath and Dinah and Hannah as friends. And now, if He wants you to belong to Boaz, then so it shall be. And if He does not, then you will settle for the people who He does give you. The people He chooses for you will be your people. No more, no less."

Ruth's eyes widened with understanding. She would abandon her life, her future, her fears into God's hands with the same all-consuming loyalty she had shown Naomi on the road to Moab.

She would walk away from the familiar. The future she knew. She would cast her life into God's hands with the abandon of a waterfall throwing itself down a cliff. This night was not merely a chance she would take on Boaz. It was a declaration of trust in the Lord. She swallowed hard.

She had been praying the whole morning for peace and favor. Without warning, that peace descended and covered her with the same delicate touch as Boaz's veil covered her head. The Lord was worthy of her abandon. Worthy of her obedience. Worthy to hold her whole life in the palm of His hand. Slowly, she nodded her agreement to Naomi.

Naomi caressed her shoulder. "Another thing. You should understand that the Lord speaks these words to *you*. He is not sending you to Boaz's presence alone. With every step you take toward that threshing floor, the Father of our people makes a promise to you. *Where you go, I will go*. He will not abandon you to go to Boaz by yourself. He will go with you.

"Can you not hear Him promising you, *where you stay, I will stay*? *He* is not afraid. *He* is not overcome by what overcomes you, Ruth. When you linger with Boaz, in those lonely, dark hours as you wait for him to fall asleep, God Himself will abide with you. He will give you His strength to do what you must. Do you understand?"

"I am trying. It seems too good to be true."

Naomi shook her head. "Do not doubt for a moment. It *is* true. The Lord also wants you to accept that your people will be *His* people. There is not one person you love whose burden you need to carry alone. Because if they belong to you, then they belong to Him even more. The Lord will take care of me and of Boaz and of Mahalath and of Dinah and Adin too."

Ruth felt the comfort of Naomi's assurance drive away the paralysis of fear. She was not alone. God Himself accompanied her. If she surrendered her life to Him, He would lavish His care upon her. With blazing and sudden certainty, she realized that regardless of the outcome of this night's meeting, she would be well. She would have the Lord all the days of her life, and that would be sufficient, even if Boaz did not want her.

Stealth did not come naturally to Ruth. She showed her heart on her face even when she did not wish to. Hiding behind a large mountain of barley, stored near the threshing floor, she waited out the evening hours as others ate and feasted. Her pulse pounded with disturbing intensity, making her dizzy.

She watched Boaz eat and a strange tenderness filled her. A single grain of roasted barley had lodged in his neat beard, and she longed to reach out and wipe it away, and to tease him about his carelessness. He noticed it and removed it with a quick smile, wiping his mouth with a linen napkin. He had beautiful manners, more like a prince than a simple landowner in a small city.

With typical generosity, he had slaughtered several sheep for his workers, and the mouthwatering aroma of roasted meat and fresh bread filled the evening. Women served platters of hot food and fresh herbs piled high for everyone to enjoy.

Boaz lifted his cup and took a deep swallow, laughing at something Abel said. The sound of his laughter was rich and deep. Ruth tried to imagine having the right to hear that laughter all the days of her life. Having the right to call him *hers*. She fought the onslaught of hopeless tears. God would take care of her, she reminded herself, whether Boaz wanted her or not. Hopelessness had no place in God's plans for her.

Boaz tipped his cup toward his mouth again and after lowering it to the floor, teased Adin with a poke in the ribs. Adin was the center of much humor that night, for after a protracted and hesitant pursuit, he had made short work of the engagement and celebrated his betrothal to Dinah the day before. Once the two had come together, there had been no wasted time.

More jovial eating and drinking followed, until exhausted but content everyone left for home, or found a private corner near the threshing floor to bed down for the night. The evening had turned chill, and Boaz, alone now, unrolled a woolen cloak, moved to a pile of fresh hay, and wrapped it snugly around his body. He turned on his side and closed his eyes with a deep sigh.

Ruth waited in careful silence for a long time, until the moon rose high and everyone seemed sunk into deep slumber. She approached Boaz on bare feet so as not to make a sound.

Help me not to fear. Help me to stand firm. Please Lord, may I see Your salvation for me and Naomi today.

Ruth reached down and untangled the cloak from around Boaz's feet and ankles, shoving the coverings and his tunic up with one movement. It was a bold gesture, redolent of a sensual offering that made Ruth turn pink.

Without making a sound, she lay down at his feet. Her heart

beat loud enough to awaken an army of men. She wondered how he slept on so peacefully. Part of her wanted to shake him awake and be finished with her torment.

Hours seemed to pass, stretching Ruth's nerves and exhausting her patience. The moon rose high. Stars twinkled in an increasingly dark sky.

She began to despair. What if he slept on, never giving her the opportunity to put Naomi's insane plan into action? If so, she concluded that would be the Lord's way of protecting her from making a considerable mistake. She would not take matters into her hands any more than she had already done.

Something startled Boaz awake. He sensed the lateness of the hour. It had grown chill and his feet were freezing. A deep stillness hung about him, and yet he could not shake the impression that he was not alone. He rolled over, eyes narrowing, wondering if a thief had slunk over to filch the threshed barley. A thief would have been bad enough. Instead, he found the supine form of a woman lying inexplicably at his feet. He stared in stunned disbelief, the last vestiges of sleep evaporating.

"Who are you?" he asked in a loud whisper, whipping up into a sitting position.

With a slow movement, the woman turned to perch at his feet. His *bared* feet, he noticed with shock. In a gesture that was ridiculously modest under the circumstances, she tucked her legs up against her hips. Long before she opened her mouth, he already knew her.

Her voice was soft and shy. "I am your maidservant, Ruth."

"Ruth?" Boaz repeated, his mouth dry, as if he hadn't already known. What was she doing here? Alone? With him? What did she mean, baring his feet in the middle of the night? Was she throwing herself at him? Had some strange waking dream taken hold of his mind? He could not credit the reality of this scene, unfolding in the deep watches of the night.

She leaned forward without touching him. "Spread the corner of your covering over me, Boaz."

His eyes widened. She wanted him to *marry* her? She had sneaked upon him, coming as close to the privacy of a bedchamber as a respectable woman could manage, in order to propose marriage to him? He was struck dumb. What drove her to this drastic and unconventional proposal? Need? Guilt? Duty? He wanted to ask a hundred questions, and yet the words would not come.

In the vacuum of his response, she lowered her eyes and bit her lips. "You are my kinsman redeemer."

He reached out a hand, noticing that it trembled, and unable to steady himself, lifted her chin and stared at her. Drenched in moonlight and starlight and the weak shadow of a distant torch, he saw the dismay on her face. Fear that he would reject her. And then he saw something else that melted his heart. She was looking at him with hunger. With longing. It wasn't duty driving her to this ridiculous length.

He almost pulled her into his arms then. He stopped himself just in time, closing his eyes tight as he brought himself under tight rein. The fingers that held her chin withdrew, lest the temptation prove too strong. She was too vulnerable, alone with him, and he refused to take advantage of her. If she were to be his, he would do it right. He would have no stain upon her character on his account.

He gulped in a great gush of air to steady himself. Steady the onrush of joy that had blossomed into the most powerful wave of desire he had ever known. He wanted this woman more than he wanted breath. And the Lord had dropped her into his arms like a ripe peach. He would treat her with the respect due her and due to the Lord who brought her to him.

"The Lord bless you," he said, and heard the trembling in his voice and couldn't even feel ashamed for his weakness. "My daughter," he added, hoping she would read his intention in those words of respect and be reassured that he would not exploit her vulnerability.

Her pale veil had slipped off her head onto her shoulders. Her hair had been arranged in a complex sweep of twining braids. A stray thin braid had escaped to lie against her cheek. Without his volition, his fingers lifted the braid. It felt like silk in his hold; he wanted to pull it until she came close enough to touch. He forced himself to let her go.

"This kindness is even greater than that which you showed Naomi."

"Kindness, my lord? What kindness am I showing you?" She drew nearer and he smiled at that trusting gesture.

"Choosing me for your husband. I could not ask for a greater blessing. You could have sought after younger men who would no doubt welcome you. Whether rich or poor, what man would deny you?"

She gave him a doubting smile and shook her head as if to contradict the possibility of such a thing. He laughed at her modesty and reached for her hand, desperate to touch her, just a little. What had she said? She had asked him to act as her kinsman redeemer. A sharp twisting pain ruptured his incandescent joy when he recalled the complexity of that request. *Jaala!*

His belly convulsed in knots. Jaala had more right to Ruth than he did. And Jaala was not a man to give up his rights easily. Boaz shook his head. The God who brought Ruth to his side in the middle of the night would help bring her safely to abide in his home for the rest of his life.

"Is something wrong?" she asked, her voice anxious.

He caressed her cheek. "Don't be afraid. I will do whatever is necessary to fulfill your request. Everyone in Bethlehem knows you are a virtuous woman. They won't be surprised to hear how much I want you."

"Do you? Want me?"

"I can't tell you how much. Not yet, anyway, for I don't have that right. It is true that I am a kinsman redeemer to you. But there is another man in your family who is more closely related to you than I am. He has the first right of refusal."

She gasped and pulled back from his touch. "*Another man?* I don't want another man!"

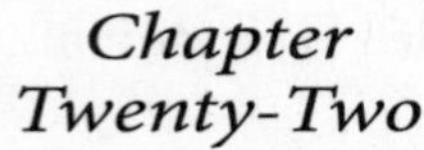

Chapter Twenty-Two

No eye has seen, nor ear heard,
Nor the heart of man imagined,
What God has prepared for those who love him.
1 CORINTHIANS 2:9

Pleasure and satisfaction heated his blood at her involuntary outburst. *I don't want another man!* Boaz felt like jumping up and shouting for joy. There may be a considerable obstacle in their path. But he intended to sweep away that obstacle, demolish it so no shadow of it remained.

"In the morning, I will seek out your kinsman redeemer. If he chooses to redeem you, very well," he said, inherent caution making him temper his words. He did not wish to give false hope when there remained even a small risk that he could not give her what she asked.

She shook her head mutely with such violence that her elaborate arrangement of braids started to come undone. He took her hand and caressed it, wanting to soothe her, wanting to impart assurance into the scepter of fear that he sensed rising in her. The vehement evidence of her genuine dismay melted him. She didn't merely want a kinsman redeemer. She wanted *him*.

"If he is not willing, as surely as the Lord lives, I will redeem you myself."

"Will he want to redeem me, do you think, Boaz?"

It was the first time she had called him by name. The sound of it on her lips made happiness coil inside him until he wanted to grin like a drunken oaf. He did not care if he appeared foolish. He had not felt so close to another human being for over a decade. He noticed that her face was stamped with dismay she could not hide. What had she asked him? The point of it, now that he remembered, was not to speak his name.

Clearing his mind of its pleasant cobwebs, he gave her a comforting smile. "Leave him in my hands, Ruth. Trust me. And trust the Lord who brought you to me." He leaned over, promising himself one last touch. His fingers grazed against her soft cheek, her temple, her ear. He noticed the earrings and bent closer to examine them, sparkling against the dainty whorls of her ear.

"You are wearing the earrings! I am so pleased."

"Naomi said you intended them for me. But I thought perhaps Mahalath made a mistake when she included them in your gifts."

"No mistake. They remind me of you. I wished you to have them."

Ruth played with one dangling pearl. "You honor me. They seem very old."

"They have been in my family for generations. Since the days of our captivity in Egypt. My fathers have presented them to their wives and passed them to their sons throughout the years. Nahshon, the leader of the tribe of Judah, gave it to his wife. And his son, Salmon, gave them to Rahab."

"And you gave them to me? Before . . . before I was anything to you."

He did not feel free to declare his heart to her yet. Not when there was Jaala in the way. "I wanted no one but you to have them."

"Naomi has told me about Rahab. How your people took her in and counted her as one of them in spite of her Canaanite heritage."

"She was much admired by all who knew her. Loyal, like you, and courageous too. Salmon's love for her is legendary in our family. He used to call her his pearl, because of these earrings. She was an irreplaceable jewel to him, sparkling like these precious pearls."

She gazed at him directly then. He was not surprised that she had picked up on the import of what he was telling her. "They remind you of *me*?"

"You are like a pearl too, Ruth. An irreplaceable jewel. I've thought of the hardships you have had to endure, and how you once told me that your life had become like an unending night. Like those earrings caught in the darkness of this threshing floor."

She ran a tentative hand over the jewels dangling against her cheek.

"They are no less valuable because the darkness hides them, are they? No less beautiful or desirable?"

She shook her head, making the pearls shiver.

"When trouble comes into our lives, we are tempted to think less of ourselves. Tempted to believe that *God* thinks less of us, or else He would not allow such pain to have rule over us. Yet, just as the darkness of night cannot overcome the worth of these jewels, your sorrows made you no less precious. Not to God. Not to others."

Her eyes widened. He could see the reflection of tears in them. Tears she held back. "Do you really see me like that?"

"Yes."

"I will never forget this night. I shall always treasure your words."

Trust her to prefer his words to his pearls. He smothered a laugh. Come morning, he would find Jaala and make Ruth his, whatever it took.

"Ruth, you bring joy wherever you go. No matter what happens, I want you to know that. Mahalath, who trusts no one, smiles around you and speaks without fear. You changed Dinah's bitterness with your kindness. You influenced Adin out of his hard-hearted attitude, and if they are now happy together, it is because of you. And Naomi, who could scarcely speak for grief, laughs again and has hope. This is all your doing. Your presence is like a balm."

Ruth made a small noise, half laugh, half refute, enjoying the words without believing them. He stared at her, unable to stop. He should send her home, but could not bear the thought of her walking alone in the dead of night lest some evil should befall her. On the other hand, if she stayed, she ran the danger of being found with him and having her reputation smirched.

"Stay here, with me, for the night. You must leave before others awake and recognize you. But until then, lie down here, and I will watch over you." He threw his cloak over her, tenderly tucking it around her, loving her closeness. She fell asleep as soon as her head touched the hay. She must have been exhausted from the stress of waiting upon him.

Boaz spent the remaining hours of the night praising, praying, and if truth be told, plotting. His approach to Jaala required careful planning. He could not rush forward and lay himself bare before that man. Jaala would only take advantage of his vulnerability. He needed the kind of calm, purposeful strategy he applied to business. Jaala needed to be handled with the greatest of care.

Before sunrise, Boaz whispered Ruth's name. She was a light sleeper and awoke at his first soft call. To his amusement, she spent no time coming to her senses but knew instantly where she was and with whom.

"Shalom, my lord."

He wanted to correct her, to remind her that she had already called him by name. Then he recalled that she did not belong to him yet. That Jaala had a right to her he did not. The thought made him grind his teeth. Not for long, he determined.

"You must leave before the sun rises, so that no one knows a woman came to the threshing floor with me."

She nodded, taking the time to fold his cloak into neat quarters. Before she could rise, he held her back with a motion of his hand. "Bring to me the shawl you are wearing and hold it out."

She gave him a confused look, but obeyed, holding the shawl open over her belly. Boaz filled it with seed. He poured six generous measures of barley and wrapped the shawl and tied it around her waist. "I don't want you to go back to your mother-in-law empty-handed."

Before she had taken ten steps, he was already on his way back to the city gate.

By the time Ruth returned home, the sky had turned a deep blue and the sun shone with comforting warmth on her face. She found herself teetering between laughter and fear. Boaz cared for her. He thought she was a pearl, precious and valuable!

Worthy to wear his Rahab's jewels.

On the darker side, there was another man who had a right to her. How great an obstacle would he prove?

Naomi, when she saw her coming down the road, ran to her, and without wasting time on a greeting, panted, "How did it go, my daughter? I spent the night praying for you and Boaz."

Ruth wrapped her arms around Naomi and laughed. "I could not have dreamt that he would be so tender toward me."

"Did I not say so? Tell me every detail."

Ruth handed over her shawl, bulging with barley, and over a meal of warm bread and cheese, she told her mother all that had come to pass the night before.

"I told you there was no mistake about those earrings. Fancy Boaz being such a poet, calling you a pearl in the night. Have I not found you a good husband?"

"The very best," Ruth said as she took a deep swallow of water. "Let me tell you the rest."

When she told Naomi about asking Boaz to act as her kinsman redeemer, Naomi clapped a hand over her mouth. "You asked him to do *what*? But I never told you to do that!"

Ruth had expected Naomi's surprise, though she found her apparent dismay puzzling. "During the day, as I prayed, the idea came to me. Do you remember, weeks ago, when I first told you about Boaz, you explained to me what a *goel* was? I remembered your words as I prayed this morning.

"It is right that if I should marry, you and your line should be provided for as well, Naomi. If Boaz marries me just for me, then the name of Elimelech will die out. But if he marries me as a kinsman redeemer, on behalf of Elimelech and Mahlon, then their names shall live on, if God chooses to open my lifeless womb, don't you see? Our firstborn son, should by some miracle God choose to bless us, shall be your grandchild as much as my son. There is small chance of it, I know, given my barrenness. But who knows what God will do for your sake, Naomi?"

Tears spilled down Naomi's cheeks and stained the front of her tunic. "It is a gracious offering, child. A gracious offering." She stood with sudden vehemence, overturning the leftover bread and cheese that sat between them. "But—there is a complication."

"I realize that now. I never knew we had a kinsman closer than Boaz who could be our redeemer. Who is this man? How is it that I have never met him?"

"We may be closer by bonds of blood, but there was no love lost between Elimelech and him. I have not seen him in years. Nor have I any wish to."

Ruth felt dread running up her spine as real as a physical touch. She came to her feet. "Does this mean that I would have to marry him if he chooses?"

Naomi turned, her movements awkward. "No. At least I don't think so. However, he is a powerful man. If he should set his mind on having you, it might prove hard to resist him."

"I will resist him," Ruth burst out, sounding more sure than she felt. "But then Boaz could not marry me. Not if this man chooses to redeem me first."

"There is that." Naomi bit her lip.

"What have I done?" Ruth asked, feeling sick.

"Boaz is cunning. He will find a way to keep you for himself."

Ruth sensed that Naomi held something back. Her heart raced harder and a bad taste filled her mouth. "Who is this man?" she asked again.

"Jaala."

Ruth felt the strength leave her legs and collapsed on the floor. "Mahalath's Jaala? The harsh lord who savaged her with his cruelty while she was his slave?"

"That one. That is why I never approached him to ask if he would act as our kinsman redeemer. I did not wish to place either of us in his power."

"I see." The silence that followed was filled with dread.

Ruth rubbed a trembling forefinger over dry lips. "It is up to Boaz, then. He alone can undo this tangle."

Naomi nodded. "He shall find a way."

With an impatient hand, Ruth wiped the tears that wet her cheeks. "I am still glad that I took this route. If Boaz succeeds, then your son may live on through us. Your name shall continue, Naomi. I want that for you, no matter what danger I need to face in order to obtain it."

"You *are* a precious pearl, Ruth. My little jewel. The Lord blessed me the day you came into my life. To think I almost left you in Moab. How grateful I am that you chose to come with me.

"Now, let us wait upon the Lord, for He did not bring you all the way from Moab simply to break your heart. He will give Boaz aid to further his cause. And knowing how Boaz dotes on you, he will not rest until this matter is settled this very day. I am certain of it."

"It's a torment to be so close to having the desire of my heart, and yet so helpless in the waiting."

"Don't give in to your fears. Together we'll wait and pray. And we shall see what happens."

Ruth tried to smile. But the turmoil in her heart almost choked her.

Boaz knew where to find Jaala. Everyone passed through the city gate at some point during the day since most of the fields as well as the threshing floors lay outside the city walls. He hoped he would not have to wait long until the man showed up, for the idea of lingering grated upon him worse than a toothache.

He found an empty bench, shielded by a narrow overhang, near the entrance of the gate. Other businessmen and leaders of the town were slowly gathering. The gate was the judicial and administrative center of Bethlehem. No other place in town boasted enough space to accommodate large gatherings. If men wished to have witnesses to a simple transaction or to conduct more complicated matters that required a court, they came to the gate.

Boaz found himself in no mood for casual conversation with his friends and neighbors. To his relief Jaala showed up uncharacteristically early. Before he could continue walking along, Boaz hailed him.

"Come over here, my friend, and sit down." He pointed at the empty space next to him on the bench.

The man gave Boaz a frowning inquiry before coming over. "You have made up your mind about that parcel of land I mentioned to you?"

Boaz had forgotten about the land. "We can talk about that later," he said, wanting to dangle that possibility to keep Jaala interested. "I do have a matter of business, which we need to discuss, first. It will need witnesses, if you agree."

The man raised bushy brows and shrugged. Boaz called ten of the elders of the town and asked them to sit near. Accustomed to such transactions, they complied with ease.

Boaz addressed Jaala. "Do you remember Naomi, Elimelech's wife?"

"Vaguely."

"She is widowed and has returned from Moab, where she buried both her sons. She has grown sadly destitute."

"Elimelech was always an idiot. I am not surprised he died in a foreign land, and his sons with him. And of course he left his wife with nothing. What's this to do with me, Boaz? I have no interest in a tale of woe."

"No, I realize. But there is financial gain for you, if you will hear me out. In her need, Naomi is selling the parcel of land that belonged to our brother Elimelech. I thought I should bring the matter to your attention."

The man sniffed. "How so? What's it to do with me?"

"I want to suggest that you buy the land. In the presence of these people here, so that we might have the witness of the elders of the people, and make it an official bargain. You are her kinsman redeemer, and if you wish, you can help her in her need. The price is more than reasonable."

Boaz stretched his legs and leaned indolently against the wall. Everything about him suggested casual interest at best. Not by one inflection did he betray how he awaited the man's response with a hitch in his breathing. He saw Jaala flush and knew that, like a fisherman, he had caught him in his net. Jaala was ever greedy for a good bargain, and he could sense one in the picture Boaz had painted. Cheap land, a grateful widow, and the respect of the community for having acted on behalf of Elimelech. All at little cost to himself.

Boaz pinned an encouraging smile on his mouth and lowered his lids to hide the coldness of calculation from Jaala's scrutiny. He wanted to feed Jaala's hungry greed. He wanted the man to burn with desire for ready land until he grew blinded to potential pitfalls. He planned to spring the steep price in such a way that Jaala would be shocked and completely put off by it. He intended to drag Jaala through a hairpin ride of emotions, up and down, and up and down again, until the man balked at the notion of being straddled with a foreign widow.

Ruth was going to belong to Boaz, and Jaala would not stand in the way.

"If you wish to redeem the land, do so. But if you do not, tell me, for at the moment no one has the right to do it except you. However, I am next in line."

The man gave a slow smile, satisfaction leaking from every feature. "Oh, I will redeem it."

Chapter Twenty-Three

Instead of your shame you will receive a double portion,
And instead of disgrace you will rejoice in your inheritance.
And so you will inherit a double portion in your land,
And everlasting joy will be yours.

ISAIAH 61:7

Boaz gave the man's shoulders a friendly tap. "Good. Good. Did I remember to mention, on the day you purchase the land from Naomi and from Ruth the Moabite, you also acquire the dead man's widow?"

"What? You mean I have to marry the Moabite to get the land?"

Boaz bit down on a smile. Here came the crucial moment when the man would back off. "I'm afraid so."

"You might have mentioned it from the beginning!"

"Didn't I?"

"Of course not." Jaala studied Boaz for a long moment, his brows lowered, tense frown lines pleating his forehead. "Well." He slapped a broad hand against his knee. "What's one more wife? Fine."

Boaz stopped breathing. This was not the response he had expected. His plan was unraveling before his eyes. "You want the Moabite?"

Jaala made a face. "If it means helping relatives. Send for her so I can have a look at her."

Helping relatives? Jaala just wanted the land! Boaz could feel sweat break out on his brow. Once Jaala saw Ruth, noted her fragile beauty, he would want her in earnest, Boaz had not doubt. The man would pounce to take hold of her. In her eyes, he would detect fear and lap it up like a thirsty viper. It would only make her more desirable in his perverse eyes. Perchance, if he intercepted her seeking Boaz's help—one pleading look, a single despairing entreaty—Jaala would not give her up for the price of three cheap fields. He would want what Boaz wanted. He had to interrupt Jaala's train of thought now. Take back control of the situation or he would lose Ruth.

"How good of you. Especially to willingly bear the burden of raising her child so that the name of Elimelech will continue," he said, forcing himself to sound bored. "That is a necessity in order to maintain the name of Mahlon. It is his property, after all. It should be his lineage who inherits it."

Jaala sprang to his feet, shaking the wrinkles out of his tunic. "Wait now. You mean, to have the land, not only must I marry this foreign widow but once I beget a son on her, the child does not even belong to me or my name? It belongs to Elimelech's lineage!"

Boaz allowed himself to exhale. "That's right."

"And the land reverts back to them?"

"Quite so."

Jaala swore. "That's ridiculous! Is this some scheme of yours? Are you trying to deceive me into taking these beggars off your hands?"

Boaz widened his eyes innocently. "I? Never."

"I cannot redeem the land at such a price because I might endanger my own estate and my own children. You expect me to pour money into land that won't even come to them? What kind of fool do you take me for, Boaz? Redeem the land yourself. I cannot do it. No wise man would. It's throwing money into a ditch."

"Will you make it a binding agreement by taking off your sandal?" Boaz asked, referring to the tradition that legalized public transactions in Israel.

Jaala rolled his eyes, impatient now with the waste of his time. He removed his sandal and held it up.

Boaz rose, his heart thundering with victory. That large, misshapen, stained sandal had just changed the tide of his destiny. He held up his arms to draw the attention of the elders. Several had already been listening and others gathered around them, curious to find out the nature of the new agreement being forged between the two men.

"You are witnesses that today I have bought from Naomi all the property of Elimelech, Chilion, and Mahlon. I have also acquired Ruth the Moabite, Mahlon's widow, as my wife. This way, she can have a son to carry on the name of her dead husband and to inherit the family property here in his hometown. Thus his name shall not disappear from among his family or from the town records." Boaz's voice dropped. "Today you are witnesses."

The elders and the rest of those gathered at the gate said, "We are witnesses."

Boaz closed his eyes for a moment. He had done it! Ruth was his, and no one could gainsay him. She truly belonged to him now.

His business concluded, his dearest wish granted, Boaz turned to race back through the city gates. He wanted to find Ruth and share his news, knowing how desperate she must feel to hear the outcome of his meeting with Jaala. Before he could take one step toward his horse, however, a wrinkled hand clasped his shoulder. Impatience making his movements sharp, Boaz swung back to find one of the city elders grinning up at him.

"May the Lord make the woman who is coming into your home like Rachel and Leah, who together built up the house of Israel," he said with a wide grin. "May she be fertile like the wombs that gave birth to a nation."

The rest of the men crowded around him. One of the youngest, the son of a favored landowner, shouted, "May you prosper in Ephrathah and be famous in Bethlehem! And may the Lord give you many descendants by this young woman!"

Boaz didn't have time to express thanks before another added his blessing. "May your family be like that of our ancestor Perez, the son of Tamar and Judah."

Boaz started to laugh. If all these extravagant blessings were to take hold, he would populate Israel with his seed and count distinguished leaders and wise men among his descendants. Surely the whole world would resound with his fame and good fortune. He laughed again, harder this time, not believing a single ridiculous thought. He had won Ruth. What more did he need?

Ruth cried when she heard the news. She cried like a child and threw herself into Boaz's arms.

He lifted her chin. "You didn't think I was going to let anybody take you away from me, did you?"

He kissed her then, finally, after waiting for what seemed like a lifetime, though it had only been a few weeks. He kissed her lingering and hard, and held her clasped against him for long moments after, settling into the feel of her willowy body against him. He could feel her heart beating furiously against his chest and kissed her again, softly this time, helpless against a desire too long denied.

They were alone in Naomi's house, for the older woman had left them discreetly when he arrived, mumbling a forgotten promise to visit a friend.

"You took out your braids," he said, to distract himself. Her hair had turned into a profusion of chestnut-colored waves. He ran his fingers through the soft length of them down her waist, relishing the knowledge that he now had a right to such intimacies. "I love you so dearly."

"I never thought to hear you say those words to me. I have longed for you in my dreams, and cried many hopeless tears. I should be really angry with you for your stubborn refusal to approach me. If it weren't for Naomi and her brazen scheme to send me to you in the middle of the night, I would never have revealed my heart to you."

"Naomi put you up to that midnight visit on the threshing floor?"

"My mother is bold."

Boaz roared with laughter. "Your mother is going to receive a magnificent gift from me. That woman is pure gold. And she can cook on top of everything else."

Ruth gave him a teasing smile. "I think you are marrying me for my mother."

"I won't deny there are certain attractions."

She thumped him on the arm. Then she gave him a melting look from her honey-colored eyes. "Kiss me with the kisses of your mouth," she said, her voice a whisper.

All thoughts of laughter and teasing fled Boaz.

Boaz told Ruth she could have an enormous wedding, if she desired. He knew a large wedding would take weeks to arrange and prayed with considerable fervency that she would refuse. Ruth teased him for a whole hour about the elaborate wedding she planned to have. Linen fabrics from Egypt, perfumes from Lebanon, a hundred lambs roasted for the whole of Bethlehem. In the end, his dismay became too obvious to hide and she laughed until her belly ached.

"Serves you right for suggesting such a thing. As if I would wait to marry you for the sake of a fancy wedding," she said. "Next week will do very well. With Naomi, Mahalath, Dinah, and Sheba helping, we will have time to spare."

Even a week seemed unreasonably long to Boaz. He thought of Jacob waiting over seven years for Rachel and pitied the poor man.

Boaz directed his men to build a wedding canopy and hung it with sky blue curtains. Mahalath and her mother draped fresh garlands of wild flowers and leaves over the top of the canopy and the sides of its curtains.

When the evening of their wedding finally arrived, Boaz went to Naomi's house to fetch his bride. Her friends had spent the day with her, accompanying her on her *mikvah* bath and helping her to dress in her bridal finery. As tradition dictated, she had dressed as a queen, though for the first few hours, her face would remain covered with an opaque veil. Their friends followed the bride and groom gaily to the bridal canopy, walking through an avenue of oil lamps lit in advance in preparation for this moment.

When they arrived at the prepared canopy, an old Levite pronounced the marriage blessing over them: "May you increase to thousands upon thousands; may your offspring possess the gates of their enemies." Then Naomi removed Ruth's veil and laid it upon Boaz's shoulder.

"The government shall be upon his shoulder," the Levite proclaimed.

Boaz hardly heard the words; he was too charmed by Ruth's ravishing beauty, finally free of its veil. Her hair had been adorned with gold beads and hung with garnets and pearls, and bracelets jangled at her wrists. "I can't believe you are mine," he said. "I never thought I could feel this happy again."

She gave him a playful smile. "Wait awhile before you say that. If my government is to be on your shoulders, you might find yourself carrying a heavier burden than you bargained for."

For seven days, Boaz and Ruth sat under the shade of the festive canopy, bedecked in wedding finery. Even though their wedding took place quickly, Boaz made sure that there was plenty of delectable food and wine available for his guests so that during the seven days of feasting they never ran short of refreshments. In the end, to surprise Ruth, he did order a hundred lambs to be slaughtered and gave half of the bounty to the poor. One thing for certain, no one went hungry or thirsty during that week.

They had come through so much, he and Ruth. They had loved other people and suffered unbearable loss. And yet in time, God had given them a new dream, a new love. He had redeemed all that sorrow. Everyone in Bethlehem celebrated the joy God had chosen to give them after such a long struggle with hardship and loss.

For many years afterward, the people of Bethlehem would remember Boaz's wedding feast fondly. It wasn't merely the refreshing wine or the delectable food that stood out in their minds. It was the simple joy of knowing that two noble people who had always done their best to make others happy had at last found happiness of their own.

When finally he held Ruth in his arms with no obstacles and boundaries between them, Boaz felt the tension of weeks sweep out of him. They had been alone for hours, and every moment of that time had felt like a balm to Boaz's bruised heart. "Are you happy, beloved?" he asked.

She caressed his face with a shy hand. "You are my home," she said. "You and the Lord. I've never been so happy. All I ever wanted was to belong. Naomi and her family gave me that. When death ripped it away, I thought I was done with joy. I thought the best I could do was to survive. Live another day. Then you came into my life and l learned to love in a deeper way. I thought death was the end of my dreams. But death led me to you."

Boaz was glad the light of the lamp had dimmed, for he could not quench the tears that filled his eyes. "God overcame death. Death itself could not conquer the Lord's plans. After so many years of loneliness, He has filled my home and my hearth with love again."

She twined her fingers into his and raised their joined hands for a soft kiss. "You know, if God can overcome death, surely He can bless a barren womb?"

"If that's His plan, I better do my part."

His wife giggled. "You just did."

"That was for practice."

She lowered her lashes and pretended that she wasn't turning red. "I don't think you need any."

Boaz gave a wide smile and pulled his wife closer. "Still, I didn't know I was helping to fulfill the Lord's purposes. I shall have to take things much more seriously now. I wouldn't want Him to accuse me of slacking on my responsibilities."

Uninterrupted joy took time to make its way into Ruth's heart and stay. In the first days of her marriage, something akin to disbelief mixed with unbearable relief dogged her hours. She could not believe that Boaz truly wanted her and that they were genuinely married. Some days she awoke not daring to open her eyes, wondering if her new life would prove a dream. As disbelief gave way to conviction, she began to wonder if Boaz would come to himself and realize that he had made a grave error. He would compare her to Judith and regret his impulse to come to her rescue. In those early days, she still expected to see disappointment reflected in his kind eyes.

It never came. Week after week, his regard for her proved steady and strong. He shared his days with her and made her laugh with his entertaining accounts of the events at work. Knowing her love of words, he encouraged her writing and began to teach her the business and household accounts. When he had initially suggested that she learn how to keep the accounts, she had been disconcerted. "Me? You want me to learn about your business?"

He laughed. "What? Do you think they will arrest me for teaching you? You have a fine mind, Ruth, and it would be a help to me."

The thought of being useful to him had overcome her doubts, so that at the end of many evenings, they sat together, reviewing the business of the day. She found him a patient and astute teacher, and learned quickly because her desire to please him surpassed her fear of failing. He taught her about the Lord, and together they made time to pray. She learned that he knew the troubles of many of those who worked for him and prayed for them with the concern of a father.

Before long, he convinced Naomi to come and live with them, assuring her that his house was big enough to handle the addition of twenty women, let alone two.

"You better not think of bringing twenty women in here," Ruth was quick to point out, and he laughed at her possessiveness.

"The one is more than enough for me," he said, kissing her with the enthusiasm that never ceased to amaze her.

Without her having to ask, Boaz took charge of Chilion's and Mahlon's lands, and cleared the fields of the debris that over a decade of neglect had wrought. For the first time in years, Elimelech's portion became ready for the plow. Boaz spent his own money on the work and the improvements, paying the wages of the workers he had hired, though none of it would return to him. There would be no gain from this investment, only loss to Boaz. Yet he never seemed to care. He certainly never brought it up to Ruth or Naomi, or held his generosity over their heads to belittle them in any way.

As days melted into weeks and autumn slipped into the early days of winter, Boaz's affection and care finally began to sink into Ruth's heart as a reality. She began to believe that this happiness would not prove false or be snatched away from her. She began to trust in the joy that the Lord had poured into her heart.

One chilly morning, as her small family gathered to have breakfast together, Ruth reached over for the warm bread that Mahalath had served and her stomach gave a great heave. Cold moisture covered her forehead and upper lip. She felt clammy as another roll of nausea washed over her. She pressed her lips together and staggered to her feet, desperate to leave Boaz and Naomi's company and find a private spot in the back of the house. She made it to the edge of the courtyard before doubling over with a violence that disconcerted her.

On her knees and shaking, she sensed Boaz's tense presence at one side and Naomi's on the other. She tried to calm her bilious stomach by force of will for their sakes. She might be physically miserable, but she knew that her sudden sickness was bound to strike fear into their hearts. She said a quick prayer and to her surprise the nausea passed. Within moments she felt completely well again.

"I must have eaten something that did not agree with me last night," she said.

She noticed that her words made no difference to Boaz's pallor or Naomi's unusual silence. Boaz insisted that she spend the rest of the morning in bed, and to humor him, she did not demur, although she felt as healthy as one of his fat ewes. By evening, the nausea returned, though it was milder this time.

The next morning it attacked her with full force again. Ruth ate sparingly that day, trying to give her belly a chance to recover. But the third morning she was sick yet again. Boaz's alarm had turned him pale and uncommunicative. He ordered her to stay in bed the whole day, and she did not argue. She could see anxiety had a hold of him.

"There is nothing wrong with me but an upset stomach," she told Naomi while Boaz rode to oversee the plowing of his fields.

"When did you last have your flow?" Naomi asked without preamble.

Ruth's breath caught. "I've forgotten. More than a month, perhaps. Do you think . . .?"

Naomi straightened the covers over Ruth. "Too early to tell, my dear. Best we keep it to ourselves for now."

Boaz arrived from the field covered in mud and came straight to Ruth. Instead of the exhilaration that his outdoor explorations usually gave him, his face looked grey, his eyes shadowed. "Shalom, Naomi," he greeted his mother-in-law with a smile as he washed his hands in the basin she filled for him. They had learned that he never waited for a servant to take care of such needs. He came over to Ruth and kissed her on the forehead. The ascetic kiss irritated his wife, though she took care to hide her irritation.

"How do you feel, beloved?" he asked.

"I feel well, Boaz. It is a strange malady that only affects me occasionally. Please try not to worry."

He removed his wool cloak, his movements abstracted, and hung the heavy garment on the hook behind the door. Droplets of water clung to it from the afternoon showers. The early rains had delayed in coming, but now they poured with a steady speed that soaked the ground with satisfying thoroughness. Without the early rains, the plows could not do their work. Their advent was a cause for relief as well as celebration. Boaz should be in an elated mood, not withdrawn and quiet. Ruth felt a tinge of guilt for being the cause of her husband's obvious anxiety.

She tried to distract him. "Tell me about the fields. How is the planting going?"

He sat at the foot of the bed. "The sowers are making steady progress behind the plows. It's been very cold and miserable for them in the heavy rains. But the work must be done if we are to have a good harvest. I was beginning to be concerned with the delay of the rains, but they have come just in time. The ground is soft and pliable. The oxen are making good time."

"What a rich blessing from God. Now all we need is the spring rains and the summer sun and we shall have another plentiful year in Bethlehem."

He gave a distracted nod and she wondered if he had heard a single word. "I've sent for a physician from Egypt," he said.

Ruth's jaw dropped. "From Egypt! For a mild stomach upset?"

Boaz stood and began to pace. "It's been going on for too long."

"Three days!"

From the corner of her eye, Ruth noticed Naomi making a calming gesture at her. *Make your gestures at him*, she wanted to say. *He is the one acting out of all sense.*

To her dismay, Naomi said, "That is a good idea. By the time he arrives, we shall give him a rich dinner and a hearty laugh to share with his Egyptian colleagues about the overprotectiveness of the husbands in Judah. But I think it would be good to ensure she suffers no serious malady."

Boaz nodded. "I hope he does laugh."

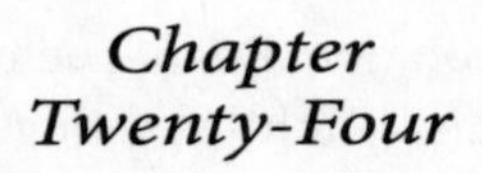

Chapter Twenty-Four

And God will call the past to account.
ECCLESIASTES 3:15

When Boaz left to meet with Zabdiel, Ruth rounded on her mother-in-law. "Why did you encourage him?"

Naomi sat next to Ruth. "If you are pregnant, he will be no less worried than if you are sick. Having a high-and-mighty physician here might bring him calm."

"Because Judith died in childbirth, you mean?"

"That, and because she had many miscarriages before she had their daughter. I doubt if Boaz has forgotten the pain of so many disappointments. They are bound to cast their shadow over him now."

"Just because they lost their babies doesn't mean I will lose ours."

"Of course not. But the heart does not reason so judiciously. You can try to reassure your heart with prudent words, but the weight of old sorrows colors our perceptions beyond reason. The Lord Himself shall have to minister to Boaz and heal him of the past. In the meantime, you must be patient with him."

"In the meantime, I might not even be with child. This might all be a storm over a piece of bad cheese."

Naomi gave a smile that did not reach her eyes. "Are you worried too, Mother?" Ruth asked.

"No. It's only . . . I sometimes miss them so. My dear boys."

Ruth winced. "I have been thoughtless. The possibility of this pregnancy must be a sting to you."

"Never think it. It would be all joy. That doesn't mean that my heart doesn't long to hold my own sons in my arms too."

A week passed with little change. Ruth still felt queasy part of the day, though she contrived to hide it better. Much of the time she felt strong and unaffected by the strange bouts of mild dizziness and nausea that gripped her without warning. She grew hopeful that she might indeed be pregnant, for her flow had yet to come.

It proved a wavering hope, however, for whenever she remembered her barren years with Mahlon, her many unanswered prayers, and the endless, monthly disappointments, her heart would sink. Had God chosen to reverse the ineptitude of her body? Had He desired to bless Mahlon's line when He had refused to do so while Mahlon lived? Was she pregnant or just wishful? Once barren, always barren. Then, against all reason, hope would poke its head out again, and the cycle of her thinking would start once more.

One afternoon, when the rains abated and the sun peeked weakly through the clouds to bring a modicum of warmth, she decided to visit the stables near the house. She knew Boaz would be there, and the sight of her, hale and hearty, would cheer him. To her surprise, she did not find him with the horses but inspecting four new oxen.

As she approached him, the sharp odor of fresh ox dung hit her with a pungent blow. It took her a moment to settle her heaving stomach. She wrapped her scarf firmly about her nose and forced her feet to move forward.

A couple of servants were cleaning the stalls where the oxen were usually kept, and Boaz, who seemed to find no job unpleasant enough to keep him at bay, was busy whispering to the restless oxen in an adjacent stall.

"Your stalls are ripe, my husband."

"Ruth! You ought not to be here, beloved. It's filthy." He came away from the oxen, lowering a rough wooden barricade to keep them from escaping.

"I noticed. Is it always like this?"

Boaz smiled. "A pristine manger means you own no oxen. But without the strength of the oxen, you cannot have abundant crops." He shrugged. "What's a little dung compared to the riches of a good harvest? If you want blessing, you must accept the manure that accompanies it."

Ruth laughed. "I hadn't thought of that. Are these new?" She pointed to the four trembling animals, bones poking out of their shoulder blades. In spite of their apparent thinness, their brown fur gleamed and stringy muscle covered their haunches.

"Yes."

"More dung to clean."

"With the new land, we needed the help."

Her eyes softened. He meant Elimelech's land. Yet more money to be spent on Mahlon's lineage. A lineage that might be growing within her even now. Ruth twined her hand into his, feeling an overwhelming sense of gratefulness that God had given this man to her as husband. "You are a good man, Boaz of Bethlehem."

By the time the physician from Egypt finally arrived, brown skinned and smoothly shaven, Ruth had grown as impatient as Boaz for his arrival. She wished for an end to this torment of wavering between hope and despair. She said nothing to Boaz of her hope. What would be the point if it proved false? He would only grow more anxious. She preferred the physician to do the talking. He, at least, would have certainty on his side.

Her stomach had begun to settle down and she felt the bite of nausea less often, though she now battled an unusual weariness that had her in bed, unconscious with exhausted sleep in the middle of the afternoon. She wondered if this meant that she was truly sick.

She shared her symptoms with the physician while Naomi held

her hand for support. To her surprise, the Egyptian spoke Hebrew fluently, though with a guttural accent that she sometimes found hard to understand. He told her that he had met Boaz on a caravan many years ago, and that he traveled to Israel regularly to visit wealthy patrons.

His manner was easy, but it became clear that beneath his charming demeanor lay a sharp mind that knew its business well.

"Congratulations, mistress. You are with child." He rinsed his fingers in the bowl he had prepared earlier and dried them on a linen towel.

"Are you certain?" Ruth's voice emerged in a feathery whisper. "I was married before for over four years and barren that whole time. I never became pregnant. Not even once."

The Egyptian shrugged a nut-brown shoulder. "Who knows why such things happen? I can assure you that you are with child now. And since you appear as healthy as one of your husband's horses, I predict this pregnancy shall progress well."

Ruth's heart soared. The Lord had blessed her. He had enabled her to become pregnant. Beyond every expectation, beyond the measure of her faith, He had given her the fulfillment of her dream. He had filled her empty womb. She would be a mother. *A mother!* Ruth of Moab was going to be a mother! No longer would people call her *barren*. They would call her blessed.

"When will he come, my baby?" She loved the sound of those words—*my baby*. For years, she had been forbidden to make such a claim. Now, these words would be a common part of her life.

The physician rubbed the smooth skin of his cheek. "Toward the end of summer, I should think. You will be large with child in the high heat. That won't be pleasant for you, but it can't be helped."

"If you want blessing, you must accept the manure that accompanies it," Ruth said, her eyes twinkling.

"Pardon?"

"Something my husband taught me. Shall we call him in and tell him the good news? And please try to reassure him. His first wife suffered many miscarriages. I suspect he shall fear the same will happen to me."

The Egyptian nodded, making the odd-shaped, starched linen covering his head shiver stiffly. "I remember that sad story."

Boaz came in looking like a man about to receive a sentence of death. His skin appeared clammy and pale. "Well?"

"Congratulations, my lord. You shall welcome a child into your home at the end of summer."

"A child?"

"We are going to have a babe," Ruth said, her hand reaching out to hold his.

Boaz did not even notice her outstretched hand. He said nothing for a long moment. He opened his mouth several times, but no sound came out. Finally, he croaked, "But I thought you could not . . . And we've only been married a few short months. How could she already be pregnant?" He turned to face the Egyptian.

The physician, shrugged, unabashed. "What shall I say? You have potent seed, my lord. It's cause for celebration, no?"

Ruth coughed and Naomi tried to hide her laughter behind her veil.

A wave of color flooded Boaz's face. He threw Ruth a sideway glance and grinned. "If a physician of your stature declares it is so, who am I to argue?" The smile faded and he put his arm around Ruth's shoulders, drawing her against his chest. "Is she in danger?"

"None that I can see. She is hale and strong. The child proceeds well."

As soon as the physician left, Boaz prayed, giving thanks to the Lord, asking for His protection. This baby was his, and yet not his. Mahlon had as much right to this child, if it should prove to be a son, as Boaz himself. Yet not by one syllable did he betray any resentment. His whole focus seemed to be Ruth's well-being. Then Naomi blessed Ruth and the babe she carried, weeping as she prayed. Ruth felt so filled with joy and thankfulness that her own prayers emerged in a jumble of words that could only have made sense to God.

"Are you happy?" Ruth asked Boaz, when they were alone.

Boaz looked down and said nothing.

Ruth's heart dropped. "Do you wish it were Judith? Do you wish it were her child?"

Boaz snapped up his head. "Ruth! How could you think such a thing?"

A tear trickled down her cheek, followed by another. She dashed at them. "I can see you are sad. Why else would you not rejoice at such a blessing?"

He wiped her tears. For a moment, he gazed at her, his eyes dark and unreadable. With a strangled sound in his throat, he pulled her into his arms, his movements rough with tension. His kiss was possessive, hard, like a stamp of ownership. Like a cry of desperation. He kissed her and kissed her until she forgot what she was crying about.

"You are my wife. My love. Don't ever pull Judith between us again. She was my past. You are my today. My tomorrow." He kissed her again, and this time he marked her with tenderness.

"Why then," she asked, a long time later. "Why aren't you happy?"

He rose and pulled his discarded mantle about him. "It's hard for me to speak of this, Ruth." With his back to her, he said, "The babes ruined Judith's health. In the end, they were the death of her."

He took a deep breath, and Ruth could tell from the rigidity of his back, from his harsh breathing and his gruff voice that he did not wish to speak to her about his struggles. But for her sake he forced himself to go on. "I know this child is what you have always wanted. I want to be happy for you. But to me, this pregnancy is like a bucket that has pulled up all the fear out of the well of my memories. How am I supposed to celebrate a child who might make you sick? Or take you from me altogether? I just found you. How shall I live if this child robs you from me?"

Ruth went to stand by him. She leaned against his side. Through the fine wool of his mantle she could feel the chill of his skin; it made her shiver. "The babies didn't take Judith from you, Boaz. Death did. And you told me yourself that death did not have the last word. Aren't they with the Lord? Didn't He have the final victory?"

In the lengthening shadows of the room, Boaz remained mute. She held him in the darkness, trying to infuse him with the reassurance of her touch. He did not hold her back.

The rain poured as though someone had ripped a hole in the sky. Each drop, the size of a sparrow's egg, found its way to the earth and soaked everything in its path. Boaz walked through the olive grove, unmindful of the cold and the wet. He had slept little the night before, thinking of Ruth's words. When had he begun to confuse his babies with death itself? When had he begun to resent them?

Reject them?

Ruth was right. They had been as much victims of death as Judith herself. Fear and grief had confused his thinking. Sometime in the dark months after Judith's death, he had begun to see those babies as the enemy. And now that Ruth carried his child, the enemy had come back to haunt him.

He had tried, in the darkness of the night, with Ruth's breaths gently stirring against his shoulder, to simply change his feelings. Rejoice over the conception of his child.

And to his shame, he could not. He could not simply decide to love that life growing inside his wife.

He could not bring himself to rejoice over the tiny creature being nourished inside her womb, drinking up her life and strength with a hungry greed that cared nothing for her well-being. He had walked the valley of death too long and knew it too well not to fear its all-consuming power. He had lost one wife to death's grip at a time that should have brought joy. He could not overcome the possibility that death might visit him again when he was least prepared for its hungry jaws.

He could not accept this child as a blessing from God.

When had he given so much ground to lies?

He pressed his palm into the gnarly bark of an olive tree. "God, help me!" His cry ripped into the silence like the roar of a madman.

Your child is a boy. A little boy, Boaz. I have plans for his welfare. Plans to give him a future and a hope. He will give rise to a great lineage. And from him shall flow rivers of living water down into the generations. Through him, the nations shall rejoice.

Boaz froze, sensing the presence of God. Sensing divine power and holiness about him. He fell to his knees, and then on his face. "Lord!" he croaked.

Open your eyes to Me, My child. See Me. Let My love cover the darkness within you. Let it wipe away the memory of grief. Set your mind on Me, not on death.

Boaz grappled with that command. Had he set his mind more on death than on God? Had he ascribed more power to death than to God? "Forgive me, Lord. Forgive me for fearing death more than I trust You."

I never left you. I never left Judith or your children. I remained near them every step of their journey. They are safe in My presence. I never abandoned you, Boaz. Death is your enemy. Not I. Not your babies. Death is your enemy and Mine. Fear not, for I have set My heart on overcoming Death forever.

A shower of warmth unlike anything Boaz had ever experienced covered him. He knew, without being able to explain, that the Lord had washed him of his sin. Later, he resolved, he would offer an unblemished lamb as a sacrifice to God. But even now, before the blood of that sacrifice covered him, he experienced a peace unlike anything he had ever tasted.

He realized that he had turned his experience with Judith into an expectation. As if God only had this one plan in mind for him. As if the past was the measure of the future. What he needed to learn was that God's plans were always a mystery. He could not predict God's intention for the future by His actions in the past. The Lord had allowed Judith and his children to die. That did not mean that He intended Ruth and her baby to suffer the same destiny.

Boaz returned home soaked through with rain and tears. For the first time in weeks he felt tranquil. He knew that he would have to fight in order to keep the peace God had offered. Fear and anxiety were not done with him.

He sensed that God was not finished with this lesson. He had more to learn about the plans and providence of God. That thought made him smile and shiver at the same time. But for now he could rest in the lingering sweetness of God's presence.

Chapter Twenty-Five

The joy of the Lord *is your strength.*
NEHEMIAH 8:10

Dinah came to visit Ruth one sunny afternoon. Since her marriage, Ruth had invited the young bride a number of times to her house. Because of Boaz's status, Dinah never felt quite at home, but she came swallowing her awkwardness. Ruth treasured each visit, knowing what it cost Dinah to come.

When they had partaken of Naomi's mouthwatering spiced honey cakes, Dinah collapsed against the cushions. "These pillows are so soft, I'm likely to fall asleep on you. Mind you, I fall asleep all the time these days. You might as well hear it from me: I'm going to have a baby."

Ruth's eyes widened. "No! Is it true?" She laughed. "I'm so happy for you."

Dinah's smile sparkled with pleasure. She reached for another honey cake and stuffed it in her mouth. "This one's for the baby."

Ruth picked a second cake. "In that case, I should also eat another."

"Wait. Does that mean . . .?"

"I am expecting a babe also."

Dinah jumped up and pulled Ruth to her feet for an exuberant embrace. "We are going to be mothers together. I am so happy!"

"How does Adin feel about your news?"

"He went a bit green and mumbled something about more mouths to feed. Then he laughed and kissed me and said God had blessed him with a good wife. Ruth, I don't mean to be rude. But I thought you were barren."

"So did I. Apparently God didn't agree."

Dinah smiled. "Lord Boaz must be speechless with delight."

"Speechless. Yes." Ruth looked down. "So, did you bring your sling? You haven't forgotten your promise to teach me how to use it?"

"Do you really want to learn?"

"More than ever. I'll teach the baby when he is older."

"What if she is a girl?"

"Then I hope she will have your aim. Let's go out and try your sling. The sun is out; we can't ask for a better day."

The two women made their way to the back of the house, beyond the barn, where a small field sat empty of animals or people.

"This will do. You won't accidentally throw a stone at some poor creature's head and injure it." Dinah pulled out a leather sling and showed Ruth how to hold it.

Ruth discovered that even holding the weapon correctly was more challenging than it seemed. A leather pouch in the center had to be balanced by the two long strings at either end. Fingers and thumbs had to hold the contraption with enough balance and flexibility to allow the sling its swinging motion without releasing the projectile too early.

From inside her belt Dinah pulled out a rounded stone the size of a pigeon egg. "You want to start collecting smooth stones about this size for your sling. You can have one of lord Boaz's men file down some of the rough edges. The best stones are found in a river."

She placed the stone in the pouch, wrapped the ends of the long strings about the fingers of one hand and swung once. Pointing to a broken branch lying on the ground twenty paces away, she released the stone. It hit the branch dead-on, making it fly into the air.

Ruth clapped. "You are incredible. As good as the young men in my caravan on the way to Bethlehem."

Dinah walked over to collect her stone. "I have many hidden talents."

"Adin must be blind to have taken so long to marry you."

Dinah smiled. "I'm not sure a man wants a woman with good aim. It might not always prove to his advantage. Now you try."

It took Ruth a number of attempts to make the sling swing properly without dropping its stone. She was afraid that if she released the stone at the wrong time, she might hit herself on the head.

"Now!" Dinah instructed, and Ruth let go. She had no aim to speak of yet, but she did manage to throw the stone without harming anyone.

"Good. Again."

As Ruth began to swing the sling over and over, Dinah laughed. "It won't make it go more accurately if you keep swinging. You're just making your arm tired. One round or two will suffice. Let the stone go. Or have you grown attached to it?"

"I'm just getting my rhythm."

"You're making me dizzy. Release."

Ruth fumbled and the stone thumped too close, bouncing twice before coming to a stop.

"What are you two up to?"

Ruth and Dinah turned in unison to find Boaz, his hands against his hips, observing them quizzically. Dinah bent to pick up the stone and tucked it into her belt with a quick motion. "I was on my way home to my family. Shalom, my lord. May you have a blessed day."

"Dinah."

"Yes, my lord?"

"I asked you a question."

Dinah scratched her head through her veil. "Did you, my lord? I thought you were addressing your wife."

Ruth laughed and hooked her arm around Boaz's elbow. "Dinah is teaching me how to use a sling."

"That's what it looked like to me. But I thought it must be a dream. Why is my wife learning how to throw a sling?"

"To defend you in case of danger, of course. There are many evil men about these days. Someone needs to look after you."

Boaz raised a dark eyebrow. "Where did you learn to use a sling with such expertise, Dinah?"

"As a child, my lord."

"Did you beat Adin?"

She scuffed her toe in the dirt. "And his brother."

"No wonder the man took so long to ask you to wife. You could put the fear of God into a man's heart."

"I suppose you will forbid me from teaching Ruth, now."

"Certainly not. Teach away. I like to know my wife can bring down a bandit from twenty paces. And I can't think of a better teacher." He turned to leave.

"Husband?"

"Yes?"

"Congratulate Dinah. She and Adin are going to have a child."

Boaz groaned. "Not another one. Is there any woman in Bethlehem under the age of seventy not so blessed?"

Ruth pulled out the old roll of parchment that contained her story, and grabbing stylus and ink, sank on a cushion near the latticed window to write. It had been some weeks since she had taken the time to work on this particular parchment. She spent most of her days learning the accounts from Boaz. Now, with the advent of her pregnancy, she felt inspired to continue her story, recording God's indescribable kindness to her.

"What are you working on?" Boaz grabbed a date, sucking on its sweetness as he bent over her.

Ruth bit her lip. "The last time you did that, you almost made my heart stop."

"Do what? Read your writing? I do that every night." He sank next to her and pulled the parchment close.

"Not this parchment."

He frowned. "These are not the accounts. Or your practice."

"No. I'm writing my story."

"Are you? May I read it?"

Ruth sighed. "If you promise not to laugh. I am not very good."

"What did you mean *the last time*? I've never seen this."

"You have. That afternoon you came to Naomi's house to pick up a jar of capers. Remember?"

"Yes. I saw you writing that day. You had an ink stain right there." He leaned over and kissed her warmly on the corner of her mouth. "I remember wanting desperately to do that then."

Ruth shook her head. "You never showed it."

"I showed it most conspicuously in spite of my best efforts. You, my love, were too blind to see."

"Well, you, my love, were too blind to see that!" She showed him his name, and her plaintive prayer.

"You cared for me even then?"

"Desperately. And you made me suffer endless torment with your show of indifference."

"When did I ever show you indifference?"

"Dutiful kindness, then. Worse than indifference."

He pulled her onto his lap and kissed her thoroughly. "I shall have to make up for it the rest of our lives. Now be still and let me read this fascinating story. If it has my name in it, it must be riveting."

He unrolled the parchment to its beginning and began to read. "You never told me much about your grandfather," he said after reading for some time. Come to think of it, you rarely speak of Moab."

"There isn't much to say. In many ways my real life did not start until I met Naomi. And yet I sometimes think even the hardness of my parents' hearts had a role to play in my happiness, for if they had been a little more loving, I might not have found the strength to leave them and Moab. I owe them a debt you see. For bringing me to you."

Boaz pulled his hand through her long hair for a reassuring caress. "How could they not have seen your worth? Were they blind?"

Ruth smiled and shook her head. "Too busy, too disappointed, too tired."

"Well, I should dispatch a messenger with my thanks, if that is what brought you to me." He gave her a kiss and turned back to his reading. She had to be patient, for he seemed to forget about her presence as he read. Once in a while he would make a small sound, a noise deep in his throat, or an exclamation of shock.

Before he came to the end of her account, he rolled the parchment closed. "How hard it must have been for you, all those years of barrenness."

She grew still. "It was like a wound that never healed. I learned not to allow it to rule my life. I learned to accept. After I came to Bethlehem, God asked more of me."

"More than acceptance?"

"Yes. He taught me to accept with joy. Accept His will, even though it meant that I could have no children of my own, not with mere resignation but with joy. The Lord taught me that even if I don't receive the desires of my heart, in Him, I can be content. That's why this baby is such a miracle. After accepting that I could have no children of my own, after learning contentment and even joy without the fulfillment of that dream, God gave me a child."

Boaz caressed her face. "Acceptance with joy. That's a lesson I wish to learn. I'm not as good a student as you seem to be. But I want you to know that I am happy God has given us this child, Ruth."

Boaz and Ruth fell into a routine of daily prayer. Often Naomi joined them. At first, Boaz's petitions tended toward a desperate kind of pleading. He begged for Ruth's health, for the babe, for the birth. Ruth realized that beseeching God helped him escape the anxiety that still plagued him on occasion.

As time passed, Boaz's prayers changed. He began to sink into an increasing assurance. The tenor of his words took on a thankful tone, as though he already counted on God's answer. He seemed more convinced that the Lord would see his family through, and that the past would not write his future. Ruth loved when Boaz prayed over her like this. His new assurance seeped into Ruth and Naomi as well. The peace of God would settle over them like a refreshing breeze.

It was during these weeks of expectation that Naomi started to rise fully out of her grief. When they prayed, her countenance would change. Ruth noticed that once again she laughed often and with ease. The haunted look that had dogged her steps for over a year left her.

By the time Ruth was seven months pregnant, her belly stretching large enough to show her pregnancy to the world, she felt well enough to attend her normal duties as Boaz's wife. Her nausea had long since abated, and with a little extra rest, she found herself equal to most of her usual tasks. Except for an occasional twinge in her back and belly, she found pregnancy easy. Boaz was amazed at her health and praised her as though she had accomplished some great task, even though she had no more to do with the state of her health than the color of her eyes.

In those months, their joy knew no bounds. They celebrated another bountiful crop. Barley and wheat grew thick and green, slowly turning golden, assuring the people of Judah that God's provision would see them through another year of comfort. Ruth could not believe that last year at this time she had been gleaning in the fields to feed herself and Naomi. Those days of uncertainty and backbreaking labor seemed a lifetime ago. Her world had changed as if overnight.

As Ruth's time grew near, however, a new fear seemed to replace the old. Boaz never spoke of it, but Ruth could sense it in him. The gloom of dread cast its long shadow over her husband once again.

Chapter Twenty-Six

He who dwells in the shelter of the Most High
will abide in the shadow of the Almighty.
I will say to the LORD*, "My refuge and my fortress,*
my God, in whom I trust."
For he will deliver you from the snare of the fowler
and from the deadly pestilence.
He will cover you with his pinions,
and under his wings you will find refuge.

PSALM 91:1–4

Naomi crooned a song under her breath as her needle flew over the edge of new swaddling cloths, hemming in neat stitches. From her seat near the window where Ruth was weaving, she joined in the song. She only knew a short snatch, and partway through the song stumbled over the words, making Naomi lose her place. They both laughed.

"You seem happy, Mother."

"I suppose I am. I miss my sons every day. They are like an ache in the marrow of my bones. And yet the Lord has shown me that I am still capable of joy. It's so odd, carrying so much pain inside, but carrying happiness too."

"What made you decide to return to Bethlehem all those months ago? I try to imagine our lives if you hadn't made that choice."

"When I heard about the bountiful harvest here, I knew the Lord had spread His wings over His people. He had visited us. I thought that I might take refuge in His provision."

"But you were so angry with Him then!"

"Angry or not, He is my God. Who have I in heaven but the Lord?"

"You tried so hard to prevent me from coming with you. I was terrified that you would leave me at the side of the road."

"I believed that you would only suffer deprivation and loss if you stayed with me. I wanted to save you from more pain."

"I know. And yet the Lord had so much good waiting for us here. You were born here, and now my child shall be born here also."

Naomi spread the cloths over her knees and straightened. "It seems no less than a miracle to me. When I consider the past year, I grow convinced that the Lord chose to guide us every step of the way. He kept us safe as we traveled. He brought you to Boaz's field. He shielded you from every harm that could have befallen you."

"You do realize, Mother, that I am the least qualified of all the women in Bethlehem to be Boaz's wife? I am a Canaanite. A nobody. And yet God chose me for him. He imported me all the way from Moab, as if I were ivory from the distant shores of Egypt, and dropped me in the man's lap. You would think there was a shortage of women in Judah."

"I only know that until you came, no woman took his fancy. He would have lived his life as a widower and been content with his lot. It was you he wanted. It was you God wanted for him."

"Why do you think that is? I cannot work it out."

Naomi pulled the fabric close to the light to adjust a stitch. "You still measure yourself by the standards of this world, daughter. God has other measures. What does He care for wealth and connections? The cattle on a thousand hills belong to Him. You have what He looks for, Ruth: Love. Faithfulness. Compassion. For such treasures, He searches the heart of man. In you, He found a treasure trove."

Ruth was large with child and Boaz was large with worry. Every day, as the size of her girth increased, Boaz's heart shrank a bit further. He realized that the second portion of God's lesson had arrived at the door of his heart.

When he had first found out that Ruth was pregnant, he had to contend with the fear that she might lose the child. Lose her grip on joy and hope and all the good things of life. Now he had to face the birth itself.

Twice, he had sat next to a woman who had travailed through the pangs of childbirth. He did not know how women bore such suffering. The first time, Judith had almost bled to death. The second time, she had succumbed to the incomprehensible affliction of birthing.

Boaz had to see Ruth through that agony! Every day brought it closer. It hung over him like a claw, ready to rip into his flesh.

This time, God offered him no gentle murmur. He extended no assurance. No promise. No words of mercy. The Lord withheld Himself. And Boaz knew this was part of his lesson. He had to hold on to faith without the great mercies of God's conspicuous presence. He had to hold on in utter darkness.

One early morning as he was riding Khaymah with a speed that would have turned Ruth white, a word came to him.

Surrender.

That was the lesson God wanted him to learn. He knew now, bone deep, that his son—Mahlon's son—would live. Thrive. Have children of his own. But it was Ruth's fate that tormented him.

That morning as he rode with the sun on his back and the wind ripping into his tunic, he understood finally that he had to surrender Ruth to God. She was the one thing in his life that he had held back from the Lord. Everything else God could have. His riches. His land. His cattle. His very life, even. But not Ruth. Not his wife, whom he loved with every fiber of his being. He had held Ruth back. She had become the prize God was not allowed to snatch.

The thought made his muscles clench until he ached. He pushed the horse to the limits of its strength. Flattening his torso forward, Boaz leaned into the neck-breaking speed, as if he could outrun the whirl of his thoughts. The thoughts kept steady pace with him no matter how fast he galloped.

Surrender Ruth! Let God have her.

And trust His will.

The horse's body moved beneath him, the muscles of its shoulders and back roiling. Boaz adjusted his crouch, his body suspended in midair as he leaned his weight on his toes and ankles, gripping the sides of the powerful beast beneath him. At this speed, his balance was precarious at best, like trying to walk a line the width of a thread. One false move and he would pitch forward or flip back off the beast.

Surrender Ruth.

Lord, can't I have this little bit of my life for myself? Can't I have something just for me? Why do You want everything?

The horse began to sag beneath him, its steps faltering. He had driven the beast hard and long. For all its power, a horse could be a delicate animal. Pushed too far, it could sicken. Die even. Boaz knew it was time to stop.

He had to slow the beast down with gradual intention. Sudden halts after a strenuous run could lead to excruciating muscle spasms and colic. From run to trot, he pulled back the horse, until they finally slowed to a lazy walk. When they came to a stop, he grabbed a rag out of the saddlebag and rubbed the animal down with steady, firm strokes. The horse stood still under his ministrations, trusting its master.

Boaz's legs shook from the long ride, the exercise having pushed him to his physical limit as much as it had pushed the horse. He laid his head against the horse's side.

God had offered him a choice. Surrender Ruth. Or continue to walk in the agony of fear. Before he returned home, Boaz made his decision.

When he came to Ruth, he was calm.

"You are soaked through with perspiration," Ruth exclaimed. "How fast did you ride that creature?"

"You don't want to know."

"You must promise me not to ride at such speeds again."

He smiled as he stripped out of his stained tunic. "No."

"No? You are about to be a father. I think you should take greater care of your safety."

"If I can live with you being pregnant and giving birth, I think you can learn to tolerate my occasional brisk rides."

Ruth's eyes rounded. "Those are not the same at all."

"Perhaps not. But they both require that we surrender one another to God's care."

"I wouldn't have to surrender anything if you would only be reasonable about the speed with which you ride."

"Think of my riding as a wonderful opportunity to draw you nearer to God." He patted her belly and grabbed the washcloth.

The birth was taking too long. The Egyptian physician, whom Boaz had brought back two weeks before in preparation for this very day, sat next to the old Jewish midwife, his pate shining with sweat and his mouth sealed with tension. The midwife had stopped speaking ten minutes before. Ruth was peripherally aware of the ominous silence that surrounded her.

Pains came upon Ruth with cruel frequency, taking most of her focus. The child would not come. She had little knowledge of childbirth. But in the midst of her misery and growing weakness, she could sense the concern that had settled in the room like a heavy shroud.

"What's amiss?" she panted between one wave of pain and the next.

"You are doing well, mistress. The child is large. He lingers. In time, he shall come," the Egyptian whispered.

Ruth rode out another pang, swallowing her screams, not wanting to fill the household servants and Boaz with dread. The midwife stood and examined Ruth. Her intrusive fingers made Ruth groan.

"This child is coming sideways. I'm sure that is what delays the birth."

The Egyptian pushed and prodded the dome of Ruth's belly. "It's likely."

Their examinations added to the pain that already ripped through her, and she squeezed Naomi's fingers until they must have turned blue. As the pain let up, she loosened her hold. "I'm sorry, Mother. That must have hurt."

Naomi chewed on dry lips. "I will fetch Boaz."

"He will only be dismayed and feel helpless," the Egyptian warned. "He can offer her no assistance. We don't need a distressed husband complicating an already difficult situation."

"Whoever heard of a husband in a birthing room, Naomi? Having a man here is bad enough." The midwife threw an accusatory glance at the physician.

"Boaz can pray for her."

Ruth tasted blood as she swallowed. "Please. Bring him to me."

Naomi turned toward the door. Ruth forgot the thread of her words as pain ripped through her belly and back. For a moment she thought that her body had torn asunder. The scream she had bit down earlier escaped her lips.

The Egyptian bent low to examine her again. He shook his head. "Her travail leads nowhere. The babe is caught." Even in her distress Ruth could sense the brittle note of doubt in his voice.

Naomi returned to take her position behind her, rubbing her aching back as Ruth leaned against her, feeling weak and dizzy.

She sensed Boaz as he sat near her and reached out to take hold of her hand. "He is slow, our son." His voice was calm. A strange peace radiated from his countenance.

Ruth smiled, relief flooding her at his presence. "Yes. I shall have to speak to him about that when he finally deigns to emerge." A low grown broke from her lips before she could strangle the sound.

"If you are trying to be brave for my sake, you should give up. I already know this child is going to be born strong and healthy. I was thinking of the name Obed. Do you like that name?"

Boaz's calm began to sink into Ruth's consciousness. She felt the tension leave her body. "Obed?"

"It means *worshiper. The servant of the Lord*. I think that would be a good name for our son. Would Mahlon approve?"

Another pain came. Yet strangely, this one did not feel like an endless wave that went nowhere. Ruth could feel her body shifting. Opening.

"He would approve," she panted. "The midwife says the child is coming sideways, with his shoulder first, instead of his head. He is caught."

"I will pray for you both, my love." He laid broad hands over her belly and began to pray. Ruth was sinking past consciousness so that his words flowed over her in syllables of noise, making no sense.

Another sharp pain crashed through her. She squeezed her eyes shut, pulling her knees closer to her chest, trying to escape the agony. Scream after helpless scream made her throat raw. Something wet gushed out of her.

"She bleeds," the midwife cried. "She bleeds too much!"

"But look! That's the head," the physician said, his voice hoarse. "I don't understand it, but the babe must have righted itself. Another push, mistress, and the head will emerge."

Boaz continued to pray, his hands on her belly, his voice a soothing murmur that calmed her. Ruth grew quiet. From somewhere she found the strength to give another mighty push. The room started to spin. She lost sight of everything but pain.

A feeble cry filled the room. Her child! That mewling sound was enough to revive her. Boaz caressed her hair back off her cheeks. She tried to kiss that beloved hand, to hold it against her. She found she was too weak to do anything but flop back against Naomi's chest.

"A boy. You have a son, mistress," a man's voice cried.

"Is he healthy?" Her voice came out a thread. She worried that they might not hear her.

"Perfectly made, and as large as a two-month-old babe," the midwife said.

Taking a shallow breath, Ruth asked, "Can I hold him?"

"Here, my dear. Let me lay him on your chest." Boaz laid the baby, wiped down with olive oil and salt and wrapped hastily in swaddling cloths, against her.

Love. She had not known it could drown you like a rolling ocean. Tether you like a rope of iron. Heal you like a balm. She held her babe and forgot the world.

A gentle touch wiped her cheeks, and only then she came to herself enough to know she was crying. "Boaz! Is he not beautiful?"

"He is perfect." Boaz leaned over and kissed her on the forehead. "Best give him to Naomi to hold now. You are weak from the birth."

Ruth did not want to let go of her son. Not even for a moment. Then she thought of Naomi and all that she had borne. Willingly, she offered up her baby, believing him to be a miraculous salve that could heal the deepest wound in Naomi's heart. "Here, Mother. You hold Obed. Hold your grandson."

Ruth began to shake violently and could not stop. Her teeth chattered. The room began to spin again and she could not collect her thoughts. She heard voices ebbing and flowing in urgent whispers around her. Boaz's face came into focus. Tears ran down his face, like spring rains, without stopping.

He bent low and whispered something into her ear. She could not hear his words. He kissed her on the lips once. She wanted another. His mouth felt warm and comforting against her cold lips. Another great gush of warm wetness emerged from her body. Her head fell back. Darkness descended like a soaking woolen blanket through which she could not breathe.

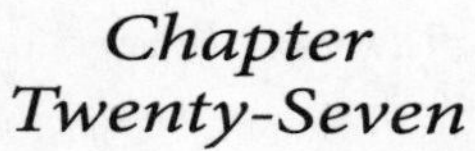

Chapter Twenty-Seven

O death, where is your victory?
O death, where is your sting?
1 CORINTHIANS 15:55

Ruth was caught in a deep sleep for three days, neither dead nor alive. She did not seem to hear them when they spoke to her. At Boaz's request, Dinah, whose own baby daughter had been born two weeks earlier, moved into the house with Adin and their children. She nursed Obed alongside her own little girl.

She was the one who insisted that they place Obed on Ruth's breast two or three times a day, encouraging him to suckle. "When she awakens, she will want to feed him herself," she insisted. "We must not allow her milk to dry."

"There's no milk," the midwife would say, grumbling under her breath.

"Not yet. But he suckles and that will help her body produce the milk in time. Besides, she can sense him, I am sure. He is a comfort to her. And when she recovers, she will be relieved that he already knows her."

No one, not even Boaz, had the heart to mention that Ruth was not going to awaken. She had lost too much blood. He sat next to her, keeping vigil. He resisted sleep as if it were a deadly plague, hating to miss even a moment of these precious twilight hours with his wife.

Occasionally, they managed to pour a thin rivulet of milk and honey or broth down Ruth's throat, keeping her nourished in her unconsciousness. On the morning of the third day, Ruth stopped being able to swallow the food. Her pulse slowed to a thread and her breathing grew shallow. She slipped further away with every moment.

Death squatted at her door, waiting like a vulture, biding its time. Boaz could sense its presence—inexorable, hungry, patient.

I surrender her to You. I surrender her to You. He meant the words. He had meant them weeks ago when he had whispered them after his wild ride. Except that surrender did not soothe the agony. He throbbed with the pain of her loss.

On the afternoon of the third day, during a rare moment when her room was empty of everyone save himself and the baby, Boaz cradled Obed and sat next to her on their bed. "Look at our son, Ruth. He is exquisite. He has your eyes, with the same reddish glint as yours in his hair." The baby fussed and he rocked him, until the tired eyes drifted shut. "Oh, beloved. Don't leave us," he begged, knowing she could not hear. She was beyond words now.

"Saying goodbye, are you? Isn't it somewhat premature?"

The harsh words shocked Boaz into looking up. Dinah stood before him, her feet planted apart, her mouth a straight line.

Boaz took a steadying breath. "Dinah. You have been good to us, moving your family here and nursing Obed. For the sake of that goodness, I will forget your outburst."

"Forget nothing!" Dinah slashed a hand in the air before planting it on her hip. "You've given up on her. You've stopped fighting for her."

With careful movements, Boaz stood and tucked the babe in his basket at the foot of the bed. "Not all of us can live in a dream world like you, Dinah."

"Since when is hoping the same as dreaming?"

"Since what you hope for is impossible!"

"It was impossible for a Moabite widow to marry the most honored man in Bethlehem. But the Lord arranged for it. It was even more impossible that a barren woman should conceive. Didn't the

Lord make that happen? Where is your faith, master Boaz?"

"The Lord Himself bid me to surrender Ruth. I have."

Dinah threw both hands up in the air. "I think you are confused, my lord. Surrender is not the same as despair. Believe me. I had to learn that distinction after years of waiting upon Adin. Surrender means you accept God's will, whatever He should choose. But you lean into hope. Into expectation. Not into discouragement. When God asks us to surrender, He only wants our full trust. His will is not that the worst should always come to pass. You have given up on hope. Do you think the Lord wanted your despair the day He demanded that you surrender Ruth?"

Boaz, who had been ready to strangle Dinah moments before, sank down on his knees, forgetting the torrent of his anger. Was she right? Was he supposed to battle for Ruth, all the way to the last moment of her time on earth? Battle for her life?

"This is cruel, Dinah. You want to awaken hope in me. How shall I survive the disappointment when that hope proves false? Look at her! You want me to anchor my soul into the expectation that my wife, who lies on that bed nearer death than life, will return to me whole and restored?"

"Better you should bear the burden of disappointment than give up too soon." She moved, her steps firm with resolve, to lift up Obed in her arms. "Come, sweet boy. Come and snuggle with your mother. She loves you so much."

Boaz watched as Dinah laid the baby carefully on Ruth's chest and sat near her, vigilant lest the baby should dislodge. Dinah had not given up. She was fighting with all her might to keep Ruth fettered to this world.

He sank his face in his hands and wept. Dinah was right. He had given up too soon. As long as Ruth breathed, there remained a chance. Boaz began to pray as he had never prayed before.

Ruth heard the lusty cry of a baby from far away.

She had been dreaming of a parched, desert land. For longer than she could remember, she had walked the sand dunes alone. Exhaustion dogged her every step. In the distance she saw the shimmer of water, and as she drew nearer, the most dazzling garden she had ever seen appeared before her.

The sight restored a new vigor to her failing limbs and she began to run toward the garden. Roses hung from white arbors; lilies carpeted the ground in a hundred different shades. Their scent perfumed the air until Ruth felt almost drunk with it. Flowers she had never seen, colors she had never imagined, filled the landscape with delight. In the midst of blue-green grass, a pathway of gold wound into the depths of the garden, and rich jewels were strewn upon the ground as if they were as common as pebbles. She detected the shadow of men and women and children milling about. Though she could not see them clearly, something about them seemed familiar, as if they beckoned to her in friendship. She laughed, her heart overflowing with joy. She felt as if she had come home. She belonged in this place.

A roar, loud as the echo of a trumpet in a canyon, brought her to a halt. A man clothed in a long robe of dazzling white with a golden sash around His chest stood before her. His hair glowed like alabaster in the eerie light. White like wool, immaculate as fresh snow. His eyes were like a flame of fire, piercing with intelligence and understanding. His face shone like the sun in full strength. He was beautiful and fearsome at once. Absolute glory shone round about Him. And He blocked her path and would not allow her to pass.

The garden beckoned with its perfect peace. A fierce desire to enter its gates overcame Ruth. Home called. Ruth took one step forward, braving the man's displeasure, and lifted her foot to take another.

The man shook His head, His hair shimmering like jewels. She fell to her knees. When she dared to look at Him again, she was overcome by the depth of kindness she found in His gaze. Had she thought Him terrifying? But He was not alarming at all. He was . . . He was love.

Fear not. I have loved you with an everlasting love;

I have drawn you with unfailing kindness.

The words reverberated in Ruth's mind, and though the man had not spoken, she knew it was His voice that echoed within her thoughts. His claim that made her skin tingle with joy.

Then Ruth heard the baby. For another moment she stared with wrenching longing at the man. She yearned to remain in the shadow of the incomprehensible love and immovable power that flowed out of Him like a river. She longed to enter the garden and find rest.

The cry came again, louder this time.

That's my baby. That's my *baby.*

The man stared with steady, unblinking eyes. She felt strength emanating from Him and saturating her own weakened limbs. She needed to go back now. The garden would have to wait.

I'm lost. I can't find my way back.

The man opened His mouth and a sound like the roar of many waters emerged from it. Despite its unnerving quality, it was a strangely reassuring sound, power and comfort mingling together in its strains. Ruth felt assailed by a desperate need to throw her arms around His powerful body and bury her face in the golden sash.

Then the cry of the baby came again, helpless and plaintive. And a man's voice, drenched in sorrow, *Come home to me, Ruth.*

Boaz.

She gave one final, longing look at the man with the burning eyes, at the garden, and turned and ran back.

"My baby." Her voice came out raw and cracked, but it was the voice of a woman living, not a dream. "Give me my baby."

"Ruth!" Boaz sounded as if he had seen a ghost.

She tried to lick her dry lips. Her eyes were out of focus. She closed and opened them again until she could see more clearly. Boaz was bending over her, his mouth half open, his eyes red.

Something of his disbelief and pain penetrated the haze that still had a hold of her mind. She was only one part here in the world of men. Some of her still lingered behind in the land of the garden. The need to reassure Boaz drew her more fully to the present. "My love," she said. "Don't weep."

Her plea backfired. He wept harder, wrenching sobs that moved his chest up and down in waves. "He brought you back to me. He brought you back."

"The man sent me."

"Who?"

Ruth shook her head. "The baby."

"I'll have him fetched. He's fine. Dinah took him away to feed. He was fussing and crying and we thought the sound might disturb you."

Jumping to his feet, Boaz wrestled the door open, banging his foot without noticing, and bellowed, "Dinah! She is awake! Dinah, bring Obed."

He returned to her side. She had closed her eyes, too tired to hold them open. "Ruth, no! Don't leave me again." He shook her, his hands gripping her shoulders, his voice pleading.

She opened her eyes with a frown, not understanding his desperation. "I didn't go anywhere."

"Thank the Lord. Thank the Lord. I thought you had fallen into that dreadful sleep again."

Ruth touched his cheek. He seemed as white as marble and just as cold. "How long did I sleep?"

"Four days. We were afraid . . . we were afraid we had lost you."

It dawned on her why he seemed so desperate. The thought of his anguish dragged her into full wakefulness. "I'm sorry to cause you such worry. Oh no! Naomi must be beside herself."

"I think she would have gone mad if not for the baby. He has kept all of us sane. We even admire his dirty diapers," he babbled. "I better send for her too."

He dragged the door open again and bellowed for Naomi.

Ruth's eyes widened at his uncharacteristic lapse in manners. He ran back to her side. "Can't believe you're awake. It's like a dream. You must be hungry and thirsty. I'll send for food." And the door crashed open again to accommodate another holler. Ruth laughed soundlessly. It made her ribs ache.

When next the door was pulled open, it wasn't by Boaz. Dinah walked in, her brows drawn together. "What's all the yelling about? Here is your son, master Boaz, as you asked. No need to . . . Oh Lord in heaven be praised. You are awake!"

Ruth held out her arms. "My son."

Chapter Twenty-Eight

My flesh and my heart may fail,
But God is the strength of my heart and my portion forever.
PSALM 73:26

Dinah laid the swaddled bundle in her arms. Ruth held on to him with puny arms, muscles shaking. Her boy. Her precious boy. She inhaled the sweet baby smell of him. He made a kitten sound and yawned, petal lips opening with abandon.

"He is so beautiful!"

"That he is," Boaz said. "Let me lift you so you can be more comfortable." With incredible care, he put his arm around her back and pulled her up. She could feel her lower belly spasm even with that gentle movement and winced. Boaz bolstered her with a few pillows and she breathed with relief. The baby rested against her chest as if it were the most comfortable place in the world.

"You've been nursing him?" she asked Dinah, without lifting her gaze away from Obed.

Dinah nodded. Ruth felt something wet land on her arm and, distracted, looked up. Tears ran the length of Dinah's face. "He is a good eater. My daughter makes a huge fuss every time she eats. Not Obed. He eats like a champion."

"Thank you for taking care of him."

Naomi came into the room and stood frozen. "Ruth?"

"Mother! Don't fret. I've recovered."

Naomi stared, words failing her. She took a shaking breath that turned into a sob, a keening noise that shivered out of her throat.

The sob turned into a wail, a loud, endless cry of pain that had been trapped inside her since the start of Ruth's illness.

Boaz rushed to her side and enfolded her in comforting arms. "Naomi!"

Ruth listened to Naomi's howls of anguish in stunned dismay. Not until this moment had she comprehended how deeply Naomi treasured her. Her pain was a measure of her love.

"Naomi," she whispered and beckoned with her fingers. "Come, Mother. Come and let me hold you in my arms."

Naomi ran to Ruth's side and, falling to her knees at the side of her bed, brought babe and mother into a tender embrace. "My daughter. My daughter, Ruth. God has brought you back to me. My precious daughter."

Boaz joined the jumble of tangled arms and added his own embrace to that of Naomi's.

By then, Mahalath and her mother as well as Adin had been drawn to the noise emanating from Ruth's room. Several other servants stood respectfully just outside the door. Everyone wept with stunned joy.

Finally Boaz stepped away from Ruth, his movements reluctant. "I'm sorry, my love. We have tired you out. You must eat. Sheba, did you bring my wife some food?"

"I fetched your own supper, master. I never dreamed the mistress would awaken. Praise be to God!" She pressed the corner of her sleeve to her wet lashes.

"No matter. We'll feed her whatever you brought me."

"Oh no, my lord! That wouldn't do. She needs something simple, as yet. I have a cup of sweet wine here. Mahalath, dip a bit of bread and give it to the mistress for now, until I go and prepare her something suitable."

Boaz took the bowl out of Mahalath's hands. "I'll feed her myself, Mahalath. Thank you."

Naomi kissed Ruth on the forehead. "We better vacate this room and allow Ruth to rest. We can all come back and visit later."

Ruth gave a tired smile. "You stay, Mother."

Naomi turned to Boaz. He nodded. "I wouldn't dream of you being anywhere but here. We need you, Naomi."

Her childhood years had taught Ruth that if she wished to be accepted, she had better be useful. She had better not be a bother to a family who was always too stretched to pay mind to one more child's needs. As an invalid, she could neither be useful, nor help being a bother. Through the first week of her recovery, she battled a constant wretched anxiety at the lingering weakness in her body. She wanted to throw off her covers and get on her feet. She expected everyone to start growing impatient with her.

Instead, her little family and faithful circle of friends encouraged her to rest, taking offense at her attempts to push herself into activity too soon. They acted as if they did not care that she was a burden to them. As if caring for her was a precious gift. If she smiled at them, they behaved as if she had presented them with a parcel of fertile land. If she asked for something, they responded as though fulfilling her wishes brightened their day.

Boaz never left her side. He fed her with his own hand, teased her when she spilled her food, combed her hair to keep it from tangling. He didn't even go to check on his horses. She could sense that he needed to be near her for now. Her mere presence, useless as she seemed to herself, gave him strength.

Naomi proved little better. If Ruth so much as shifted, a new pillow found its way behind her back. Her tongue had no sooner run over dry lips than a bowl of warm milk rested against her mouth. Ruth was stunned at the fuss everyone made over her. She had little comprehension of how close to death she had truly come, or how her survival seemed no less than a miracle to those who had witnessed her slide toward the grave.

She only knew that she was loved beyond her wildest dreams. She belonged to this small band of people. They had made a home for her with their constant affection. Slowly, love began to repair Ruth's broken body. She was surrounded with it, drenched by its healing powers. Although she continued to experience lingering pain, she felt hopeful that she would be restored.

One evening, as she held Obed, staring into his sleepy eyes, a promise sprang to her mind.

I have loved you with an everlasting love.

I have drawn you with unfailing kindness.

She remembered the words of the man whose voice roared like many waters, remembered them with rare clarity, for her dream had faded more from memory with each passing day. With the recollection of the words came other memories, and her heart was flooded by the man's steadfast affection for her. She remembered His power, and the desire she had sensed in Him to keep her safe. To shield her from harm.

She told Boaz of her strange dream, and the lingering experience of the man's love that at times overwhelmed her heart. "When I cradled Obed in my arms just now, I remembered that sweet presence. Not that He was docile, mind. He scared me half to death with His wildness. But He loved me too, the way I love Obed. More even, though that's hard for me to imagine. There were no limits to His love, and no fear either, the way sometimes I fear for Obed."

Boaz pulled his fingers through Ruth's unbound hair. "Perhaps it was the angel of God."

"I think not. He seemed . . . more, somehow."

"More than an angel?"

Ruth shifted on the bed. "I cannot describe Him adequately. It was like being in the presence of the sun. He is the one who sent me back to you."

"Then whoever He was, I owe Him my life." He bent to peek at Obed, lying against her chest. "Our son has fallen asleep. I better put him back in his cradle so you can eat." He lifted Obed with care and placed him in his padded basket. Wetting a napkin with tepid water, he wiped the milk trails that stained the baby's cheek. Ruth straightened her clothes and sat up against the pillows. Dinah, to everyone's surprise, had proven right. Ruth's milk had come in and she had been able to feed Obed herself for some days now.

"What did you mean when you said sometimes you fear for Obed?"

Ruth sighed and rubbed her sore breast. "I fear I might not be a good mother and fail him. I fear he might grow sick. I fear I might lose him. I fear I won't teach him what he needs to know to be happy. To be a good man. My parents taught me little that I can pass on to him, Boaz. I didn't grow up like you, in the shadow of the Lord."

Boaz sprawled on the bed next to Ruth. For an active man, more often on the back of a horse, inspecting his land and attending to business affairs, he had shown great ease with being stuck at home for days on end. "I may have grown up in the shadow of the Lord, but I have similar concerns."

"You have?"

He nodded. "No more than a handful of weeks ago, I did not even wish for a child. My fears were too great."

"And now?"

"God has given me the desire of my heart. The desire I did not even know I had. When you came into my life, I thought having you as my wife was all I wanted. God understood my heart better than I did myself. I had buried my longing for a child out of fear. But God would not let that longing remain buried. He knew that in order to resurrect that dream, I had to face those fears. If He had left it to me, I probably would not have chosen that battle."

"Too hard?"

He nodded and kissed her gently on the lips. It was the first time since her sickness that he had kissed her this intimately. She felt heat rise up her chest and suffuse her cheeks. He still wanted her, in spite of the fact that ill health had reduced her body to an unappealing stick and robbed her of beauty. She blinked back quick tears of relief. Since awakening from her deathlike sleep, he had made it clear that his love for her remained strong. But she had begun to wonder if he had lost interest in her as a woman. His kiss, gentle and brief though it had been, carried a definite promise. She gave a small, satisfied smile.

He smiled back and kissed her again. "Remember that night on the threshing floor?"

"It was the best night of my life and the worst. How could I forget?"

"I never could have imagined, that night, the gift God wanted to give me. Having you seemed more than enough. Yet the Lord had a plan for us. He wished for this son to be born from your flesh and mine. Sometimes, I am overwhelmed by the enormity of my love for him."

"I feel the same."

"One day, Obed will grow and have sons of his own. Grandsons. Great-grandsons. You have given me a lineage, Ruth. Flesh of my flesh to continue through the generations. I had long since given up hope on such a possibility. Now, when I hold Obed in my arms, I know that he will continue my name as well as Mahlon's. I will live on in him."

Ruth leaned her head against his chest. "The Lord wanted *me* to be the mother of your sons. He used you to redeem Naomi and me. To give us a future. But what is even more incomprehensible is that He used *me* to redeem your future from extinction. He brought me all the way from Moab so that through me He could give you a future and a hope."

Late one morning, just after Ruth had improved enough to go below stairs, she walked into the guest chamber in search of Naomi, Obed resting against her shoulder. She found Naomi surrounded by a dozen of her friends and the women of the neighborhood. They rushed to their feet as she entered, cooing to the baby and vying for his attention.

Miriam plumped several fat pillows and drew Ruth to sit near her. She offered a squat finger to Obed, who grabbed it in a confident grip. She laughed. “Strong fellow. Watch you don't break this old finger of mine. Is he not the most handsome baby boy you have ever seen?” she asked the others.

Naomi beamed. “I would agree, but then I might be partial.”

Obed chose that moment to burp with gusto. Ruth giggled. “Pardon my son. I just finished feeding him.”

Amid smiles and nods of approval, one of the women said, “Blessed be the Lord, who has not left your side, Naomi.”

Naomi's eyes filled with tears. “There was a time when I accused Him of turning His hand against me. Now I know He never left me. See for yourselves.” She gestured toward Ruth and the baby. “He has continued to bless me. He has not abandoned me.”

Sheba, Mahalath's mother, proclaimed, “Praise the Lord who has now given you a redeemer, Naomi, for this sweet boy shall be as redeemer unto you and your family. Your son shall live through him. You will be remembered throughout the generations because of him. May his name be renowned in Israel.”

Another of the women, whose name Ruth did not know said, “May he restore your youth. May he care for you in your old age.”

Miriam added, “For Ruth, your daughter-in-law who loves you, has been better to you than seven sons. Better than a perfect family. And she has given birth to this winsome child. She has brought joy back into your life.”

Naomi's face broke into a wide smile. Ruth lifted the baby toward her. “Here, Mother. He is happy now that his belly is full. Do you wish to hold him?”

Naomi took the baby in her arms and laid him on her lap. “He is such a delicious bundle.”

“*Obed* is the perfect name for this little one,” Miriam said. “We declare his name before all Israel this day, for he shall be a loyal servant of the Lord and worship Him faithfully.”

Sheba managed to squeeze her wide hips between Naomi and

Miriam. "A son has been born to Naomi. Never shall you be lonely again."

Naomi dandled her grandson on her knee. "Listen, now, little boy. Your mother was a barren woman who had never even set eyes on Judah. Your father was an honored man of Bethlehem with no plans ever to marry again. There were many obstacles against you being born. God must have really wanted you in this world. He went to a great deal of trouble to make sure that you lived. Never forget how important you are to Him."

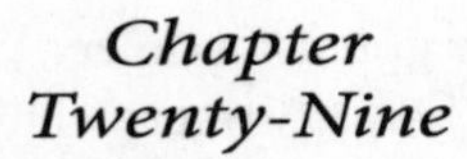

He has sent me to bind up the brokenhearted,
To proclaim liberty to the captives,
And the opening of the prison to those who are bound;
To proclaim the year of the LORD*'s favor.*
ISAIAH 61:1–2

Months passed and, to her distress, Ruth still did not regain her former vigor. Often, she contended with debilitating headaches that would last for hours. She had never experienced serious illness before, and the weakness of her body became a constant source of frustration in spite of her happiness. Naomi proved invaluable during those months, for Ruth could not manage the care of Obed alone. Naomi saw to him with tender love, as if she were nurturing her own son.

"What if I never get better?" she asked Boaz one night after he had extinguished all the lamps save one. They were already in bed, cocooned between the feather mattress and the quilted covers. Ruth clung to her side of the bed, too hesitant to draw near to Boaz. "What if I remain weak the rest of my life?"

"Then we shall cope, as we do now, beloved."

"I shall be such a burden to you, Boaz."

"Burden? May the Lord bless me with a hundred burdens if they are like you. How can you believe such falsehood?" He reached for her and pulled her against his chest, encircling his arm around her back to keep her from wriggling away. "It's been hard on you, this illness. You tire easily, and even though you never say so, I know that you are often in pain."

Ruth drew in a steadying breath. "Is that why you won't touch me anymore?"

He went still against her. She could hear the thud of his heartbeat beneath her ear. "You need time to recover. If you think I have lost my desire for you, think again. I want you, more than ever. But I won't risk your health. We will wait on God."

Ruth tried to control the tears that spilled down her cheeks. They kept coming like Noah's flood, with no sign of an end.

Boaz kissed her on the mouth. "Hush, beloved. You'll make yourself sick. Why all this sorrow? Do you think I cannot wait?"

"I fear you'll have to wait forever."

"Then I will. As long as I have you and Obed, I can bear anything."

Ruth remembered how God had once taught her the lesson of acceptance. Acceptance with joy. Did He want her to accept her sickness? To be joyful in spite of it? It seemed an impossible requirement.

In the ensuing weeks, she found herself battling anger. Why had God allowed this illness? Why had He intervened to save her, only to let her sink into pain and weakness? The Lord did not seem in the least interested in answering her questions. Her whys remained between them, a silent indictment in Ruth's heart. As the rest of her family and friends returned to the normal routines of everyday life, Ruth had to contend with a shrunken world.

Naomi, who had had her own battle with the Lord, understood.

"Is this the life He wants me to have? This half existence?" Ruth cried one afternoon, after crawling into bed when what she wanted most was to go outside and play with Obed in the sunshine.

"I don't know the answer to that question. But I have learned one thing. He has not abandoned you, Ruth. The Lord is near to the brokenhearted and saves the crushed in spirit. God may not always answer our questions, but He walks with us in the midst of them, lest we get lost in the wilderness of our minds. Invite the Lord into your pain. Invite Him to be your sufficiency in the midst of it. I promise, He will sustain you."

"That isn't enough, Naomi. I don't want to be sustained! I want to be healed."

Naomi gave a gentle laugh. "I understand. You want what you want, not what He is willing to give. It's an awkward spot. In my experience, He usually wins. Try to remember, daughter, time does not work the same in the hands of the Lord as it would in ours. Sometimes, out of the delays of life, He calls forth a blessing."

When Naomi left, Ruth decided to pray. Not only to beg and cajole the Lord into giving her the desire of her heart. This time, she prayed with her hands open, willing to let Him choose her destiny for her.

"Sustain me, Lord, through the best of life and the worst. Help me cling to You. Help me remember that although my flesh and my heart may fail, You are the strength of my heart and my portion forever. Carry me and rescue me even when I fight You. Overcome my struggles. Quiet me until I become like a weaned child with his mother."

For the first time in months, Ruth experienced peace. Her storm-tossed thoughts grew still and she felt quieted.

The assurance, when it came, was inward, more a sense than words. And yet she knew that the Lord had spoken to her.

I am He who will sustain you. I have made you and I will carry you; I will sustain you and I will rescue you.

Not long after the anniversary of Obed's first birthday, Ruth weaned him. It had been difficult to nurse him this long because of her sickness. She was sad that she could not nurse him as long as other women nursed their infants. But her milk had been decreasing, and she found herself weak after every feeding. Boaz and Naomi had both insisted that weaning Obed would be the best decision for her health.

As was common in Israel, they celebrated the occasion with a great feast. The morning of the festivities Ruth awoke without pain and weakness. Over the past year, she had on many occasions experienced short stretches of well-being, sometimes lasting several hours. Other than a flash of relief, she thought little of her reprieve that morning. She spent the day helping to prepare the food, joining Mahalath and Sheba and a few extra servants hired especially for the occasion as they made honey cakes and decorated large platters of dates and nuts. She crushed mint and garlic for the roasted lamb and spooned out Naomi's pickled capers into the lentil stew boiling in a large pot.

By that evening when the guests began to arrive, Ruth had still not experienced even a twinge of pain. She felt as strong as in the old days. Too busy to think of the aberration, she changed into a green tunic, her narrow waist cinched in by a silver belt Boaz had given to her as a gift to celebrate Obed's weaning. Mahalath twined her hair into bejeweled braids before rushing out to help with final preparations. Ruth had not had a chance to don her light veil when Boaz came in.

"You are so lovely," he said, kissing the side of her neck.

She shivered. "I missed you." He had been away from home for two days, dealing with a caravan carrying goods that had been stuck in bad roads outside Bethlehem.

"They tell me you have overworked and refused to rest all day. I came to scold you. Now I find you looking lovelier than a new lily. Do you not feel tired?"

She frowned. "Not even a little. I feel strong and well, as if I had never been sick."

Boaz lowered his lashes. "I am glad you are having a good day. Best not overdo it, though. You might pay for it tomorrow."

The surge of health lingered through the night. Ruth chatted with her neighbors and chased after Obed who had begun to walk in earnest two weeks before. She noticed that he loved being in the midst of so many admirers, and did everything in his power to charm their guests. His antics made everyone laugh, and Ruth looked on with pride. She ate more heartily than she had in months and never once felt the need to crawl into bed, overcome by exhaustion.

In the morning she awoke, still free of pain. The sheer bliss of uninterrupted physical well-being overwhelmed her senses. It was pure delight not to be sick. She stretched her hands above her head and arched her back like a contented cat in the sun.

"How do you feel?" Boaz stood near a window, sunlight revealing the tense expression on his face.

"I feel wonderful."

"Not sick?"

"Not at all." She went still as a realization settled into her heart. Pushing the covers back, she ran to him and wrapped her arms around his neck. "Boaz, I think the Lord has healed me."

He smiled down into her eyes. "I pray you are right."

At Boaz's insistence Ruth left the cleaning to others in the household. Husband and wife spent the morning playing with Obed. Boaz brought them into the barn and let Obed tangle his chubby hands into the horses' manes. The little boy screamed with delight and the horses bore his enthusiastic assault with admirable aplomb.

In the evening, Naomi joined them for a supper of leftover roast lamb and fresh bread. "Daughter, do my eyes deceive me? I have worried for you these past two days, noting how hard you've pushed yourself. I must admit, however, that you look recovered."

Ruth grinned. "I have not had a moment of discomfort or sickness since yesterday. The Lord has healed me, I am certain. But this husband of mine is too cautious to believe it. He won't agree unless the Lord were to send him a personal letter, declaring me restored."

Boaz pushed his sleeves up over his elbows. "It has only been two days. Let's wait a month."

"A month! You called a physician after three days when you thought I was sick. Shall we not hold the reverse true? Three days, and you can declare me healed."

Naomi laughed. "She has you there, Boaz."

He held up a hand. "I never thought I'd see the day when the two of you convened against me."

Convinced of her healing, Ruth waited patiently for five whole days. She felt no surprise when she remained free of any nagging symptoms. Every passing hour seemed to add to her vigor and she began to put on a bit of healthy flesh. Still, Boaz would not budge and acknowledge that she was cured.

On the fifth night after the feast, when Boaz drew Ruth into his arms for a comforting peck on the cheek, she kissed him on the mouth and kept on kissing him, until with a groan, he gave in and kissed her without holding back.

"You should ask yourself, husband," Ruth said much later as she leaned against her pillows, her arms crossed over her chest, unable to quash a smug smile, "when it comes to the important moments in our lives, why is it that I always have to make the first move?"

Boaz roared with laughter. "You ought to have known, that night on the threshing floor, when you had to throw yourself at me, that you would have a rough life ahead of you."

"I did not throw myself at you!"

"As I recall, I opened my eyes in the dark of the night, innocent as a babe, to find my feet naked and a brazen woman cuddled up to me."

She leaned in for a deep kiss. "I don't think we should tell Obed about that story."

"About what a hussy his mother is? Too late. I already told him. I'm sure he will tell our grandchildren as well. I fear the secret is out. The whole world will probably hear about it before the next harvest."

She thumped him on the arm. "No one shall find out. I'm very good at keeping secrets."

"Beloved, I am afraid one day you will be famous. Everyone will hear about your story, for you are far too extraordinary to remain forgotten. As long as there are people in this world, they will speak of your faithfulness and courage."

"If anyone is going to be famous in this family, it is you. You are already well known in Bethlehem. And in the years to come, many will speak of your extraordinary goodness."

"I care nothing about fame, Ruth. I only know the Lord has blessed us beyond what I could imagine. He has spread His wings over us. Remember how I prayed that over you the first day I met you?"

Ruth bolted up with excitement. "I had forgotten the blessing you spoke over me that day. He honored your prayer, Boaz."

"And by blessing you, He blessed me."

"What do you mean?"

"He has given us a glorious lineage. A child of our flesh. We had to wait both of us, for many years. But those years weren't wasted. God built our character in the waiting times. In the despairing seasons. The Lord has given us happiness. But He has given us something more important still. He has matured us in the invisible things of the soul. We learned the power of obedience as we waited. No matter what we go through now, that inner strength will undergird us."

"I look forward to a boring old age, with no adventures and no need to exercise extraordinary inner strength."

"He has restored you to me. That's as much adventure as I need."

"Does this mean that you are convinced I am healed?"

His hand tangled in her hair and pulled her forward in a blatantly possessive move. "I'm convinced. With all my heart, I love you, Ruth of Moab."

She trembled in his arms. "I am my beloved's and he is mine."

Seven months later, Boaz took Ruth with him on a trip to Jerusalem. After concluding his business, he brought her to a stretch of land at the foot of the mountain ridge east of Jerusalem. He had arranged for a servant to bring a rug and some cushions as well as a basket of food. "I thought we could have lunch by ourselves," he said.

She extended long legs over the rug and, flopping on her belly, lay against a cushion. "It's beautiful here. Whose land is this?"

He ignored her question. "Do you know what today is?"

She frowned. "The day I eat too much and fall asleep in your arms?"

"It's the anniversary of the day you arrived in Bethlehem. Three years ago on this day, you came to Israel."

Ruth gasped and sat up. "I had forgotten. Has it truly been that long?"

Boaz nodded. "My life changed the moment you stepped foot into Judah and I did not even know it. I was in my house, having supper, washing my hands, having a conversation with Mahalath. Going through the mundane routines of my normal life. And the whole while, my world had turned on its head."

"And I thought my biggest longing was to fix the holes in Naomi's roof and find a way to feed us so that we wouldn't starve. Think of the shock in store for me. The Lord must have laughed hard that day."

"I bought you a gift. To celebrate."

"A gift?" Ruth, who had received so few presents in her early years, had become spoilt with a husband who loved to give freely. "What is it?" She looked about for a package wrapped in fabric and saw nothing.

Boaz spread a hand in front of him. "This. This land is yours now. You know I own fields all over Judah, and not only in Bethlehem. Parcels like this aren't available for purchase every day. As soon as I saw it, I thought of you."

Ruth gasped. "The land?" She had never owned land of her own before. Not even a patch the size of a pillow, let alone land that spread beyond the horizon. "This beautiful place? You bought it for me?"

"I plan to make it an olive grove."

"Boaz!" Ruth threw herself into his arms and covered his face with tiny kisses.

Boaz laughed. "I thought you might approve. We shall call it the Mount of Olives. What do you think?"

"It's perfect!"

"It will be many years before the trees will mature and bear fruit. But they will be here long after we are gone. They will be a reminder of our lives, yours and mine, of the hard stony years, and the sweetness that God created in spite of them."

Ruth reached for his hand. "I could not imagine a better way to be remembered. I hope our descendants will understand that without the stones, there can be no oil. I pray they will learn fortitude and faith when they look at these trees you dream of planting."

"Who knows? Perhaps, one day, hundreds of years from now, a great-great-great-great-grandson of ours might sit under the shade of those trees and find comfort in his hour of need."

Epilogue

Though the fig tree should not blossom,
Nor fruit be on the vines,
The produce of the olive fail and the fields yield no food,
The flock be cut off from the fold
And there be no herd in the stalls,
Yet I will rejoice in the LORD;
I will take joy in the God of my salvation.
God, the LORD, is my strength;
He makes my feet like the deer's;
He makes me tread on my high places.

HABAKKUK 3:17–19

Time was running out. David examined his face in the smooth surface of a polished copper mirror, seeing the shadow of death hanging over him. His once robust body had lost its vigor, muscles melted like wax, skin hanging loose and wrinkled off his fragile bones. All his beauty and might stolen by the passing of the seasons. Forty years had flown since he had become king. He had lived through uprisings and betrayals; he had seen his sons die and his daughter disintegrate by the shame of rape. He had overcome powerful enemies and established a secure kingdom for his people. He had caused an innocent man's demise.

Let death come. It held few terrors for him. He had tasted of the best and the worst. What could death do to him?

Though I walk through the valley of the shadow of death, I will fear no evil, for You are with me.

It was the unfinished business of life that devoured his peace.

Pulling his blankets more securely around him, David shivered in spite of the fire that burned in the hearth. Summer held the land in a fierce grip. Everyone in Jerusalem sweated, but the trembling in the king's limbs persisted. It never stopped. Warmth had eluded him for months.

Abishag ran over to add another blanket to the ineffectual heap already suffocating him. He waved her away with a weak hand. She was new to her duties, the latest brainchild of his wily advisors who intended to keep him alive and in power as long as possible.

"Fetch my box," he said with a wave of his hand.

They hadn't trained Abishag properly. Just stuffed her into silks and linens, painted her eyes with kohl and shoved her into David's chamber, hoping for the best. As if the comely lines of a woman's body could drive the old age right out of him.

In her ignorance, she fetched David's linen casket. David squelched a wave of impatience. "Not that one." He pointed a crooked finger toward a carved chest at the foot of his bed. "My personal writings."

The cedar box was heavy. It wobbled in the girl's slim hands as she hefted it over to him. He hoped she would not drop it on her henna-stained toes, and sighed when she managed to bring it without incident.

He waved Abishag away, then pulled out a thick sheaf of parchment from the carved box. Somewhere buried in the bowels of that chest lay a few of his deepest secrets. He studied every sheaf with an intensity that belied the infirmity in his body. Age had not robbed him of his brains. Some pieces he set aside immediately. Others, he lingered over. By midnight, he had found what he sought. His bed looked like a library after a war, with bits of parchment and rolls of papyrus scattered in every direction.

Abishag had long since fallen asleep at his feet. Pity prevented him from waking her to bring order back into his room. Instead, grasping the scraps of parchment he had searched for with such diligence, he lay back and fell into an exhausted slumber.

The sound of a gasp dragged David out of an uneasy dream. For a moment he blinked in confusion at the beautiful young woman who stood, her hands in a knot, studying his bed, her doe eyes wide with shock.

David wondered if an assassin had loosed an asp in his covers and looked around with concern, trying to pinpoint the source of her dismay. His gaze fell on the disarray he had caused earlier.

"I was searching for something," he said, trying to make his voice sound soothing.

"Your maidservant will clean it up." Abishag knelt by his side and reached for the stray sheaves that had landed on the floor. When she had finished, she noticed the piece of rolled parchment he still held in his hand and reached for it.

David pulled his arm back. "This stays with me."

That night the girl lay next to him, as she had done most of the evenings since they had brought her to serve his needs. She slept next to him to try and warm his shivering body. He had never touched her; she was nothing more than a living blanket. In the morning she awoke early and helped him out of bed. When she reached to anoint his hands with scented oil, she noticed that he still held on to the faded parchment.

Her plucked eyebrows shot up. "My lord! Let me put that away."

"No. I want to hold it." He clutched the roll in his fist. "Now send for my son Solomon."

It had been a week since he had declared Solomon his successor. Even though Adonijah was older, David had chosen Bathsheba's son to be king after him, upholding a promise he had made to her long ago.

The young man arrived, and with the grace of a gazelle, prostrated himself before David. How old was he now? Seventeen? Eighteen? David signaled Solomon to rise and studied the handsome face for a few moments.

"Soon you will be king," he said without preamble.

"May the king live forever!"

"Well, he won't. You will be king come winter, and I will sleep with my fathers."

He detected a sheen of tears in his son's large brown eyes. "I would rather have you, Father."

David's mouth softened. "Sit with me awhile. I have not spent enough time with you. I regret that. Matters of state and the troubles of rule always seemed more urgent than the need to be with my family. I haven't had a chance to be a real father to you."

Solomon sat at David's feet, like a child. Then he lowered his head. "I am afraid. I am afraid I won't be a great king like you. You were a success even before you were my age. Already a hero."

David guffawed. "I was the eighth son of a farmer in Bethlehem. At the bottom of the pile. A nobody. My family sent me to keep the sheep company; that's what they deemed me worthy of. I played my wooden harp and made up songs, and no one heard me but the sheep. Then Samuel poured the anointing oil on my head and told me I would be king. And even as the Spirit of the Lord rushed upon me, I looked at him as dumbly as one of my father's cattle.

"No. I have but one success and it is not the throne, for God Himself gave me that. If you want a true hero, you will have to look farther up our family tree." He held up the faded roll of parchment.

"What is that?"

"My secret. And yours."

"A secret?"

"This is an account of my great-grandmother's life. Some say the prophet Samuel wrote it. But it is not so. Ruth wrote most of it by her own hand, for her husband taught her to read and write. Through the years, my great-grandfather Boaz and his son Obed added more details to her story, as they remembered it."

"What secret does it contain?"

"For one thing, she was a Canaanite. Born and raised in Moab."

Solomon's back snapped up straight in astonishment. "Never!"

"It's the truth, I assure you."

"But . . . how can this be? The king of Israel bearing Moabite blood in his veins? Moses taught that no Moabite may enter the assembly of the Lord. Even to the tenth generation, none of his descendants may enter the assembly of the Lord. Everyone knows God chose you, my father, handpicked you from all the men of Israel, to be our king. Would He have put you on the throne if you had the blood of Moabites?"

"Apparently."

Solomon stood. His ivory white hands shook. "That is a great reproach to our family. I won't tell anyone. I promise."

David laughed so loud the sparrows resting on the windowsill took to hasty flight. "I am very proud of my great-grandmother. She loved the Lord better than the rest of us and served our people with unmatched loyalty. That makes her a true Israelite."

"Not so loud, I beg you, Father! Do you wish people to find out that you approve of your Moabite lineage? Best keep that shame buried somewhere in a dark place."

"I've kept it buried too long. The best part of our family, and we act as if it were the plague that blighted the seed of Jesse. The few who know about it advised me never to speak of it after I ascended the throne. But it proved to be foolish advice."

"You must admit our heritage presents a problem, my lord. She belonged to Moab!" Solomon pronounced the word *Moab* with the same distaste he would have shown an army of locusts.

David took a calming breath. "Why don't you read it? We can speak of the matter after you have." He held out the parchment for Solomon. "Stay here in my chamber while you read. Perhaps you will understand better once you know her story."

"Read it, my lord?"

"I trust you know how? With all the money I spent on teachers, you should at least be able to decipher a simple script."

Solomon grabbed the parchment. "I know how." He sat down again and unrolled the parchment to its beginning, his fingers stiff with reluctance. David hid his smile and waved away the serving boy who came in bearing a tray loaded with wine and fruit. He wanted no interruptions. Solomon was about to come face-to-face with a few interesting facts about his heritage. David needed to know how his son would respond.

Time trickled by as Solomon read. Then with an abrupt move, he let the scroll close. "A young boy with a sling, facing a giant? That sounds familiar," he said.

"Ruth is the one who taught me to use a sling, though she was quite old by then."

"An old woman taught you to use a sling so well that you felled a giant?"

"It was her sling I used on Goliath; she gave it to me as a gift on my tenth birthday. She was surprisingly adept at the use of it. I loved that old woman dearly."

"You met her?"

"She was still alive when I was a boy. My parents had little interest in me. They had seven older boys to see to and were too tired to take much note of the runt of the litter. Ruth took me under her wing. The year Ruth died, Goliath challenged Israel's army. Mind you, he was truly a giant, not merely tall and broad-shouldered. I remembered Ruth's story, of course. And I knew that with the help of the Lord I could do as well as that young man. Better. I could rid Israel of a great enemy. I could show our people that with the Lord, everything is possible."

Solomon ran a hand through his short beard. "So the Lord used you. Made you His champion for Israel."

"What was it Ruth liked to say? *The Lord uses odd instruments to fulfill His will.* The weaker the vessel, the better He likes it. It only proves His strength. I want you to understand. I wasn't the hero in that story. God was."

Solomon gave a puzzled frown and returned to his reading. Hours passed. David ordered food, which Solomon was too distracted to eat. At one point he murmured under his breath, "*Kiss me with the kisses of your mouth*. That's poetic. I like that. Must remember it."

Later, he slapped a hand against a muscular thigh and laughed. "That's true, for certain. Without oxen your stable remains clean. Your great-grandfather was a discerning man, my lord. He saw wisdom at work in the ordinary things of life."

Still more time passed. "What a poet she is!" he said with enthusiasm. "*I am my beloved's and he is mine*. I could not have expressed it better myself."

When Solomon finally set the scroll away, David took a deep breath. "What did you think?"

Solomon ran agitated fingers through his curled hair. "She was loyal. Hardworking. Admirable even. That doesn't change the fact that she was a Moabite."

David took a deep breath, trying to stamp out the ire that rose in his gut, threatening to overwhelm his patience. "You said I was a success even before I reached your age. I was never as great a success as Ruth. Or Boaz. Because true success doesn't come from what you accomplish. It doesn't come from my riches, my crown, or the people I rule. True success only means one thing: obedience to the Great Shepherd. Loving Him. Following Him. Abiding with Him.

"If I did anything right in my life, it was this. I trusted the Lord to deliver me. Even in this, I sometimes failed. But at least I tried to remain close to my God."

"But your wealth, your fame, your numberless talents . . ."

"Were all from God. They were His gifts. Sometimes I used them to His glory. Sometimes I squandered them. No, I don't measure my success by these things. There is only one measure of true success, child. How close you remain by His side. Does the dust of His feet get on your cloak because you follow so close? Does the sound of His whisper reverberate in your ear because you have drawn so near? Are you obedient to that voice, day after day, hour after hour? That's how I measure success. Do you understand?"

His son looked at him with blank eyes. David swallowed his

sigh. Perhaps it was too much to expect that what he himself had learned so late in life would become accessible to a young prince in the course of a few hours. What he wished to impart to Solomon stood in bitter opposition to the counsel of the world. His greatest advisors would brand him an idiot. Why should Solomon be any different?

"Go home, son. I will send for you another day." David found himself unable to keep the disappointment from his voice.

Abishag had built up the fire in the king's chamber. In his absence, she busied herself with cleaning the room, making certain every corner remained spotless. She jumped when the door burst open without an announcement. The king's son Adonijah lingered at the threshold for a few moments.

"Aren't you a beauty," he drawled. "And which of his wives are you?"

"Not his wife, my lord. I am Abishag, his servant."

"Ah. The one who keeps him warm at night. I only get a hot brick in my bed."

Abishag pressed her lips and said nothing.

"Where is he?"

"The king is in royal counsel."

Adonijah threw himself on a purple couch and stretched his feet with careless ease over the low, cedar table. "I'll wait here."

Abishag hesitated. She had no authority over a prince of Judah. She could not order him out or reprimand him for his rudeness. With a stiff bow, she returned to her duties. From the corner of her eye, she saw the prince pick up the parchment that had so completely preoccupied the king of late. With a careless flick of his wrist, he opened the scroll and began to read, his face a mask of boredom. In a few moments, he sat up straighter, his eyebrows knit in the middle as he became engrossed in the text. He did not even hear Abishag ask him to move his feet in order to clean the tabletop.

After about an hour of reading, Adonijah hissed out an expletive. "What is this seditious rubbish? This kind of false propaganda could ruin our family and destroy the royal line of David." Without hesitation, he walked to the fire, which burned with raging enthusiasm thanks to Abishag's earlier efforts, and with a flick of his wrist flung the scroll into the flames. Immediately it caught fire. Abishag watched in dismay as the parchment began to burn, the black words turning to cinder within moments.

"Tell my father I did him a favor," Adonijah declared before leaving.

"I tried to save it, my lord. But it was too late." David looked at the charred remains of Ruth's story and his heart sank. It was gone. His great-grandmother's history and life-changing wisdom, gone forever. He should have known that his sons would want to destroy Ruth's account. All they cared about was that she hailed from Moab. They could not get past that reality. They feared it would pull them off the throne.

"Bring me my writing materials," David told Abishag, determined to repair Adonijah's damage. He would not be able to remember all the details of the story. But he could put down enough of Ruth's account to capture her extraordinary faith. Faith that might yet save his progeny from walking away from the destiny God wished to give them.

"Adonijah burned the book," David told Solomon the following week. Solomon did not blink once; he registered no shock or regret on his impassive features.

"Do you approve of his actions?" David pressed.

The long curling eyelashes, so much like his mother's, lowered. "I considered doing so myself."

"But you did not destroy it. Why?"

"You seemed convinced of its importance. I thought I had best wait and consider the matter."

"At least you are honest."

Solomon shrugged. "I know I am young and I have much to learn. Adonijah is older. More determined."

"Adonijah practically declared himself king not three months since. He did not have the decency to wait for me to die. Or even to ask. He just thought to take the throne while I still lived. If not for me, you would be dead, boy. You still might be, when I'm gone."

Solomon fisted his hands. "I'll be sure and watch my back."

"That's the third son now who has betrayed me. My greatest failure, staring me in the face. I should have learned better from Boaz."

Solomon leaned forward, his hands tented between his knees. "What failure, my lord? You are a legend among our people, great beyond dispute. No one compares with you."

"You call it greatness when a son rises up against his own father? When one brother kills another? When a house is turned against itself and ambition rather than godliness rules the new generation?"

"Every nation has suffered through the same struggles. It's the way of royalty."

"It's the way of fools. No, don't be offended. I count myself as one of them. I should have learned from Boaz. I should have married one woman and stayed faithful to her. Instead I went the way of kings. I married every woman who pleased me. I sired half brothers who hate each other and plot to kill one another for the sake of rule. I love every one of them. When they bleed, I bleed. When they hurt, I weep. But I have not disciplined them. I have not taught them the ways of the Lord.

"That is my failure. How can my kingdom last? The Lord has promised an everlasting covenant with me. But I think it will take a miracle for that covenant to come to pass. It will take a move of heaven to bring forth a kingdom of righteousness and peace out of the fruit of my loins."

A dark flush stained Solomon's face. His square jaw clenched. David remembered that in spite of his youth, Solomon already had three wives and more than one concubine. "Marrying numerous wives is expedient for a king," he said, his voice defensive. "It eases political tensions within the nation and without. Who wants to attack his own son-in-law? Besides, having many sons secures the throne and makes sure it does not remain empty."

"Empty? It seems a little overpopulated from where I stand. Your brothers aren't desperate to support you. That is not what I call security. How will you hold this nation together? How will your sons? How will you protect it from larger powers rising up, hungry for land and slaves? You will not, without the Lord. That is what I want you to understand. That is the legacy Ruth and Boaz left you. It doesn't matter what other people think about you. It doesn't matter how hard times become. Don't lean on your own understanding. Trust in the Lord and He will make your paths straight."

"I do trust the Lord, Father. You needn't worry. You have brought stability and prosperity to our nation. I will guard all you have done."

"All the Lord has done, Solomon."

"Yes, Father."

David sighed. "I have written Ruth's story to the best of my recollection. I haven't the time or strength to add many details. But eyes wise enough shall see that the Moabs of life need not remain your home. We all have a choice to move toward the Lord or away from Him. The past need not be the measure of our future."

"I wrote some of the words down, myself. They were worth remembering."

"Yes. I used them in my psalms as well." David fetched the new scroll from its hiding place. "I am going to entrust it to you, Solomon. I am going to rely on you to keep it safe. Protect it from destruction. Let the world see this book. Understand it. Who knows? Perhaps there is another Ruth somewhere who needs to be encouraged. Another Naomi who needs to turn back to God. Another

Boaz who shall become a kinsman redeemer."

Solomon reached his hand for the scroll. For a moment David hesitated. "Will you promise not to destroy it? Promise to share it with the people?"

Solomon hesitated before nodding gravely. "I promise."

David knew with an inexplicable certainty that the account of Ruth's life would survive. What he could not ascertain was whether his throne would also survive throughout the coming ages. Would his sons be able to keep Israel unified? Would they manage to protect the nation from rising powers? Would the Lord send another David in time of need? The king realized that these were questions only God could answer. For all his experience, the future remained a mystery to the king.

Though my dreams be crushed, though my throne be plundered, yet shall I trust You, he promised. And with a sigh gave up his fears into the hands of the Lord one final time.

THE FOREBEARS OF BOAZ:

"Abraham was the father of Isaac, and Isaac the father of Jacob, and Jacob the father of Judah and his brothers, and Judah the father of Perez and Zerah by Tamar, and Perez the father of Hezron, and Hezron the father of Ram, and Ram the father of Amminadab, and Amminadab the father of Nahshon and Nahshon the father of Salmon, and Salmon the father of Boaz by Rahab . . .

"The descendants of Boaz and Ruth:

"And Boaz the father of Obed by Ruth, and Obed the father of Jesse, and Jesse the father of David the king.

"David was the father of Solomon, whose mother had been Uriah's wife, Solomon the father of Rehoboam *(during whose reign the nation of Israel was torn into two, resulting in Rehoboam ruling over the southern kingdom of Judah, only)* . . .

"Rehoboam the father of Abijah, Abijah the father of Asa, Asa the father of Jehoshaphat, Jehoshaphat the father of Jehoram,

Jehoram the father of Uzziah, Uzziah the father of Jotham, Jotham the father of Ahaz, Ahaz the father of Hezekiah, Hezekiah the father of Manasseh, Manasseh the father of Amon, Amon the father of Josiah, and Josiah the father of Jeconiah and his brothers at the time of the exile to Babylon.

"After the exile to Babylon: Jeconiah was the father of Sheltiel, Shealtiel the father of Zerubbabel, Zerubbabel the father of Abiud, Abiud the father of Eliakim, Eliakim the father of Azor, Azor the father of Zadok, Zadok the father of Akim, Akim the father of Eliud, Eliud the father of Eleazar, Eleazar the father of Matthan, Matthan the father of Jacob, . . .

"And Jacob the father of Joseph the husband of Mary, of whom Jesus was born, who is called Christ." (Based on Matthew 1:2–16.)

Author's Notes

Using a deceptively simple story, the book of Ruth reveals the power of God at work in the daily life and toil of human beings. To me, this is one of the Old Testament's most moving stories, demonstrating the sovereignty of God in the midst of sorrow and loss. The first word in my novel is death. The last word is Christ. God has the last word—even over death. That says it all, as far as I am concerned.

Choosing the right language for biblical fiction has something in common with the conundrum of the Bible translator. A linguist's main grammatical choice revolves around one central decision: What is more important—sounding closest to the original language, or trying to convey an accurate *sense* of the words to today's reader? You might present modern readers with a very close approximation of a Hebrew text, using word-for-word interpretation, but they may not necessarily understand it, whereas a more contemporary translation might grab the reader's heart and mind more powerfully.

As a biblical novelist, I must contend with a similar choice. Ultimately, I want to create a world that feels like the biblical era and yet connects emotionally to my reader. There is no point in being literal if my readers come away feeling unmoved; untouched, because the world is too alien and the words too foreign. You might say my language resembles more of a New Living Translation vibe than the literal accuracy of a translation such as the English Standard Version. It's a balancing act and one that I don't always get right. I have tried to walk this tightrope in the story of Ruth as best I can.

Just as some readers resonate more deeply with the KJV and others with NIV, readers of a biblical novel will experience the linguistic choices of the author through their own personal preference of biblical language.

Some notes more specific to this novel are in order. The author of Ruth is unknown. The story thread dealing with the authorship presented in *In the Field of Grace* is a product of my imagination and has no basis in historical facts. The concept that some of David's and Solomon's writings were inspired by Ruth and Boaz is also due to literary license. However, as we are aware that some of the material in the Bible was preserved in oral fashion for long years before being written down, the idea that David and Solomon might have been quoting their great-grandparents is not entirely unthinkable.

Most readers familiar with the story of Ruth remember that according to the genealogy in the final chapter of Ruth, Salmon fathered Boaz. There is a practical challenge with interpreting the genealogy in this way. If you count the years in the book of Judges, during which era the story of Ruth takes place, you will find that there is almost three hundred years between the time of the conquest when Salmon lived and the period in history occupied by Boaz and Ruth. This would make Boaz's age quite advanced, especially when you take into consideration that the age of extraordinarily long life spans is now over. According to David, only two generations later, the average age of a man is around 70, not 250.

As readers, we must recall that the original Hebrew for the word *father* used in Ruth is flexible. It need not mean that Salmon and Rahab gave birth directly to Boaz. It could just as easily mean that they were his great-great grandparents, because the word *father* works more elastically in Hebrew than it does in English. For example, Jesus warns the Pharisees and Sadducees about saying, "We have Abraham as our father" (Matthew 3:9). Obviously He does not mean this literally; He is exchanging the word *father* for *forefather*. (For a more detailed account, please refer to John Reed's commentary on Ruth in the *Bible Knowledge Commentary*, edited by John F. Walvoord and Roy Zuck.) It is possible that the generations in between the names mentioned in the genealogy were not considered worth preserving in Scripture because historically or theologically they made little difference to the kingdom of God. In any case, I have tried to write this aspect of the story with vague enough language that the reader can make his or her own decision on the matter.

According to some sources, ancient wedding rituals in Israel contained the phrase *the government shall be on his shoulders*. Clearly, this is a quote from Isaiah, who lived several hundred years after the story of Ruth took place. However, it is possible that an oral tradition may have already existed, using this proclamation in the marriage ceremony, prompting Isaiah to use it in his prophecy of the coming Messiah, indicating that He would be as a Bridegroom to His people. Since that imagery occurs in the Bible already, I felt that the possibility of an older-existing oral tradition was not unreasonable, and chose to use the quote in Boaz and Ruth's wedding ceremony.

There are no examples of animals being named in the Bible, although this is a common practice among other ancient cultures. In the end, I chose to name a few animals in the story because my scholarly sources pointed out that it would make life awkward if none of the animals were named.

As I often do, I have made reference to the work of other authors in this novel. Ruth's assertion that horses are dangerous on both ends and uncomfortable in the middle is a quote from Oscar Wilde, although Wilde's original statement is somewhat more colorful in language. I have used the phrase *acceptance with joy* from Hannah Hurnard's classic *Hinds Feet in High Places*.

Every chapter begins with a biblical quote. Readers familiar with the Bible will be instantly aware that these verses are anachronistic. I am using them as a lens through which the chapter can be read, rather than an accurate representation of Scripture in Ruth's world.

The best way to study the Bible is not through a novel but

simply to read the original. This story can in no way replace the transformative power that the reader will encounter in the Scriptures. For the original account of Ruth, please refer to the book by the same name in your Bible.

Author Acknowledgments

The gracious expertise and help of many people made this novel possible. I would like to thank my agent, Wendy Lawton, whose efforts on my behalf continue to pave the way for me as a writer. I was blessed the day we met. To Deb Keiser at River North Fiction, simply, thank you. It's been such a joy to work with you, brainstorm, pull out our hair mutually over title woes, have delicious dinners together, and celebrate the challenges of the writing life. You have been a generous and supportive resource, one of the foundational blessings in my writing life. In the same way, I wish to thank Michele Forrider, whose gentle, sweet nature can make any day look good, and whose belief in these books has been a rock of encouragement. What an amazing team to work with.

Few writers are blessed with faithful and encouraging critique partners who genuinely make a difference in the outcome of a book's life. Lauren Yarger's friendship, incredible book launches, events, and brilliant editing has left a lasting imprint in my life. Cindy McDowell is always a rich source of encouragement and hope when hope is thin. And she can make one mean flower arrangement! These women occupy a special place in my heart.

I deeply appreciate the unstinting support provided by Deryk Richenburg, who as a pastor understands the Bible better than most scholars, and as a farmer knows how to properly wrestle a ram to the ground—a rare skill. He also knows what it feels like to go flying through the air and earn a fat lip when said ram is feeling rambunctious. What more can I ask of a proofreader? Except for his insightful ideas that made *In the Field of Grace* a better book.

Thanks to my dearest friends, Rebecca Rhee, who is always there, graciously allowing me to moan about plotline problems, and Beth and Rob Bull who never cease to encourage and support me along this path, recommending my books to everyone they know. As always, my sister Emi Trowbridge's undeserved faith in me sustains me every day.

Special acknowledgment is due to Tegan Willard for her astute suggestions and incredible proofing, and Molly Chase who graciously brought her fantastic editing knowledge into this novel and made it better. I am grateful for the Reverend Halvor Ronning's suggestions regarding Ruth's travel arrangements. I spent an invaluable evening with Judy Franzen, pouring over her photos from her recent trip to Israel in order to make the world of Ruth come alive for me.

A book's life is complicated, and there are many who are essential in the process of its birth and release. My profound thanks to Jeane Wynne and the Moody sales force, who manage to land these books in the most astonishing locations. You folks are marvelous. A special note of appreciation is due to Janis Backing whose exceptional support helps to release my novels into many hands. Thank you for giving up your Saturday for me, Janis!

And to my fans, who write Facebook messages, emails, and best of all read my books, you are a true joy to me—my beloved companions on this adventure.

IMPACTING LIVES THROUGH THE POWER OF STORY

Thank you! We are honored that you took the time out of your busy schedule to read this book. If you enjoyed what you read, would you consider sharing the message with others?

- Write a review online at amazon.com, bn.com, goodreads.com, cbd.com.
- Recommend this book to friends in your book club, workplace, church, school, classes, or small group.
- Go to facebook.com/RiverNorthFiction, "like" the page and post a comment as to what you enjoyed the most.
- Mention this book in a Facebook post, Twitter update, Pinterest pin, or a blog post.
- Pick up a copy for someone you know who would be encouraged by this message.
- Subscribe to our newsletter for information on upcoming titles, inside information on discounts and promotions, and learn more about your favorite authors at RiverNorthFiction.com.